MOTHERS
and SONS

PAUL HOND

MOTHERS
and SONS

A Novel

RANDOM HOUSE

NEW YORK

Copyright © 2005 by Paul Hond

All rights reserved under International and Pan-American
Copyright Conventions. Published in the United States by
Random House, an imprint of The Random House Publishing Group,
a division of Random House, Inc., New York, and simultaneously
in Canada by Random House of Canada Limited, Toronto.

RANDOM HOUSE and colophon are registered trademarks
of Random House, Inc.

Library of Congress Cataloging-in-Publication Data
Hond, Paul.
Mothers and sons : a novel / by Paul Hond.
p. cm.
ISBN 0-375-50805-8 (acid-free paper)
1. Triangles (Interpersonal relations)—Fiction. 2. Manhattan
(New York, N.Y.)—Fiction. 3. Parent and adult child—Fiction.
4. Mothers and sons—Fiction. 5. Women musicians—Fiction.
6. Male friendship—Fiction. 7. Dramatists—Fiction. I. Title.
PS3558.O466M67 2005
813'.54—dc22   2004046817

Printed in the United States of America on acid-free paper
Random House website address: www.atrandom.com
2 4 6 8 9 7 5 3 1
First Edition

Book design by Victoria Wong

for K.

MOTHERS
and SONS

1

FOR THE FIFTH STRAIGHT MORNING, MOSS MESSINGER was awakened by noise: deep, infernal grunts, toad rhythms, a throbbing, a frenzy, an orgy, an infestation. The monsters! They were killing him. Moss removed his earplugs, which were made of a specially engineered foam, guaranteed to block out snoring, car alarms. Yet useless. The noise bored right through them, to the root of Moss's brain. His sleep was ruined. He heaved himself up in his bed, pulled open the curtain and saw on the window ledge two plump gray pigeons, the head of one tucked under the other's wing. They appeared to be asleep. Moss tapped the pane, but the lovers didn't move; instead came the flapping and screeching of other birds, exploding from their sanctuaries in the narrow air shaft and falling upward through the canyon of blackened bricks toward daylight.

In Moss's life in that apartment, there had been many annoyances—busted boilers, banging pipes, leaks, bad smells—but never this, never pigeons. Had someone dropped bread out a window?

Moss suspected one of the old Ukrainian widows that you often saw in the park, standing in a roiling sea of strutting, pecking, filthy birds, tossing crusts from under her tattered shawl. A few of them lived in Moss's building and in the tenement next door, on the other side of the air shaft: they sat in their windows like faded portraits. Every so often, one would die, and before the body was cold the contractors would be hammering away, renovating the place so that Moss's cheeseparing landlady, Mrs. Bulina, could rent the unit for five times the money she'd been getting before. Moss knew that his own apartment was similarly undervalued. He also knew that Mrs. Bulina knew this. Moreover he was aware that a few unscrupulous building owners had taken to harassing long-standing tenants in an effort to drive them out, and sometimes not just harass: the murder of a tenant at the hands of his landlord on Norfolk Street had been big news in the wake of recent battles in the state legislature in which laws protecting tenants like Moss from sudden and dramatic increases in rent had mercifully been upheld. Sometimes he felt that his landlady viewed him mostly in terms of money lost, and why wouldn't she? The logic was inescapable. Now Moss wondered, not too seriously, if Mrs. Bulina might herself have dropped some bread, as part of a plot to drive him out. Moss, it was true, had a tendency to create elaborate dramas around himself, but it was hard to overestimate Mrs. Bulina, who, seen carrying her small heft tidily up and down the stairs in floral-print dresses and white sneakers to deliver rent notices, had been a notorious slumlord in her day. Even now, she refused to make improvements to the building, and when Moss's upstairs neighbor, a dandified Pole with a Hitler mustache

above a moist quivering lip, had gone on rent strike over Mrs. Bulina's continued failure to install an intercom system, so that guests
and couriers and deliverymen could be admitted at the push of a
button instead of your having to go down to open the door, Moss
had kept a low profile, declining to add his name to a petition that
the neighbor had circulated. Moss was all for an intercom, but did
not want to antagonize his landlady, and besides, he rarely ordered
in. Still, he was unnerved by the example made of his neighbor, who
was eventually removed from the premises by three cops and a psy-
chiatrist.

Moss now noticed the droppings on the windowsill: green and
white spatterings covered with wormy ash-colored coils. You could
get respiratory diseases from breathing that stuff, Moss had read.
Maybe he'd already contracted something. Hadn't he been coughing lately? Wheezing? Of course, the main problem was the noise.
Whenever the pigeons got agitated and burst from a ledge, a high-
pitched pulsing sound rattled in their fat throats, like the trill of a
car's starter on a freezing day.

Moss got out of bed and went to the toilet with a book of poems
by Keats, a gift from Danielle on his last birthday. Moss had resisted
these poems because Keats had died at twenty-six, and Moss, at
twenty-seven, felt threatened by the genius of men younger than
himself. If he and Keats had been friends, which of them would get
the girls? That was the real question in life, and the fact remained
that Moss had yet to have a single one of his plays produced.
Danielle once mentioned that Keats had died a virgin, and that was
of some consolation. Danielle always knew what to say. Moss saw

that she had marked a poem for him—"Ode to a Nightingale."
That was eerie, a further encroachment of birds. Moss read the
poem skeptically, feeling certain that Keats, for all his problems,
had never been ravaged by pigeons. And while an Old World song-
bird was a different thing from what was roosting in Moss's air
shaft, Moss made no distinction. *Thou wast not born for death, im-
mortal Bird!* Moss's great-grandfather had raised pigeons for food
on the roof of a tenement on Avenue C, and so maybe there was
some justice at work. More to the point, Moss himself had eaten
pigeon for the first time just ten days before. This was at Beaujoli,
a slick new eatery that had opened up a few blocks away in what
was once a Salvation Army outlet where Moss used to get his shirts.
Moss's dining companion, Boris, had ordered the *pigeons au Sancerre*. A culinary-school dropout, Boris suspected it was not a Sancerre that had been used but a California sauvignon blanc, which
he claimed was a common substitute in that dish. The kitchen confirmed this upon inquiry. Moss thought that the discrepancy ought
to have been explained beforehand by the waiter, a waifish blue-
eyed hustler who reeled off sumptuous descriptions as long as your
arm but couldn't remember to bring a glass of water. Moss would
mention all of this in his review. In addition, Boris thought that the
bouquet garni overwhelmed the other flavors. Moss saw his point.
Moss himself had ordered the loin of hare, cooked in wine and butter and blood. Boris tasted it and thought the sauce too bloody. Moss
made a note.

Moss's opinions about Beaujoli—which were largely Boris's—

had appeared a week later in *Eat New York,* and that night—three nights ago—he had come home to find a frightening message on his answering machine: a low, breathy voice, obviously disguised, saying, "Sweet little [unintelligible], why did you die?" Moss listened to it over and over, nibbling on his thumb. Sweet little *what?* Red Fee? Reffie? Referee? Suddenly, Moss knew: it was Nik Cattai, owner of Beaujoli. *Referee.* Cattai, a foreigner, might have meant this in the sense of "judge," as a synonym for "critic"; and his "why did you die?" seemed almost a parody of a threat delivered in sinister broken English. Moss had met Cattai briefly at the restaurant's opening-night party a month or so before, and was impressed by his charm, a product of vampire good looks, a streetwise solicitousness and several million dollars. There were rumors that he'd made his fortune as a youth in Croatia, funneling weapons to the Irish Republican Army. Moss didn't ask. All he knew was that Cattai had invested a huge amount of money in what he hoped would become the next sensation on the downtown restaurant scene. *Eat New York,* though subheaded "What's Yummy and What's Crummy," was concerned less with serious food criticism than with Who Was Eating Where, and promoted the celebrity of chefs and owners, combining interviews and sexy photos with industry gossip and recipes of the stars. Nik Cattai was determined to become a star in his own right, and Beaujoli, with its antique ceiling fans and tile mosaics, to say nothing of chef Billy Pipp, was to be his key; and with a view toward a major cover story, he'd been terribly gracious to Moss (who, like some reviewers, forswore his anonymity in exchange for special treatment), taking him through the kitchen, introducing him around and generally making him feel that he was being asked to do a favor.

Moss had mentioned this too in his critique.

Now, from the bathroom, he heard the pigeons shrieking as they flew from ledge to ledge.

Of all the times to be single, Moss thought, recalling Danielle's quiet top-floor studio on Bank Street, which had afforded him so many peaceful sleep-filled hours. He had ended that relationship weeks ago, long before the pigeons. He could not have seen them coming. Not that having a noiseless living space had been Danielle's chief attribute—far from it. Aside from her beauty—older people compared her to Grace Kelly—she was probably the most selfless and giving person Moss had ever known. There was nothing she would not have done for him. Well, there had been one thing. She wouldn't leave him. He'd given her every chance—told her he couldn't be "trusted," that he wasn't "ready," that he feared "intimacy"—anything to get around the painful truth, which was that he had turned off to her sexually. He hardly understood it, but there it was. And because he could not abide the effect his flagging interest might have on Danielle's self-esteem, he took the blame: I'm confused, he would say, I'm afraid of getting too close, I don't want to lose myself, and on and on. Danielle had no choice but to believe him—the alternative was too horrible. Occasionally she tried to seduce him. He feigned sleep, illness. Frustrated, she suggested—tolerantly—that he might be gay. "It's okay if you are," she told him with compassion. "I just want to *know*." Moss denied it, but not categorically. Meanwhile he lusted after every pretty girl he saw. For months he lived like this, celibate in the prime of life, all because he could not bring himself to betray a woman who loved him so much that she was willing to wait years for him to realize what a precious thing he had.

He realized it now. Love! He had traded love for freedom. Didn't every pop song of the past fifty years warn expressly against that? "Let's hang on to what we've got." "Don't turn your back on love." Christ! It was all true. He'd never understood those songs before, and wondered if they'd been penned and sung from the same anguish he himself was feeling, or if he was merely responding, in his heightened state, to bland imitations of sentiment—as if the simplest, most timeworn phrases had a power that revealed itself to those whose experience made them receptive to it, the way believers find religious significance in ordinary events.

He flushed the toilet and stepped into the shower, sick with longing for Danielle, who had recently turned thirty and begun threatening to get a dog. "Why do I need a man or a baby?" she liked to say, pretending to have come to a more mature, more realistic point of view. It killed Moss every time. When they first met, she'd just moved to the city, bursting with plans to take acting classes and audition for *As the World Turns*. Moss got a bad feeling. Danielle had exactly the sort of résumé—small town, big dreams, a *nurse*—that made her a natural target for homeless schizophrenics with bricks, though more likely she'd be crushed by high rent, self-centered men, stiff competition and phone calls not returned. On their first date Moss learned that she'd been treated badly by her last boyfriend, a dashing young gynecologist from Bombay. "I gave him a blow job," she said, glumly stirring her drink, "and then he broke up with me. Like right afterward." Moss was offended by the boyfriend's cruelty and felt that he must make it up to her somehow, even as he calculated the odds of himself receiving a blow job. He was beginning to like his chances. "That guy was a disgusting jerk," he said, and speculated that a man who chose to examine vaginas for a living must have pretty complicated feelings about women. This drew an appreciative laugh from Danielle. A wonderful laugh—sweet, shy, held back in the throat as though in ladylike restraint, bringing out her dimples and setting her tense nostrils fluttering. A snapshot of the soul. Moss fell in love with it. Already he sensed that she had chosen him, and his only response was to let himself be claimed. He held doors, pulled out chairs, praised her clothes, hair, eyes, nose, walked her home through dark streets and kissed her tenderly goodnight. Soon they were sleeping together. Moss would mount her from behind like an animal, turn her over and come on her face (her idea), and then take a shower. It was nothing personal, he'd tell her, the shower. He averaged three a day, even without sex. He washed his hands constantly. He avoided doorknobs, public bathrooms, people with colds. He loved condoms. Only when drunk could he really enjoy himself in bed. Bodily smells repelled him, especially his own. He wanted to be of the angels. *Pure*. With soap and mouthwash and antiperspirant he waged endless war with his body, striving for godliness. One of the great things about Danielle was that she always smelled clean, even when she came home from work. Moss would sniff her neck, her hair. "You're a flower," he'd tell her, and she would blush and assure him that she hadn't *always* smelled so good after work, a reference to her stint in Labor and Delivery, which was still her first love. Moss had never been present at a birth (not counting his own, which his mother had once described as "something I'd never want to go through again"—and she hadn't), but he'd seen footage of one on television, and that was enough: the mother seemed to be ridding herself of some horrible bloody thing that had invaded her. Danielle saw it differently. To her, a human birth was the foremost event in nature; in her rubber gloves and blue mask she had bent herself at the volcano's edge.

Now she worked in Intensive Care. Instead of birth, it was death she attended. She wanted to become well-rounded in the field. More than once she suggested to Moss that they have sex in the hospital morgue. She was getting in touch with things that were beyond Moss. If one of her patients died, it was her job to remove the jewelry. "It was inscribed, Moss, on the inside—'Harry and Ruth,' and the date. Fifty years. That ring hadn't come off in *fifty years*"—conveying, Moss knew, her own desire for a lifelong bond; for she had seen what it was to die alone, without love. "How infinitely depressing," Moss would say, whenever she described a patient who had no visitors. It made Moss think he should volunteer his time, talk with these people, hear their stories, remember them. But then the feeling would pass. In the meantime, the sick were fortunate to have someone like Danielle, who, when she had some free minutes, would massage their swollen feet.

God, what had he done? How would he survive without her?

Maybe he wouldn't. He stood in the shower like a statue in the rain, picturing her face; it was all he could do to turn off the water. He dried himself and put on his blue bathrobe—another gift from Danielle—and settled at his desk, where he began typing his letter of resignation to his editor at *Eat*. His tenure there, so brief and fateful, could be traced to the day two months before, when Boris, a subscriber to that magazine, came across an intriguing ad in the back:

SPERM DONOR WANTED,

$10,000 Reward:

Are You a Young, Handsome, Brilliant,

Talented, Healthy, Potent White Male?

Boris had called Moss to tell him about it, knowing that Moss could use the money, especially as how Moss had been complaining lately that he couldn't afford to give Danielle any of the things she wanted, even though she insisted she didn't want those things ("I only want *you*—I don't care if we're poor"). But Moss knew better. She was always reading mail-order catalogs, coveting furniture and clothes in shop windows, dreaming of vacations to Provence or the Amalfi coast. How often did he dream of striking it rich, just so he could buy her a house in the country, with a yard and a garden and a wraparound porch, and send her to picturesque seaside places, and enroll her in the top acting programs in the city?

And so it took little prodding to get Moss to answer the ad; ten grand was ten grand, and with one phone call he scheduled an interview with the needy couple, Joel and Gail Faber, at their Upper West Side apartment. A personal-claims lawyer who dealt in evidence, Joel Faber told Moss to bring his college transcripts, medical records, photos or videotape of himself as a child, and a sample of any "creative work." Moss gathered what he could, but decided against telling Danielle, to whom the idea of his impregnating another woman in exchange for money with which to buy material goods intended to pacify her desire for a child of her own would seem grossly insensitive at best. Besides, his chances of being chosen were slim; according to his understanding of the *Eat* demographic, he'd be competing with highly educated professionals in their thirties and forties who could afford to dine out. And while he was in good physical health, his GPA had been in the low twos (he'd never even graduated), and the only pictures he could find of himself—his mother having been a less-than-avid chronicler of his childhood—revealed a sullen little person with his thumb in his mouth, looking distrustfully at the camera, or else caught unawares in startling tableaus of orphan solitude: sitting on a barren floor, as if left there by drug dealers, or petting a dog on the street, with an expression of childlike wonder at a creature that was miraculously free of the disease of human cruelty. Whether or not the Fabers would infer the worst from this evidence was unclear, and so Moss threw all his hope into his latest play, *The Scavengers,* which concerned a young man who combs the city for sex in the aftermath of a massive nuclear attack. Of course, the key would be the interview itself: his lack of accomplishment and pedigree might be forgiven if he made a strong personal impression. To that end, he decided against cutting his hair, which had grown over the months into a thick brown bush that swayed lavishly atop his head: high above him it carried on its own wild fertility, heaving in the wind, collecting particles that Danielle would sometimes pick out while they watched TV. The Fabers might appreciate a thriving head of hair.

Joel Faber wore a welcoming smile as he greeted Moss at the door. He was tall and broad-shouldered, with a meticulously trimmed beard and small, book-blurred eyes that moved around in hypnotic circles behind round wire-framed glasses. "You must be the stud," he said. His handshake was too firm, as if in compensation for his deficiency. Moss felt the death in his grip, the evolutionary death. And yet his first impression was that he himself was too young, slight and incompetent to serve as this man's surrogate.

"Hope this passes muster," said Moss, handing Joel a folder that included his baby pictures and a fresh photocopy of *The Scavengers*. As Joel thumbed through the materials, Moss looked around. The place was huge, and barely furnished, as though the Fabers were waiting to resolve their problem before really making the place a home.

A woman appeared.

"This is my wife, Gail," Joel said, closing the folder.

Gail Faber was tall and big-boned like her husband—what Moss thought of as a "handsome woman." She had blue eyes, pale freckles and chestnut hair with strands of gray. Moss could picture her in khaki shorts and a sun hat, working with gorillas.

"Good to meet you," she said, extending her large hand.

"Likewise," said Moss, feeling Gail's blood galloping in his palm, heading beyond the boundaries of her marriage and into the vast genetic universe now available to her. Moss assumed the insemination would be done artificially, but either way, he was a prospective partner for a union so momentous that between himself and the mother-to-be there had sprung a small but crucial tension.

"How about some wine," Joel said to Moss, with an air of gentle correction. "That way you can tell us more about yourself."

In the kitchen Joel opened one of the many bottles of wine that were stored in the pantry (a Pinot Noir from Burgundy, he announced, eliciting from Moss a grunt of uninformed approval, the transparency of which Moss felt was being silently computed), explaining, as he worked the corkscrew, that he and Gail had tried every weapon known to modern science to reverse his condition, without success.

They moved to the living room. Moss sat on the blue velvet sofa, with Joel and Gail opposite on matching chairs. On the glass coffee table was the current issue of *Eat New York*.

"I'm the managing editor," said Gail, noticing Moss's attention to the magazine. "That's why we placed the ad there. It keeps it in the family."

The conversation turned to medical matters. Moss, under informal oath, vowed that there were no patterns of major disease in his family. This wasn't entirely accurate—he didn't know who his father was, and his mother's parents and grandparents had all died horribly of cancer—but ten grand was ten grand.

When the wineglasses were empty, Gail gathered them up and returned to the kitchen.

"So," said Joel. He looked at his watch. "Would you mind taking off your clothes?"

"Excuse me?"

"We'd like to check for any defects or irregularities. Unless you'd rather leave it to our imaginations."

"It's just that I wasn't expecting this," said Moss.

"Did you think ten thousand dollars would come so easily?" said Joel, smiling blandly.

Moss had to admit that perhaps he'd been naïve in that regard. He said, "Does your wife need to see me too?"

"If you don't mind," said Gail as she came into the room, one of those alert and magnificent people who hears everything. "But if you'd rather just have Joel look at you, we could work around that."

"I'm sorry," said Moss, a warm humiliation creeping over him. "I'm not comfortable with this." Moss had no serious flaws to hide, but there was the principle of the thing, and also he had a partial erection.

"That's fine," said Joel, as if surmising the nature of Moss's reluctance. "We don't want you to be uncomfortable." He patted the folder on his lap. "We'll deal with what we've got."

Moss saw his prospects fading. "I'll do it for eight thousand."

Joel crossed his legs. "Sperm donation aside, if you want to make a few extra dollars, you should talk to Gail."

"Six thousand."

"Do you like to eat out?" Gail said.

Moss had to think. "Sure. Once in a while."

"Because we're starting a new column called 'The Layman's

Lunch.' Food reviews written by regular people. It pays thirty dollars per review, three to five hundred words, and of course the meals are on us. Can you eat food and then write about the experience? What you liked, what you didn't like?"

"Sure," said Moss, thinking that this was their way of getting rid of him without hurting his feelings. But he needed money, any sort of money, if not for Danielle then for himself. Ever since his mother left, he'd been moving from one odd job to the next. This would be one of the more respectable ones.

And so he accepted the offer, never imagining that he would soon become the target of a restaurateur's vengeance.

HE FINISHED TYPING his resignation letter, and was reading it over when the phone rang. He set the page aside and picked up.

"Hello?"

No answer.

"Hello?"

Nothing. Yet Moss sensed presence. No audible breathing, but a suspense, a closeness, an intimacy—it was like being watched.

"Who is this?" he demanded.

The line went dead.

2

A FEW MINUTES LATER, THE PHONE RANG AGAIN. MOSS LET
the machine answer. It was Fran. "If you're not busy tonight," she said, "do you want to get a drink?" Fran was Moss's
closest friend, a talented singer with a borderline drug problem
whom Moss had known since high school. She could sing anything,
from jazz to country to Schubert lieder. Most recently she'd fronted
an all-girl band called The Bushtits (leather boots, hot pants, studded leather bras), but then the drummer got married and moved to
Park Slope, and Fran had a freakout about never finding the right
guy, never leaving the city or having a family, and decided that she
was wasting her life trying to be a singer, when she should put her
degree to use and help people. And so she got a job teaching first
grade at a public school in the Bronx. Within weeks she was saying
things like, "Animals treat their offspring better than these people,"
and "When you have seven-year-olds threatening to kill their
teachers, it makes you really think about forced sterilization," and
then she'd start to cry. She wanted to switch to a private school, but

those were the gigs everyone wanted and it was hard to break in. Instead she began writing Appalachian folk songs and trying to sleep with anyone in the record business. What she needed most, Moss felt, was to find one style and stick with it. "I'm eclectic," she'd say, as though it were an eating disorder. Nowadays when she called Moss for a drink it usually meant that her junkie boyfriend, Zak, the bass player for Diet of Worms, was being an asshole, and Moss knew that she would want to flirt with other guys and ask Moss repeatedly if he thought Zak was cheating on her. Moss looked forward to the diversion. He called her back and they agreed to meet at ten at the Grasshopper. He then left a message for Boris, inviting him along. Fran had met Boris several times and often asked Moss if he was sure Boris wasn't gay. She thought that about any guy who didn't instantly drool over her.

Once, as a teenager, she'd tried to kill herself with aspirin and tequila.

Moss arrived at the bar at ten-fifteen because Fran was never on time. He took a table at the back and ordered a beer. Fran walked in twenty minutes later. "Hi," she said, her eyes raking the crowd as she pulled out a chair. She wore a short black dress and fishnets— even on a freezing cold night—and had inserted her gold nose ring, which lent her the menace of a small charging bull. Her bleached blond hair was cut in a pixie; green eyes were wide from appetite suppressants and possibly cocaine. On one round shoulder was a tattoo of a pair of smoochy red lips, which Moss had urged her not to get, on the grounds that she'd soon outgrow it. That had been eight years ago. Now she talked of getting another one on her ass.

She sat. "What's the matter?" she said. "You look tired."

"I'm besieged," Moss groaned. "I haven't slept."

"Besieged with what?"

"Pigeons."

"Pigeons?"

"In the air shaft," said Moss. "They wake me up at five every morning. You can't imagine the noises they make. It's diabolical. I can't take it. I can't take it for another day." He could hear them now, in his head. "They fuck each other right on my windowsill. Feathers float into my room. There could be lice. Disease. Have you ever heard of psittacosis? Parrot fever?"

"No."

"Bubonic plague?"

"I thought that was from rats."

"What are pigeons?" Moss coughed and patted his chest.

"What you should do," said Fran, "is complain to your land-lady."

Moss shook his head. "She won't do anything."

"So use poison."

"On my landlady?"

"No. On the pigeons."

"And end up with an air shaft full of dead birds?"

"They'd be dead, at least," said Fran. "That's better than noth-ing."

"I'd rather kill my landlady."

"Maybe you should."

"What I *should* do," said Moss, "is get back with Danielle. She had such a quiet apartment."

"How's she doing?"

"She's depressed."

"God, Moss. You really ruined her." Fran stirred her drink. "But don't worry. I'm sure she'll be okay."

"She must curse the day she met me," said Moss, recalling that warm spring night three years before, when he'd checked himself in to the emergency room with shortness of breath and chest pains. Danielle happened to be on duty, filling in for someone, and so it was left to her to explain to Moss, after listening to his heart, that he was only hyperventilating. She then gave him a brown paper bag, the kind used by drunks, and showed him how to breathe into it, just as she would later teach him the Heimlich maneuver and CPR. "Like this?" he said, sticking his nose into the bag. "Excellent," she told him. When his normal breathing pattern was restored, he asked her, half-jokingly, if she'd like to have a drink, to celebrate. To his surprise, she said yes.

"She'll get over it," Fran was saying. "She just needs to meet people."

"She's shy," said Moss. "She's introverted. She's heartbroken. It makes me sick to think of her alone in her apartment. She doesn't deserve to suffer. All she ever did was love me."

Moss reflected on the wonder of that. Someone had loved him. What were the chances?

"But you didn't want to have sex with her," Fran pointed out, in

that vaguely accusatory way she had when discussing Moss's problems. "And all because she wants a baby." She turned and ordered a
vodka tonic from the waitress.

"She loved me," said Moss, ignoring Fran's analysis. Fran had
an explanation for everything in Moss's life.

"She's a beautiful woman," Fran said, as if someone had implied otherwise. "Guys'll be all over her."

Boris came in.

"Look who it is," Moss said, grateful for the diversion.

"It's a bird, it's a plane," said Fran. "It's Super Yuppie."

"Be nice," said Moss. "He can't help it if he's rich."

"Hey, Moss," said Boris, sliding smoothly out of his black
leather coat. "Hi, Fran. Nice dress." He pulled out a chair, draped
the coat over the back of it, took off his black ski cap and sat. "Man,
it's cold tonight."

"It's because you're bald," said Fran. "Grow some hair."

"You think?" said Boris, signaling to the waitress. He was a
good two inches shorter than Moss, and had shaved his head pre-
emptively, to "lose my hair on my own terms." It looked great. He
had thick black eyebrows over quicksilver eyes, and a nose like a
hanging rock. Moss had first met him two years ago, at a bar on
Fifth Street—Moss was working on *The Scavengers,* and Boris,
drinking alone at the next table, had asked him about it, saying that
he'd spent time in L.A. as a screenwriter, without success, before
coming back home and starting an elite online fertility agency
called LittleEinsteins.com, which represented Ivy League sperm
donors, including himself, and which he eventually sold for three

million dollars. It seemed that Boris, thirty-five and single, had been looking for a friend with whom he could drink and carouse and talk openly about women—apparently he'd lost a string of such confidants to marriage, one after the next, and had still been licking his wounds when he recruited Moss, whom he instantly recognized as a brother. "You and me, we're poets," he took the liberty to tell Moss after several Glenlivets. "We understand the relationship between God and alcohol, alcohol and beauty. We love beauty. It's that simple. *We love beauty*. The day we apologize for that is the day we stop living." And he bought more drinks and talked about how important it was for a man to stay single as long as possible.

"So what's new?" said Fran, grinning wickedly at Boris.

Women were often attracted to Boris, but Fran treated him more as an amusement—"He's got nice biceps" was the best thing she'd ever said about him—and Boris, whose tastes in women ranged from young Puerto Rican mothers to fifty-year-old ex-ballerinas, dismissed Fran as "too crazy" whenever Moss asked him if he found her attractive. If Moss was disappointed that two people he cared about didn't particularly care for each other, he was glad, at least, that he could bring them together without having to worry about complications.

"I just saw a terrible movie," said Boris, and named a title Moss hadn't heard of but that Boris assured him had been breathlessly hailed by the critics. "Awful script, awful performances—a complete waste of time." Whenever someone loved something—a movie, a book, a person—Boris took it as an attack on himself. "How does this crap get made?" he demanded, but no one had an answer and Boris's face crimsoned a little as his ardor reverberated in the silence. When his scotch arrived a moment later, he cupped it gratefully in his hands. "Anyway, don't bother."

"Speaking of hatchet jobs," said Fran, "did you read Moss's review in *Eat?*"

"You saw that?" said Moss, surprised that Fran followed his work that closely.

"There was a copy at my shrink's," Fran said. "You really stuck it to that place."

"It was a fair review," said Boris. "The food was crap and the service was nonexistent."

"Exactly," said Moss, glancing at Boris. "We even saw a roach."

"I just feel bad for the owner," said Fran. "He probably put his whole life into that restaurant."

"Maybe he'll take revenge," Moss said lightly, wanting to be reassured that the idea was as comical as he hoped to suggest.

"Revenge?" said Boris, eyeing the waitress as she passed. "You mean like put out a hit on you?"

"I'm sure it's happened," said Fran. "Restaurant owners can be real thugs. Believe me, I've worked for enough of them."

"It's funny," said Moss. "Because I've been getting these crank calls."

Boris looked at him. "You mean in connection with the review?"

"What do they say?" said Fran.

"They don't say anything." Moss regretted bringing it up, yet he kept going. "The last time, they just stayed on the line, in perfect silence."

"Did you check for the number?" said Boris.

"It was blocked," said Moss. He finished off his beer.

"It's probably nothing," said Fran. "Things seem worse when you're not sleeping."

"You're not sleeping?" said Boris.

"He needs a woman," Fran said.

"It's a noise issue," said Moss.

"He had a woman," said Fran.

"Right," said Boris. "The nurse. She worked nights. That's why I never met her."

"She was nice," said Fran.

"She's not dead," said Moss. "I just need to get her off my mind."

"I wish I knew someone," said Fran, all of whose friends were male.

"I should probably just marry her," said Moss, "and get it over with."

"Why not just castrate yourself?" said Boris. "That's what marriage is, essentially."

"That's ridiculous," said Fran, whose war against conformity ended mysteriously at the marriage question. "Not every marriage is like that."

"No, not every," said Boris. He turned to Moss. "What kind of noise?"

Moss looked heavenward. "Pigeons."

"Pigeons." Boris nodded. "Have you tried earplugs?"

"Of course I've tried earplugs," Moss said. "I'm not an idiot."

"You should try sleeping pills," said Fran. "They always work for me."

"Maybe I'll take a whole bottle," said Moss. "That'll solve everything."

"Don't say things like that, Moss," Fran said, looking strangely concerned. "Not even in jest."

AS MOSS WALKED home, he noticed the people on the street. Every few paces he looked back to make sure he wasn't being followed. He considered calling Nik Cattai, to try to smooth things over, but it was too late for apologies. The damage had been done. Better to call Danielle; she'd tell him he was overreacting, being paranoid, which was exactly what he needed to hear. She knew him. But he couldn't call her. They'd agreed to suspend all communication for a month (so far it had been three days), and then see how they felt. Moss had sworn himself to the bargain; refraining from contact was the best, most humane thing he could do for Danielle. And frankly, he was surprised she hadn't called him. What did it mean? Moss wasn't sure what was worse—the idea of her having met someone (a doctor?), or her sitting alone all night in front of the TV, puffy-eyed, eating chocolate. *God, Moss. You really ruined her.* And how she'd cried, that day he'd made it final ("You should be with some-one who can give you what you want," he'd told her, meaning a baby, and though she insisted that it wasn't *that* important, that she still "had time," Moss shook his head, as if to say that they both knew better); how he'd held her, kissed her, stroked her hair, how he'd promised her that everything would be okay!

Moss had his keys in his fist as he reached the door to his building. No one had followed him. He went inside. It was almost two A.M. and people were still awake—Moss heard a muted dance beat coming from upstairs, and the clack of mah-jongg tiles from the Chinese people at the back.

The stairwell was covered with old footprints and cigarette butts. Moss went up to the third floor.

He opened the door to his apartment and turned on the light. Inside it was quiet; the pigeons wouldn't start trouble for another three hours. Moss went to the phone to see if anyone had left a message. No one had.

He picked up the phone, thinking how easy it would be to shatter the wall that he and Danielle had put up. And why shouldn't he? All he wanted was contact. The world wouldn't end. Sure, it'd be a moment of weakness. So what? He was weak. He steeled himself and dialed her number.

She answered on the first ring.

"Hi," said Moss. His voice was low, infinitely remorseful.

"Hi," said Danielle. She sounded as if she were peering around a corner.

"I guess you're not working tonight."

"Moss. You promised you wouldn't call."

"I know. I'm sorry."

"You can't do this."

"I know. You're right." Moss shuddered; nothing could soothe him as completely as the miracle of her voice. She was there; salvation was still possible.

"I have to go, Moss," she said throatily. Moss's heart dropped: she was suffering, she was in pain, and Moss, horrified, lashed out at that pain, which he felt as his own.

"Why does it have to be like this?" he said.

"It's how you wanted it, Moss."

"No, I didn't."

"Yes, you did."

"Have you met anyone yet?"

"That's none of your business."

"It *is* my business," said Moss, noting that Danielle seemed to have rebounded some. "I love you."

"You're not ready to love, Moss."

"What the hell does that mean?"

Danielle sighed like the older woman that she was, intimating that she'd given the topic a lot of thought, but hadn't planned on talking about it, at least not with him.

"You're young," she said. "I wasn't ready to love, either, at your age. I thought I was. But now I realize how little I knew. Three years ago I didn't know anything. Maybe that's how it is with you. And that's okay, Moss. It's normal. It's life."

Moss had never heard her so sure of herself, so serenely philosophical. It alarmed him.

"You've met someone," Moss said. It was all he could think of.

"It's late, Moss."

"Did you?" said Moss, reasonably sure that she hadn't, but inclined to skepticism, and aware, too, of how nicely his vulnerability was reducing Danielle's sense of her own victimization.

"Moss. I have to go."

"And since when is twenty-seven too young to love?"

"It's not the age, Moss. It's you."

"You just say that because I'm not ready to have a baby."

"It's not just that."

"What else, then?"

"I don't know—you're damaged or something."

Moss took heart: by ascribing his shortcomings to some emotional handicap, she had absolved him of any moral failing.

"I'm not *damaged,*" he said, having to put up some argument, since if he agreed with her he'd appear to be taking the easy way out. Conveniently, a denial did nothing to disprove the charge.

"I don't have time to discuss your problems," said Danielle. "It's always about you. That's why it's better for me to get out of this."

"That's a lie," said Moss, who was never so defensive as when he was accused of selfishness. The record would show that he'd spent far more time and energy on her problems than she'd spent on his. But he knew he couldn't convince her of this without making her feel even more self-conscious and unstable than she already did. And so they lapsed, as they often had of late, into a long, agonizing silence, confronting—or rather, refusing to confront—the unendurable fact of *the end.* Moss had expected that they'd have gotten beyond these paralyzing struggles, which, draining as they were, stood nonetheless as a refuge from the risks of language, a place to rest, breathe, wait. Usually it was Moss who rescued them by offering some shred of hope or reason ("Look, we can work this out"); and he could feel, each time, Danielle yielding to that semblance of authority, pretending, just as she hated herself for always doing: *I'm sick of pretending that everything's okay, Moss, when it's not. I'm sick of it!*

Finally, she gathered herself and said, "I've got to go to sleep, Moss. Okay?"

Moss was grateful to her for having assumed command over the situation, and did not want to spoil the effect by drawing things out further.

"Okay," he said. "We'll continue this later. Okay?"

"Don't call me."

"Okay."

After another several minutes of hairsplitting negotiations over who would hang up first—during which much of Danielle's newfound supremacy was squandered—Moss's impatience leapt up from him: "This is just *stupid*!" he yelled, thinking that when *she* said things like that, it was okay, but when he did, it was like bringing a hammer down on her head. Her final "'Bye" came out like a meek apology, and when Moss hung up he felt worse for her than before. Didn't he understand that he could never, ever win?

He went to the kitchen and warmed some milk in a saucepan, half expecting the phone to ring. It didn't, and it followed that every sound he made seemed amplified, significant: the tick of the stove, the poof of the flame, the clank of the pan, the squeal of the cupboard door. He recalled performing this ritual alone at night as a child (his mother out at a gig), and imagining—no, feeling, *believing*—that he was being watched by God, that his every sound was being registered in Heaven like a string of prayers. And while Nina Messinger could hardly be said to have indoctrinated her only child, it was possible that her oft-told joke about Moss being the fruit of an immaculate conception might have led in some way to these spasms of piety: Moss at nine and ten was convinced that God was watching over him, so that even as a teenager, late at night, choked with ineffable longings, he would address God aloud, saying, with great humility, "I love you, God. I may not always say it, I may do bad things, but I want you to know that I love you and believe in you, and always will." These confessions stopped around the time his mother left—he was nineteen then.

He sat at the kitchen table in the stark light and held the cup of milk like a chalice in his hands, blew gently across the surface, then closed his eyes and sipped.

3

ANTON STOOD HUNCHED OVER THE MAHOGANY SHOULDER of his bass, his head like a cold sun setting, strands of grizzled hair falling over his tightly shut eyes. One hand fingered the long neck, the other stroked lower down, bringing growls from the hollow womb. His thin blue lips mumbled a secret language, copper eyebrows twitched and hopped. Only a few of the tables were occupied, but Anton, much to Nina's admiration, played with no less feeling than had they been performing for Hollywood royalty. With the solemn attentiveness of a chamberlain, he'd accompanied her for the past five years, sensitive to each note she played, pushing here, pulling there, stepping dutifully aside as she passed.

They were supposed to leave Tuesday for Cabo San Lucas to celebrate their first wedding anniversary, but in light of this morning's developments, the trip would have to be postponed, and Nina's mind, as she played, was focused on how to break the news to Anton. Mexico had been *his* idea; he'd brought it up in bed one morning, while Nina was half asleep and would have agreed to anything. Like a child, Anton exploited her moments of weakness, and like a mother, she let him do it. He made the arrangements while she was still in bed; in a dream she heard him book the flight. If he wanted to make such a big deal out of it—Nina had already told him that she'd be fine with a nice dinner at home—if he wanted to draw attention to their moribund sex life by creating such obvious expectations, then he must accept the risks. Sex had never been the point anyway. The point was security. Spiritual calm. Having a kid at seventeen had screwed up everything for Nina, and she'd been trying to put things right ever since. It wasn't easy. She had shamed her family, lost her freedom, killed her own future. She was *tainted* (her mother's word), and in an effort to obliterate the stain, had tried to negate herself through the very act that had gotten her into this mess, losing herself in sex with anyone she could. But when she finally woke up one morning and decided she wanted something more from a man, she was destined to learn what she had already feared, which was that a small child was not exactly an enticement to marriage. After a depressing series of Moss-centered rejections, Nina gave up on love and threw herself entirely into her music, and didn't come up for air until Moss reached adulthood; at which point she packed her bags and took off for Europe, to fulfill a lifelong dream that circumstances had denied her. And if she didn't exactly conquer the world, as she hoped she might, she at least got to see a bit of it. She played clubs from Milan to Berlin to Copenhagen, recorded a mix of standards and novelties for a small German label, met famous expatriates whose records she'd listened to as a kid, and lived pretty much like a gypsy, sometimes literally playing for her meals or a place to sleep. One night, at a club in Göteborg, Sweden, she met a tall, reserved American who came to the town every couple of years to drink aquavit at his grandmother's grave and play jazz with the locals. With his long gray-gold hair, he rode his bass like a warrior, a Viking Jesus. After the set, Nina introduced herself to him, and they had drinks at the bar, where he recounted his years on the American road, wheeling his instrument across the decks of riverboats or down the piss-stinking steps of subway stations, into the elevators of posh waterfront hotels and through the dim wood-paneled lounges of Holiday Inns, where there lurked in perverse anonymity some of the best players alive, soft-spoken men who had drifted, faded and resurfaced as quietly as exiled mullahs, now living out their musical lives in the dead zones off lonely interstates. He had no wife, no kids. When the place cleared out, Nina went over to the scarred piano and played one of her own arrangements as he watched her from the bar. She dared to look back at him. He didn't blink, didn't smile. Later, they went back to Nina's hotel room, and the following morning Nina convinced him—he was an agreeable, easygoing type, like every bassist she'd known—to stay in Europe for a while and play music with her (he was living at a friend's "guesthouse" in Long Beach, California, and had no serious obligations). And so they gigged their way south for half a year and ended up in Barcelona, where they got a steady job at the Harlem Jazz Club, playing four nights a week, and then Sundays at Le Meridien. After several days in a cramped pensione, they moved into a sunny high-ceilinged apartment that floated above a steep, narrow street in Gracia: calm by day, with ghosts of blue sea and white mountain wavering in the open windows, siesta breezes passing lightly over their faces, and an overlapping clang of church bells that reached them through the gauze of their sleep like voices in the next room; and later, outside, the buzz of the evening crowds, the *cerveza* crowds, and kids launching firecrackers in the square. Together they'd cook an early dinner of fish and vegetables bought fresh that day from the market, and then, afterward, prepare for another night: Anton smoking dope and packing his fiddle, and Nina, in a red dress, frowning in the mirror, fluffing her dark curls.

One morning, as Anton slept, Nina looked around their bedroom and noticed how their clothes were jumbled on the floor. Boots, jeans, socks, shoes—everything tangled together, a poem, unexpected and real.

Eventually they had to go to the States to pick up Anton's things from the guesthouse (it turned out to be a small converted garage, crammed with old LPs and sci-fi novels and books on conspiracies and unexplained phenomena), since the owner was moving out, and it was on the marathon flight to L.A. that Nina suggested they get married. They'd tossed the idea around before, not too seriously— Anton had been through it once—but now that they were coming home, perhaps for good, Nina felt a panic, a sense of incompleteness, as if she'd left something behind and was now exposed, unprotected.

"Baby," she said, throwing her arms around Anton's neck. "Let's get married. Just to see."

He looked at her. "Yeah?"

"I want to take care of you." Nina felt the truth of this and it surprised her. "You take such good care of me."

Anton's pale eyes grew moist, and he took Nina's face in his cold hands and kissed her devoutly on her forehead.

They were married a month later at sunrise on the beach near Carmel by a friend of Anton's who was an ordained minister of the Universal Life Church—it was just the bride and groom, and the sandal-wearing minister, and a few large honking gulls—and after putting a down payment on a small condo in Santa Monica (Anton had some inheritance money put away, and wanted to stay in California), they threw a party, where Nina was introduced to twenty of Anton's friends and relatives. Nina had urged Moss to come out—had offered to pay his way—but he invoked (conveniently, Nina felt) his flying phobia, which was as good as saying he would *never* visit; and though his tone was one of regret and apology, Nina heard behind it the desire to punish her for having sprung the news on him after the fact (she'd seen no need to tell him beforehand; she should have been able to call him and say, "Guess what, baby? I got married," and have him be happy for her); and so she'd had to face Anton's people alone, and make excuses for her son's absence.

And now, a year later, she was settled into a regular gig with Anton in the lounge of the Beverly-Bonaventure. It was a grand old hotel, prewar, with marble floors and a waterfall in the lobby. Usually it was quiet and uneventful in the lounge, but every so often you saw a celebrity.

. . .

OVER ANOTHER STUMBLING chorus of "Embraceable You," Nina wondered what Anton would say. Maybe he'd tell her she was overreacting. She herself had been inclined, at first, to dismiss Fran's e-mail, received that morning as she ate her breakfast, as an overreaction, on the grounds that its author, the last time Nina had seen her, had had pink hair and a safety pin going through her face. Nonetheless, Nina was struck by the effort Fran had taken to locate and contact her without Moss's knowledge, which gave her account of his condition a chilling veracity:

HE IS HIGHLY DISTRESSED BY HIS BREAKUP WITH HIS GIRLFRIEND AND BY SOME PIGEONS THAT HAVE BEEN FLOCKING IN HIS AIR SHAFT. ALSO, HE THINKS A RESTAURANT OWNER IS STALKING HIM IN REVENGE FOR A NEGATIVE REVIEW HE WROTE IN A MAGAZINE. PERSONALLY I THINK HE'S HEADED FOR A BREAKDOWN. ANYWAY, I THOUGHT YOU SHOULD KNOW. BUT IF YOU TALK TO HIM, PLEASE, PLEASE DON'T TELL HIM I WROTE TO YOU. HE'D KILL ME. OKAY?

Nina had read the message several times, trying to make sense of it. Breakups? Breakdowns? Pigeons? Restaurant owners?

She had decided to step out onto the balcony (she'd heard Anton coughing upstairs in the bedroom) and call Moss, to feel him out. It would be just before noon in New York.

The balcony faced east, and on a clear day you could see the downtown skyscrapers and the snowcapped peaks beyond. Day and night, helicopters buzzed across the basin, dipping into the brownish haze that loafed over the molten flow of the freeways. And yet the sky overhead was a heavenly blue, the sun was warm and loving, and pink and white flowers blazed from boxes on every veranda. Nina liked to characterize herself as a cranky New Yorker in exile, but in truth she'd developed a real affection for the place: the relentless blue skies and ornamental palms and pink stucco and the turquoise leather of the ocean reminded her, as it was meant to, of the Mediterranean coast.

She closed the sliding glass door behind her and dialed Moss's number. Someone picked up on the third ring, but said nothing.

"Moss? Is that you, sweetie?"

"Who's this?" came Moss's voice. He sounded wary, though that wasn't unusual for him.

"It's Mom. Can you hear me?"

"Mom," Moss said, with noticeable relief. "Are you okay?"

"I'm fine," said Nina, alerted by his question to a shiny buoyancy in her voice, like a toy in a bathtub that won't stay down. "And you?"

"Me? I'm all right."

"Were you sleeping?"

Moss sighed. "I know you think I sleep all day because I don't have a regular job, but in fact, I was wide awake."

"I don't think anything," said Nina. "I just worry about you. What if something happens? With a regular job you'd have benefits."

"There are no jobs," said Moss. "And I have no skills. And work is slavery. Do you know what my girlfriend called me? A prince. In the pejorative sense. I took it as a compliment."

"Moss—"

"A prince. My coat has holes. I eat peanut butter and rice. I've tried to sell my bodily fluids. Now I'm writing restaurant reviews for a food magazine. The layperson's view. Free meals. I take what I can get."

"I'm not attacking you, Moss," Nina said. "I just worry."

"Don't," said Moss. "I'm a survivor."

"What if you get sick, or get hurt, and you need care? How will you pay for it?"

"You know, if you keep thinking something's going to happen to me, it probably will."

"That's not the point."

"Maybe I'll move to Canada. Or Sweden. Don't they have free health care?"

"Is everything okay, Moss?"

"Not really."

"Do you want to talk about it?"

"Not now. I have to eat my sandwich."

Nina could hear that he really did want to talk, but not on the phone, not from three thousand miles away; and knew, instinctively, that she must see him, tend to him, because who else would? He was a grown man, true, but he was still in many ways a child, and she was still his mother. Before she knew quite what she was doing, she said, "The reason I'm calling is that I'm coming to New York for a few days."

"When?" said Moss, his voice rising. "Why?"

"An old friend called and asked me to play on a recording session," Nina improvised, not sure where she was going with this. "I thought it might be fun—and I'd get to see you."

"What about your trip to Mexico?" said Moss, pouncing on the thing she'd pretended wasn't there. "Your anniversary?"

"Oh, that," Nina said fumblingly, not even remembering having told him about it (she must have mentioned it in their last conversation, weeks ago), and imagining that his lightning recall of what for him must have been a minor detail was somehow tied to his broader disturbance; and it was her sense of this hollow-eyed lucidity, this epileptic discernment, that made her further explanation, called up from the depths, seem all the more daring: "Anton and I," she said, "had a little fight," already regretting the "little" for its smell of condescension, "and we agreed that we could stand a few days away from each other," aware too of the compounding diminutive of "a few" and how the whole thing must have translated to Moss as a full-scale marital crisis—and thinking, in her own defense, that it had been necessary to distract Moss as best she could from the *real* reason for her coming.

"Sounds pretty grim," Moss said with sober reverence.

"It'll be fine," Nina said. She knew how susceptible he was to her moods; or at least he had been, when he was small. "In general we're very happy together."

Moss said nothing.

Nina couldn't interpret his silence. She knew he thought she was being less than honest with him, but in which direction? Did he think she was making the whole thing up, or downplaying something more serious?

Moss said, "Are there lots of pigeons where you are?"

"Pigeons?" said Nina, remembering the word from Fran's e-mail. "Sure. We've got pigeons. Not like in New York, though."

"I would like them all to die."

Through the glass doors Nina saw Anton, already stoned, enter the kitchen in his yellow jogging shorts and orange headband, to start the coffee. He used to be an avid runner, but his knees were shot, and now he wore the outfit with the dopey nostalgia of an old soldier in his uniform.

She said, "I've got to go, sweetie. But I'll call you soon and let you know when I'm coming in."

"Are you staying *here*? In the apartment?"

"Where else?"

"Just checking," Moss said. He didn't sound disappointed.

When Nina hung up she stayed on the balcony for a moment, wary of Anton. She decided to tell him later, after their gig, over drinks at the hotel bar. He was always pretty mellow at the end of a night.

"WHAT'S ON YOUR mind?" said Anton, tapping his fingers on his beer bottle.

They had been sitting in silence for five minutes. The lounge was almost empty.

Nina sipped her bourbon and soda. "It's my son," she said, and was struck by the intimate sound of that, and the formality of it with regard to Anton.

"Your 'son'?" Anton said. "You mean Moss?"

Nina blushed: *Moss.* She'd given him that name, a bastardization of the "Moses" she'd originally conceived, thinking she might float him, figuratively, up the Hudson, toward the shores of Riverside Park, where he would be found by a barren princess of the Upper West Side, but in deciding to keep him had dropped the "e," and to the extent that to name one's child was to invent him (what a thrill it was, watching him write his name, lovingly tracing the lines of his identity: what a strange and powerful thing to give), and that he had ended up, all these years later, broke, uninsured, and possibly nuts, she might wish to avoid the association. Yet referring to him as "my son" felt more carnal, there was blood in it, and flesh, and bone—it was, she knew, deeper than any name.

"Yes, I mean Moss," she said. She paused, wondering how to phrase it. "Apparently he's having some kind of breakdown."

"'Apparently'?" said Anton. "What do you mean?"

Nina set down her glass and recounted the key points in Fran's e-mail, and her subsequent conversation with Moss, theorizing that he was depressed over his breakup.

Anton listened with his usual subtlety and patience, then nodded thoughtfully (he never nodded while you spoke) and took a long pull on his bottle.

"People break up," he said. "It happens. I went through a divorce at his age. He'll be all right."

"He's not you," Nina said. "Things don't roll off his back."

"Why are you getting mad?"

"I'm not mad. It's just that he's my son, and he's suffering." The emotion in her voice surprised both of them, but Nina felt righteous now. Anton had gotten too comfortable with her distance from Moss and he ought to know that a mother still had responsibilities. "I've decided to go see him."

"Sure," said Anton, humbled by this force in her, which he had never felt.

"I know we have plans," Nina said, more gently now, "but I can't just fly off to Mexico and leave him like that."

Anton nodded, absorbing the blow, trying to see her point.

"You know best," he said. "If he needs you, you should go."

Nina could see that he wasn't just placating her; he was facing facts, appreciating, for the first time, the true dimensions of what he'd signed on to: they might end up having a child after all.

"I wish you'd come with me," Nina said, as though it were assumed he wouldn't. As with a woman with two lovers, her choosing of one induced sympathy for the other.

Anton sensed this, but to dignify himself, he treated her statement as a sincere invitation, which for generous reasons he couldn't accept.

"Sounds like the kid has enough on his mind," he said. "This probably isn't the best time for him to meet me."

Nina heard a trace of self-pity there, and to ease her guilt chose to hear his words as a rejection of her offer.

"Maybe it *is* the best time," she said, fostering a notion that

Anton had no interest in meeting Moss. "Maybe it would help him, seeing you. You know? Maybe that's part of what's bothering him. It's not normal, that you two haven't met."

"I doubt," said Anton, "that his problems have anything to do with me."

Nina saw, to her surprise, that Anton thought she was indulging him, trying to make him feel needed rather than responsible; and this was such a startling sign of his insecurity—of his sense that Moss was the indifferent one—that Nina moved instinctively to his defense.

"It's true, baby," she said, grabbing his arm. "He asks about you."

"That doesn't mean he likes me. After all, I'm the one who took you away from him."

"If that's true, then he probably thinks you did him a favor."

"Unlikely," said Anton. "You were already separated for a long time. I'm sure he misses the hell out of you."

"We'll see," said Nina, taking heart in the suggestion that Moss, in missing her, might be more forgiving of her neglect, if that's what it was, than she might have hoped.

"How long do you think you'll be, then?"

"Not long." Nina's voice was suffused with the humility of the victor. "Just long enough to make sure he's okay." She looked at Anton. "A few days at the most."

But she had her doubts. How would Moss react to her? How erratic was he?

"I just hope," she said, "that he's not dead by the time I get there."

"Did he say something about hurting himself?" said Anton, his formless anger seizing on the idea that Nina had withheld crucial information.

"I was *kidding,*" Nina said.

"But you think it's possible," said Anton. If she was going to miss their anniversary, he seemed to be saying, then the reason had better be as dire as that. "You're worried about him."

"I am," Nina said quietly, and realized that it was truer than she'd known.

4

MOSS WAS DOZING ON THE COUCH WHEN HE HEARD THE jangle of his mother's keys in the hall. He sat up, not sure whether to go to the door and open it for her or feign sleep to give himself extra time to decide how to act. He didn't believe her story about a studio date with a friend. She was here because her marriage was falling apart.

He decided to get up and let her in, but as he reached for the door, it came toward him, causing him to step back, so that his first live contact with his mother since her marriage took the form of a startled encounter: her eyes flashed with fear before she saw that the thin, bushy-haired man standing before her in his boxers and a T-shirt was in fact her adult son.

"I didn't think you'd be home," she said, as if to explain her initial reaction to him. She wore jeans, black boots and a leather bomber jacket, and her curls were wild and bountiful, as if they were excited to see him. As a child, he loved to pull them and watch them spring back. Nina loved it too. She never wanted him to stop.

"Hi," Moss said, his voice clotted with the veneration he always felt at seeing his mother after a long interval. She always looked beautiful and powerful, which was how he needed her to be. He did not want her to get old.

"Hi, baby," she said, smiling now. She had a sunny California glow that made Moss aware of something gray and unhealthful about himself, and also about the apartment, which formed the backdrop to him, a commentary on his appearance. He'd swept and mopped and scrubbed and wiped, but nothing could erase the *sameness* of the place, which had barely changed since Nina had lived there. He wished he'd gotten rid of everything and started over. He wished one of his plays was up at a theater, and not in a folder in his drawer. Should he let her read one, then? But no: all the plays needed work, and he did not want to embarrass himself. Nina's opinions meant everything to him, and often he felt that if he ever met with her complete approval he'd have nothing left to live for.

He moved toward her as she set down her suitcase, knowing that their embrace would be what he made it, that all he had to do was show her how much he wanted from her, and that she would give accordingly. He bent slightly and kissed her left cheek, hesitated over whether to kiss her right cheek, then did that, causing laughter to spill between them, affirming their awkwardness and obliging them to fall clumsily into a giggling embrace, in whose sleeves they snuffed their incompetence and communicated their love without having to face each other.

"How was your flight?" Moss said into her neck.

"Long," said Nina, separating from him.

They looked boldly into each other's eyes, assured for the moment by the lingering vibrations of their contact.

"Your hair," said Nina. She reached up to touch it, frowning. "You'll let me trim it later. You look like a tree."

"I like trees," said Moss.

"So do birds—you should be careful."

"Speaking of birds. Pigeons have invaded the air shaft."

"You mentioned that on the phone," said Nina. "Did you call Mrs. Bulina?"

"Why would she do anything? She only wants to get rid of us. Do you know what she could get for this place?"

"If she really wanted money, she'd sell the building."

"Maybe," said Moss. He admired his mother's logic, so lacking in himself, but he didn't always trust it.

He picked up her suitcase and they headed to her bedroom, which was opposite his, away from the air shaft. Moss could have slept there, to escape the pigeons, but certain events from the past precluded that. The first had occurred when he was three or four. He was lying in his bed; the room was dark; the door was closed because his mother, after kissing his head, had shut it on her way out, which she did only rarely, leading Moss to make harebrained connections between her closing of the door and the strange rhythmic noises that invariably followed. Soft cries, and the squeal of bedsprings, which also sounded animalistic. This time he heard two male voices, and Moss, as he lay there in Spider-Man pajamas, imagined that one of them was their neighbor Jack, who had dark, slicked-back hair and long sideburns and wore black jeans and boots, who chatted and laughed with his mother when they bumped into each other on the stairs or on the street, and who would crouch in front of Moss in an easy cowboy way and touch his cheek with the nicotine knuckles of a scuffed fist and call him "Stirling Moss," with what Moss was too young to appreciate as an English accent, but whose inflections of camaraderie pleased him and enlarged his sense of the world. He had felt the attraction between Jack and his mother, and some of that energy reached him now under the covers. He got out of the bed, and had to go on tiptoe to grasp the gold hunk of doorknob and turn it with both hands to let himself out, the noises growing louder, until it seemed they were occurring inside his head. He stood in the dark, narrow hallway and faced his mother's door, noticing that it wasn't closed all the way. Softly he pushed it open. In the darkness he saw figures moving on the bed. The bed itself seemed alive. There were arms and legs and heads. Moss did not understand what the people were doing to one another. But whatever it was, there was probably a reason it was being done in darkness and at a secret hour. He covered his ears, feeling that he was not supposed to be witnessing this, but that he'd been led to it by some invisible hand and was allowed, by virtue of his red and blue pajamas, to be there under laws of his own. A bar of streetlight slanted through the window, so that Moss could see the dark outlines of his mother, who was lying on her back with her legs spread and a man on top of her. Moss thought she was being hurt in some way, yet he knew it was by choice, and so he did not fear for her safety. She was doing this because this was what she did—*that* was the discovery: she had this other life. A second man was kissing her breast; his face came into the light, and Moss saw that it was Jack. Moss opened his mouth. Did this mean Jack was his father? What was he doing here, without clothes? Jack then saw him. Moss stared. Jack's eyes looked funny, rolling back like he'd been hit in the head. Then, with his finger, he made a slow slashing motion across his throat. Moss took it as a signal to disappear and never say a word. He and Jack had a secret, then. Moss backed out of the doorway and padded back to his room, feeling less omnipotent and certainly less stealthy than a good superhero should, yet privileged with new knowledge that was beyond him but that would, he sensed, strengthen him against his enemies. He crawled into his bed and tried to listen for the sounds of his mother's pleasure—he understood it as pleasure, a dangerous pleasure that he himself could never give her. Something had been lost.

When Moss was fourteen, and deemed old enough to take care of himself, Nina began staying out all night, so that Moss would go to bed without the comfort of knowing for sure if she would be there when he awoke. She always was—up early, on four hours of sleep, sometimes less, packing his lunch for school (more from a fear of what he'd do to the kitchen than from motherly devotion, but still, he loved the way she made a sandwich, two neat triangles, and the stuff in between—peanut butter and jelly, tuna salad— flush with the bread, perfect as a slice of pie in a window) and asking if his homework was done; and when he got home from school she would still be there, napping or practicing piano, and before she went out again she would leave him a few dollars to get takeout from China Star or Mamoud's Falafel, and in the morning returned early enough to fill a brown bag with a snugly wrapped sandwich that had the plump pliant weight of a living thing. Moss, then, when he had the place to himself, soon felt impelled to enter his mother's bedroom, wanting only to explore, to open drawers and peek under soft folded fabric, move his hand around in the silky pool of her underwear in hopes of discovering something, money, pot, letters, he didn't know what, but in finding these things, he still wasn't satisfied—there was something else, something he would never find, and one day he lay on her bed and masturbated into the yellow-stained cotton panel of her red panties, imagining that they belonged to a girl from school, and afterward felt empty and ashamed and bitterly free. What could he ever do that was worse than that? What crime? What punishment? And what had made him do it? He had no idea.

When Moss was nineteen, Nina went to Europe. Her plan had been to go away for a year, but one year blurred into the next, and the next, her absence interrupted only by visits that were as brief as they were infrequent. Moss took to using her room for his mastur-batory experiments, wanting to preserve his own room, and indeed the rest of the world, from the corruption that he associated with the act. One night he got drunk with Fran and they began confess-ing their secrets, and after learning that Fran had been molested by her stepfather when she was twelve ("It's not like I was *raped,*" she said, when Moss tried to hug her consolingly), he told her about his mother's room, what he had done there and what he had seen, and Fran told him that he had "serious problems" and should "defi-nitely get some help," which hurt Moss, who felt not only that Fran had betrayed his trust by judging him ("That's *sick*," she said, when he told her about the panties), but that she might have a point; and this idea, that he was a fetishist in need of counseling, a genuine sexual deviant, terrified him into vowing to never enter his mother's room again for any reason, with the belief that someday, through years of such abstinence, his deeds would be erased.

NINA PUT THE suitcase on the bed and began unpacking it, aware of her son flickering in the doorway. She had expected to find the apartment a mess, a reflection of Moss's state of mind, but when she opened the door and saw that everything was in order, it struck her obliquely as vindication.

"So," she said, without looking at him, "how are things with your girlfriend?"

"We broke up," Moss said. "I wrecked her life."

"Moss."

"She's in pain. We both are. It's the worst thing I've ever felt."

"I'm sorry," Nina said, struck afresh by the idea that Moss was old enough to suffer from love.

"She wants to get married and have a baby," Moss said. "*My* baby. She doesn't care if I'm poor. I told her once that even if we *did* get engaged, I could never afford a ring, and you know what she said? She said, 'I'd take a twist tie, Moss.' I'd go to her apartment and she'd open the door and I'd come in and we'd hug each other for the longest time, and I'd see her face in the mirror, and her eyes would be closed and she'd be smiling the purest, sweetest smile you ever saw, like this was all she'd ever wanted out of life." A tear rolled down the side of Moss's nose and onto his lip. "You know what she told me once? That she thanked God for me every day."

Nina had no idea what to do. Should she go over and hold him?

"I feel so responsible for her," he said. "She gave herself to me. She trusted in me. And I let her down. I don't want to let her down."

"I know, baby," said Nina, with an empathy she hadn't been aware of until she heard the rasp of it in her voice. Moss had never confided in her like this; and she couldn't help but feel that his words had been repeated many times, that he had spoken them to any number of people, some of them strangers, and maybe, she thought, this was the only way he could speak to her, with this momentum, this inclusion of her among the many, that it wouldn't feel as personal and threatening to either of them as it might have, had he singled her out.

"But when things were good between us," he said, "we were amazed by what we had. Everywhere we went we saw couples who obviously weren't as in love as we were. Old people on benches would smile at us. It was her beauty that did it. Her light. No one held our happiness against us."

Nina wondered about this amazing, radiant woman who had come to have such power over her son, to the point of making him feel responsible for her life. Her instinct was to hate her, for tormenting her son. But she felt there was more to the story.

"So you're saying it's the marriage issue that's caused this?" she said.

Moss stood inside the door frame, pressing his hands against the sides.

"What if she changed her mind?" Nina said. "What if she dropped her demands? Would you stay with her?"

The words had a physical effect on Moss; he sighed and crouched down slowly, rested his thin arms on his knees. "You're right," he said softly, staring at the floor. "We're not compatible. We're not the same kind of people."

"What do you mean?"

Moss shook his head, as if unsure what he meant, or unwilling to say it. "I want her to have the best of everything. And I can't give her that."

"What she wants is *you*."

"She wants what she calls a 'normal life.' Who does she think I am?"

"Then let her go, Moss. Don't string her along."

Moss looked up at Nina, then stood, as if to better defend himself. "I'm not 'stringing her along.' Give her some credit. We broke up."

"Then she'll move on. And so will you. I know it's hard to see that now. But believe me—you'll both get through this."

"But I don't *want* to get through it," said Moss, with pleading eyes. "If I find out that I can live without her, it'll be like I lost something. My sadness—I don't know who I'd be without it."

"I know, Moss. You just need some time."

"But what if she's right—what if we *should* be together? What if she knows something I don't? What if she knows the truth?"

"*You* know the truth," said Nina. "Don't you?"

Moss shook his head, but not to her question. "The thought of us fading from each other's lives, of dying out forever. It's unbearable to me."

NINA SHOWERED AND put on her jeans and a long-sleeved top. She was too tired to go out—she would do that tomorrow. Besides, it was better to stay with Moss. He shouldn't be alone.

In the living room she pulled out the piano bench as Moss lay on the couch. She'd bought the piano years ago from a dealer on Ludlow Street—a Winter & Company spinet, the best she could afford at the time. It had served her well enough. Her fingers dug in, drawing their nourishment, like the roots of bent trees. When Moss was small, he would sit on the floor doing his homework while she played. Nina loved that: loved the lull into concentration that her playing induced in him, how it calmed and comforted him without his realizing it. Both of them had gained something from the other's presence. Playing for him, Nina could feel that she was spending time with him while cultivating his sensibilities.

She played some chords, melodized with her right hand. Her sound had become more lyrical with age—long, unbroken lines that rose and dipped and slithered over the changes, falling behind them, as if not wanting to be caught. As a teenager, her pursuit had been the crisp, articulate phrase, the fashioning of elegant questions and logical answers blooming into whole coherent paragraphs, and finally into an orderly, self-contained narrative spread over four or five choruses. In those days she'd come into the city and stay out all night at the blowdowns on Avenue A, where she'd wait through the endless sax and trumpet solos of thin, bloodshot black men getting payback for lives of struggle: you had to cut them off if you ever wanted to take your own, and though they usually lowered their heads and abdicated in a fading flurry of notes, there were times they would glare at you and play another chorus. But when it was Nina's turn, they gave her respect, they listened, they nodded, and no one tried to take advantage of her—there was an understanding that came down from the elders in the room. "Her pop's in the Mafia," they'd joke. Actually he was in plumbing supplies, and, having remembered the way his sister played piano as a child, had started Nina on lessons when she was seven. Soon she was playing Bach and Mozart, but she preferred to make up pieces herself. One night when she was thirteen and in bed fooling with her radio, she tuned in to a jazz station playing an up-tempo piano trio number. She'd never heard such a breathless stream of notes, such thrilling syncopations—they grabbed her and held her like an older boy's hands, while someone else's fingers crawled up her leg. The DJ later identified the pianist as Elmo Hope. It was the most exciting thing she'd ever heard, along with Glenn Gould playing the *Goldberg Variations,* and she could hear the Bach in Hope's playing, too. She quit her classical lessons and began studying in the city with Don Feldman, a Bill Evans disciple who taught her jazz harmony. She started attending jam sessions. She watched the badasses enter with instrument cases in hand: they attached reeds, emptied spittle, tightened screws. The scene was drug-free, as far as she could tell— most everyone was in a program of some kind, though not necessarily clean. Nina didn't care. She was there to play, to feel the engine of a rhythm section beneath her, bass and drums, sustaining her. One night, having missed the last train home, she went for pierogies at the all-night Ukrainian, where a guy sitting alone at the next table started talking to her. He was eighteen, with dark wild hair, pink cheeks and a scraggly pubescent beard, and was reading the Book of Ecclesiastes. He said his name was Nebuchadnezzar and that he was heading to the desert, and then maybe to San Francisco to start a comic book. He took her back to a room on Sixth Street, where he was crashing. That was it. By the time she figured out she was pregnant, he had already disappeared.

THE PHONE RANG in the kitchen. Moss opened his eyes and Nina stopped playing: it was after ten, time had passed without their realizing it, the spell of the evening was broken. But before Moss stood up, the next ring failed to sound. Moss froze.

"That's him," he said.

"Who?"

Moss looked at his mother, surprised to have captured her attention from the piano—she always used to ignore him when he tried to talk to her while she played. Quickly then, he told her about the review in *Eat* and the "death threat," as he characterized it, from Nik Cattai. "Since then," he said, "there've been three calls where he doesn't say anything."

"How do you know it's him?"

"He's got motive."

"Oh, don't worry," said Nina, who never conceded the worst

for others, only for herself. "Pretty soon he'll get another review somewhere else, and then he'll obsess about that one for a while, until the next one comes. How bad was this review, exactly?"

"It was fair," Moss said. "My friend Boris—" The phone rang again, and this time Moss went to the kitchen—suddenly it seemed unlikely that Cattai would become manifest in Nina's presence and prove Moss's claims.

Moss picked up on the second ring, hoping, suddenly, that it was Danielle.

"Hello?" he said.

There was a pause on the other end, and then a male voice: "Moss?"

"Who's this?" said Moss, but he already knew.

"It's Anton. Is your mom around?"

"Hey, Anton. Yeah, she's here." Moss had only ever spoken to Anton over the phone, but they had established a friendly rapport based on a mutual understanding that they had nothing to say to each other.

"She said she'd call me when she got in," said Anton, "and I haven't heard from her."

Moss looked up and saw Nina standing a few feet from him with her hand out. She had a guilty look.

"Here she is," Moss said. He handed the phone to his mother, who took it from him without a word.

"Hi, baby," she said into the phone, then walked out of the kitchen and down the hall to her bedroom, her voice trailing apologetically. "I know—I was just about to call you . . ." She shut her door.

Baby. How old was the guy—sixty? Another few years and she'd have to start taking care of him, like a real baby. Did she even realize that?

Moss paced the kitchen floor, waiting for her to come back. Minutes passed.

He went to her door and listened for her voice. He heard nothing.

He knocked hesitantly. "Mom?"

No answer. He turned the knob slowly and opened the door just enough to peek in. She was on the bed, stretched out on her back with her eyes closed and her shoes off and one knee slightly bent. The phone was by her hand.

"Mom."

Nina spoke without opening her eyes. "I just need to sleep for a while," she said in a faraway voice. "Are you going out?"

"Why?" said Moss, not sure if she wanted him to go or stay. "Did you want to get dinner?"

"That's okay," said Nina. "You probably have things to do."

Moss saw that behind this pretense of accommodating him, she really did want to be alone. He knew she was tired and having marital difficulties, but still, it hurt him.

"Is everything okay?" he said. "With Anton?"

"Yes, Moss," she told him. "Everything's okay. Now can you just give me a little peace and quiet, please?"

5

DANIELLE HAD NO STRENGTH TO GET OUT OF BED, MUCH less go to work, but things had reached a point where a twelve-hour overnight in Intensive Care, wiping asses and drawing blood, was more appealing than another night in front of the television. If nothing else, she thought, work would take her mind off her problems. She was wrong. The usual presence of death, far from "putting things in perspective," greeted her with a peculiar vengeance the moment she got off the elevator, when her nurse manager informed her that Bea Sirkin had died. The death came as no surprise; Bea Sirkin was a frail almond-eyed little lady with inoperable cancer who two weeks before had squeezed Danielle's hand and mouthed the words "Kill me"—this sweet, kind, tough old woman, always smiling, always holding your hand, reduced to this indignity, this hopeless appeal for mercy: she had never married, had no children, no family, no one to comfort her but the nurses, and certainly no one to fight to remove her from the ventilator. Instead she was shipped to a nursing home in Queens, where, some-time last night, blind and alone, she passed quietly away. Danielle wanted to cry—really, how else could news of a death affect her if not by reminding her of the death—and it *was* a death, like any other—of her relationship with Moss?

She could only hope there was a Heaven, and not just for the Bea Sirkins of the world. The only trouble with Heaven (or so she'd learned as a girl, attending First Baptist with her mother) was that you couldn't get in by killing yourself. You had to endure. Maybe that was why, unlike her colleagues, who would rather work with unconscious patients so that they could chat with one another across the beds, she preferred the "walkie-talkies"—even the worst com-plainers were good now and then for some word or observation that *did* put things in perspective; and she was aware, too, as she headed down the corridor to the nurses' station, clamps and scissors hitched to her pants, stethoscope around her neck, of how her sadness over Bea Sirkin served handily as a cover for her deeper grief, a grief that showed plainly on her face, as her emotions always did. Because what could she say? That she'd been screwed over, yet again? It was her own stupid fault. She'd gotten too clingy. She couldn't help it. She wanted promises. She wanted a life. Meanwhile, everyone—her colleagues, her mother, her sister—told her she was crazy to stay with a guy who was not only broke and unemployed, but who didn't want the things she wanted. They were right—she saw that now. Why should she expect Moss to change? Was there anything anyone could do to change another person? Especially one as emotionally and morally backward as Moss? More than once she had considered contacting his mother and telling her how her sociopathic son had put her through hell with his refusal to make a decision about the future ("You can't *plan* the future," he once said; "you can't *plan* your life")—clearly he was afraid of serious attachments. Maybe he even hated women and went out of his way to hurt them.

Of course, her worst fear was that he would marry the next woman he met.

No, she did not want to end up alone like Bea Sirkin, but sometimes she thought it might be easier than leaving a loved one behind, or worse, being left behind herself. The widows and widowers. Poor Mrs. Wasserman, married sixty-three years—how would she survive? It was just a week ago that her husband, Sidney, an elegant grouch who was convinced that a band of thieves had sneaked into his room and beaten and robbed him, suddenly became very lucid, as people will in their last hours, and looked into Danielle's eyes and said, with his sweet Yiddish accent, "Thank you, young lady." Danielle smiled down at him and stroked his hand, but when she got home that morning she broke down and cried long and hard, not only for the Wassermans, but for herself, knowing, by the old man's words, what she had long suspected— that the meaning of her life lay in nothing more romantic or interesting or significant than the small unsung comfort she brought to the sick; yet crying, too, from a bitter solace in the knowledge that there *was* meaning.

And it was Moss, more than anyone, who recognized this—

who loved her for what she did, who was proud of her. She would have to try not to think about that.

HE TOOK THE bus up First Avenue and got out at the hospital. He'd made several unannounced visits to Intensive Care, usually after a nasty fight ("Why can't you just *commit* to me?") wherein Danielle left for work in tears and Moss went drinking and then resolved in his drunkenness to go by bus or on foot to the hospital to make peace. And no matter how bad the fight had been, Danielle always lit up at the sight of him, moved that he had poisoned himself for her and then come to her, forlorn and penitent, in the middle of her own difficult night. She was merciful, but so was he. Unless it wasn't mercy, but a way of prolonging the agony. Maybe it didn't matter. Maybe they would just go on like this, and realize, in another three years, that the lives they were so worried about getting right, or at least not getting wrong, had already happened to them. Maybe this was it.

But that was wishful thinking; Moss knew he was living on borrowed time, knew he might already be dead. He'd always believed that someday she would find the strength to resist him.

He entered the building, checked in at the security desk and proceeded to the elevators. Inside the elevator was a sign telling personnel not to discuss patients' cases aloud.

He got off on the fifteenth floor, turned left, and pushed open the imposing double doors of Intensive Care.

A nurse in light-blue scrubs was standing in the middle of the corridor, writing on a clipboard. Moss's facial muscles tensed. Danielle—beautiful, beautiful Danielle! How many times did he picture her like this when he was alone, and smile to himself, and mumble her name, and get tears in his eyes? She was in profile, unaware of him. She wore her hair in a braid—Moss loved watching her braid her hair, the way she separated the three parts with a comb and wove them together, with the slightest tic of impatience that made you realize that her hands had always been her tools, that she did not think of them as objects of beauty, and in fact they were not beautiful, but they performed extraordinary deeds for people and Moss loved them.

She looked up and saw him, and as always there was that flash of disbelief in her eyes, as though she wasn't sure it was him. And then, seeing his condition, his need for her, her eyes filled with a love that forgave him everything. She came to him, her head tilted in concern: he might have been a patient who had slipped from his restraints.

"Moss," she said. "What are you doing here?"

"I miss you," Moss said, and then the tears came. He'd been saved again, spared again, and he knew he didn't deserve it. He held out his arms to her; and though she was on duty, she broke her own rule and hugged him, and Moss could feel, in her touch, the hope he was giving back to her. But it was his hope, too. He hugged her closer, nuzzled her neck, felt the hard bone of her stethoscope between them. As usual, she smelled clean and fresh. How could he live without the smell of her neck?

She withdrew from him and searched his face. "You're drunk," she said, with mock disapproval. In fact she wouldn't have expected anything less. She was raised in a milieu where men drank and got violent to prove their love, and though she didn't expect rage from Moss, the rare times when he did lose his temper and call her a bitch she seemed to like it, as though it confirmed a passion that was in doubt.

Moss wiped his eyes, smiling in wonder and infinite gratitude. "God, your eyes are blue."

"What are you doing here?"

"I've got this pain in my heart." Moss tried to renew the embrace, but this time Danielle was rigid.

"I'm working, Moss. No more hugs."

Moss wouldn't let go. "Hugs."

"Moss. Stand up straight."

Moss obeyed. "I can't stop thinking about you," he said.

Danielle seemed to have an inkling of the risk this posed to her. "You promised you wouldn't do this," she said.

"I think about you every minute," said Moss. "I keep thinking I see you on the street."

"How do you expect me to react to this, Moss?"

"I don't know. You have every right to ask me to leave."

Danielle looked down at the floor.

She said, "I've had the worst night."

"Tell me." Moss touched her arm, his touch saying that he was here for her, that he was back.

"Come with me for a minute," said Danielle, and led Moss through the double doors and into a room around the corner.

The room contained lockers, a coffee station and a long table with folding chairs. Moss sat in one of the chairs while Danielle made coffee and told him about a patient, an antiques dealer in her sixties, a wonderful woman who had been making a dramatic recovery from cancer, and who, earlier in the night, during a routine test, had suffered, from nowhere, a pulmonary embolism, which stopped her oxygen flow and caused her jaw to clench, with her tongue caught between her teeth. Within minutes she was brain-dead, and not even the brilliant and muscular Dr. Schwartz could part her jaws. The tongue, clamped by the teeth, began to fall apart in liver-colored bits, and Danielle had spent a good part of her night picking up the pieces.

Moss knew that his own problems must seem minor in comparison, but he told Danielle about them anyway: the review in *Eat* and Nik Cattai's ensuing threat; the pigeons; his mother's unexpected arrival.

"Your mother?" said Danielle, who hadn't much comment about the other two subjects but sprang to life at this one. She brought the coffee to the table where Moss was sitting. "Where's she staying?"

"With me," said Moss, feeling protective of Nina, even though Danielle had implied nothing against her. He stared into the brown plastic coffee mug. "I think she had a fight with her husband."

"What?"

"A fight," Moss said. "On their one-year anniversary." He was always happy to thrust under her nose an example of a troubled marriage.

"It must have been pretty bad," Danielle said, her shoulders tensing. She began stirring her coffee. "How long is she staying?"

"I'm not sure," said Moss, who had been wondering the same thing. A few days? A week? Forever?

"Maybe," said Danielle, "she'll move back in with you."

Moss heard sarcasm there—the insinuation that living with his mother was appropriate for him.

"I hope not," he said. "I'm used to living alone and I'd like to keep it that way."

"I'm sure you will," said Danielle. "Your whole life."

Moss nodded in appreciation of her wit. "We'll see about that."

"Well," Danielle said. "I know if *I* were getting threats, *I'd* want someone around."

"I guess you'd call them threats," Moss said. "I mean, I feel threatened."

"Oh, sweetie," said Danielle, her eyes getting all worried and sad—he might have been going off to war. "If anything happened to you, I swear, I'd never get over it." She came over and sat on his knee and wrapped her arms around his neck. "Hey," she whispered. "Let's have a quickie."

"What?"

But Danielle was already unbuttoning his pants. Then she stood up and loosened the drawstrings of her scrubs and lowered them along with her thong and gripped the edge of the table and bent over. "Come on," she said. "Hurry."

Moss knew that this was an abiding fantasy of hers—doing it at the hospital, from behind—but he hadn't expected her to act on it.

"What if someone comes in?" he said, getting behind her, caught up drunkenly in her need. He assumed it was hers.

"No one's going to come in," Danielle said. "Just do it—just this once. I've had the worst night."

"This is crazy," said Moss, thinking that in doing this, he was atoning for the things he had never done for her, all her ideas that they had discussed but let fade away, like going to Italy, or taking a bath in the dark with floating candles, or driving up to Boris's house for a long weekend. Danielle would have driven them, since Moss had never gotten a license. She was a great driver. Twice they'd rented a car and driven to the country. Danielle held the wheel in one hand and a Coke in the other, while Moss changed the stations. She wore sunglasses. She cursed at other drivers as she left them in her dust. She liked having Moss as her passenger, in his seat belt. But that was over now. And they had never gone to Italy, or even to the bathtub. Moss could get depressed thinking about the smallness of her dreams; marriage aside, she had only ever asked for so little, and he had given her so much less. I *owe* this to her, he thought as he humped her. Where would he come? In his coffee cup? He then heard—thought he heard—a noise. He stopped moving.

"Moss?" Danielle said, casting a bleary eye over her shoulder. "What's wrong?"

"I'm sorry," Moss said, withdrawing. "I can't do this here. I heard a noise. I keep thinking about that dried-up crumbling tongue." He buttoned his pants.

"You're just a tease," Danielle said sweetly, pulling up her scrubs, evidently pleased by his willingness to have gone as far as he

did, which was, after all, so much farther than he'd gone in a very
long time.

"Sorry," said Moss. "I've been drinking."

Danielle turned to him and put her hands on his shoulders,
looking into his eyes as if trying to cast a spell. "You can sleep at my
place," she said. "No scary phone calls there. No pigeons either. You
still have my keys, don't you?"

HE LET HIMSELF into the building and bumped through the narrow, tilting hallway to the stairwell and grabbed the banister for
support, not so much going up the stairs as hauling them down. So
many times he'd groped his way up these stairs, or down them, or
lingered on a step after leaving her room in a rage, waiting for her
to call for him to come back up.

At the top of the stairs he opened Danielle's door and turned on
the light. The place was a mess: clothes strewn everywhere, fashion
and fitness magazines covering the floor, fudge-stuccoed dishes
scuttled in the sink. That she hadn't warned him about these condi-
tions meant that she had already stopped noticing them. Moss tried
not to read into it.

He shed his coat and shoes and sat on the embroidered white
linen of the bed, reacquainting himself with the room: the Matisse
art posters on the walls (a green and yellow woman with a fruit-
filled hat, a bottle-shaped girl in a yellow dress), the sheer white
curtains and the colossal oak dresser that had cost far too much
(Danielle's tastes were well beyond her means, and when she
bought things she couldn't afford—*nice* things, she called them,

with a tone of resentment aimed at his own low material ambitions—Moss felt it as an attack on his conscience, as though she were forced to acquire a different sort of permanence from the one he denied her, even if it meant ruining herself financially). Moss then noticed that a photograph of himself, which Danielle had kept on her desk, was gone. The absence startled him. Had she torn it up? Burned it? Hidden it away? A sadness filled him as he tried to imagine the poignant ceremony that must have taken place—her looking for the last time at the image of the person to whom she'd given her heart, whose features she'd superimposed upon the faces of her children, and who had failed her. It was worse than if he had died: in death, photographs are brought out and lovingly displayed. Here, they were taken down.

God, why couldn't she just get it together, make some friends, find a passion, and stop depending on him to save her? He found the remote control, aimed it. Television: how she must rely on it these days, he thought. How it must comfort her when she came home to her empty apartment, when she cooked her lonely meals.

Christ.

On the screen, a pack of mangy hyenas was roaming the savannah, all low hindquarters and massive heads, walking slowly with that loathsome gait, moving both legs on one side of the body together. They had fresh blood on their faces.

Moss fell asleep on the bed, and when he opened his eyes hours later, he was under the blankets, another pair of arms enclosing him from behind. Dull afternoon light entered through the curtains; the radiator ticked. Danielle slept. Through the murk of his waking,

Moss recalled her straddling his leg, loosening his buttons with nimble nurse's fingers. He had reached out to her from his sleep, thinking that she was someone else, one of the women he'd leered at or talked to in bars, the faces and asses filed away like baseball cards in his brain. But soon after his pants had been pulled from him, he'd stirred with anticipation, lying there like an anesthetized patient, manacled by surface dreams as Danielle eased herself atop him.

"What are you thinking?" Danielle said presently, divining his wakefulness, since his back was to her and she couldn't see his eyes. There was sorcery in it, Moss believed.

"I'm thinking," Moss said, "that I should call my mother. She has no idea where I am."

"So call."

"Or maybe I'll just head home." Moss then had an idea; he turned to Danielle. "Come with me," he said, not wanting to face Nina alone, and drawing subversive pleasure from the idea of showing up with Danielle after having told his mother about their breakup.

"That's okay," said Danielle, with the false nonchalance she took up when she felt an offer was insincere. "I don't want to intrude. I know you two haven't spent much time together—"

"No, no," said Moss. "It's fine. Seriously. You two should meet."

"What does she know about me?"

"I think she'll be surprised when she doesn't see a halo over your head."

"I'm sure you told her what a bitch I am."

"Never," said Moss, and he kissed her cheek with harsh affection. "I think you're the best person I've ever known."

"Thank you," Danielle said softly. She couldn't meet his eyes.

They showered, got dressed and walked across town, holding hands, the way they used to.

WHEN THEY REACHED Moss's building, Danielle got cold feet.

"I can't go up there like this," she said. "I look so ugly."

"Don't be crazy," said Moss.

"Are you sure?"

"I'm sure."

Moss led the way inside, jingling his keys. He hoped the two women would hit it off. But why wouldn't they?

He opened the door and turned on the light.

"Mom?" he called. No answer. He looked at Danielle. "I guess she's out." He was surprised by his disappointment.

He led the way to his bedroom, where they could lie down for a few minutes. His door was closed: he had shut it before leaving last night, on some impulse of privacy or concealment. Now he opened it, and there was a loud clatter all around his head—he jumped back, and found himself face-to-face with a sight so unearthly that he couldn't move: there were two of them, one resting atop the half-open closet door, the other scratching for purchase above the window, which had been left open just enough to allow them to wander in stupidly from the ledge. Moss covered his mouth. Blobs of greenish slime were splashed everywhere—on the bed, the floor, the blinds, the dresser. The pigeon on the closet door, stunned with pure unthinking fear, leaked more of the stuff—it dribbled thickly down the face of the door and congealed there, a gleaming guacamole.

"Dannie!" Moss yelled. "Danielle!"

Danielle, who had been a few paces behind, now appeared beside him, and in response to that second presence the pigeons beat their wings in terror, then detached themselves from their perches and blew about the room, wailing as their lost feathers swirled in the wind: they crashed at the windows, flapping for their lives, then returned to their original spots and froze, as if they'd never moved.

"Moss!" Danielle said, laughing. "This is awful!"

Moss, stricken, held his nose.

"Get me a broom and a towel," said Danielle, looking from the birds to the windows and rolling up her sleeves.

Moss wanted to fall to her feet. In the most aberrant of circumstances, she kept her head. Moss went to the kitchen to get the supplies. When he returned, the windows were open wide. Danielle took the broom and tried to shoo the birds out, touching off another squall of screams and feathers and knockings against glass. Moss thought the birds might simply die of fright. Instead they collected themselves and landed together atop the frame of the same window, inches from freedom, but too stupid to know it. Their eyes projected nothing: black dots in discs of burnt sienna, insensible. How birds and humans occupied the same planet was beyond Moss. Danielle, who accepted such things at face value, had dragged Moss's desk chair to the window, and was in the act of stepping on it when she remarked that pigeons, for all their faults, were beautiful creatures—

the blue-gray crown, the snowy, black-banded wings, the green and purple iridescence of the neck and the mulberry-colored feet.

"Yes," Moss said. "Now please kill them."

He grabbed the broom. The birds were looking off in different directions, motionless.

"Be careful," Moss said, thinking the creatures might attack. This seemed eminently possible, up till the last second, when Danielle gathered one up in her towel-covered hands and tossed it out the window: it rose and was gone. The second one went quietly too, and all that was left were floating feathers and numerous hardening puddles of spattered birdshit. Moss made a quick inventory of what would have to be destroyed: his comforter, a shirt, the blinds, the towel. Everything else would have to be scrubbed and disinfected by professionals.

"Thank you," Moss said as Danielle came down from the chair. "I think you saved my life."

"I'm so sorry, Moss," Danielle said with real sympathy, knowing what the ordeal must have taken from him. "You can stay at my place tonight, if you want."

DANIELLE WAS AT her desk, checking out million-dollar apartments on the Internet, a hobby of hers. Moss sat on her bed, watching the evening news. Another humdrum day of religious and economic warfare. Moss picked up the phone and called his mother.

"I was hoping it was you," Nina said when Moss identified himself. "Are you at Danielle's?"

"How did you know?"

"The way you were talking about her yesterday, I kind of figured you'd end up seeing her." Nina did not sound disappointed, but there was something pointed in her insight. "Oh, listen," she said. "I'm playing tomorrow night at The Black Rose, with Sam Silvestri. Ten o'clock." Sam Silvestri was an old friend of hers, a jazz guitarist with a pencil-thin mustache who wore Western-style shirts and cowboy boots. "I called him to say hi, and he said his piano player was sick, and would I mind filling in. Anyway, it'd be great if you came."

"Ten o'clock?"

"Bring Danielle. Bring anyone you want."

Moss could not account for Nina's expansiveness (had she reconciled with Anton?), but he was glad for it, and felt it pass into him, even as he told her about the pigeon incident and advised her to keep his door closed so that any toxic dust from the droppings wouldn't drift into the rest of the apartment.

"Everything okay?" Danielle said, after Moss hung up. Her eyes were still on the monitor.

"Are you off tomorrow night?" said Moss.

"Yes. Why?"

"Because my mother's playing and I want you to come."

Danielle turned to him. "I'd love to," she said in a subdued voice, as if taking care not to upset whatever fragile balance had permitted this miracle. Moss decided to invite Boris, and Fran, too, though Fran usually went to bed early on school nights. Danielle didn't object to any additional guests; to her, it meant that Moss wanted to integrate her, it spoke to the long term. And Moss looked forward to showing her off, particularly to Boris. He'd wanted to do that for a long time, but the nature of that friendship, with its fixation on a single topic, coupled with the fear that Boris's charisma and financial success might take more from Moss in Danielle's eyes by comparison than it would lend him by association, had kept him from ever bringing them together.

6

NINA ARRIVED EARLY AT THE CLUB, WEARING A LONG BLACK skirt and tight red top, and feeling a few butterflies. Sam Silvestri was a brilliant musician and a little dictator of a bandleader; nine years ago they'd had a fling, and Nina, who had long since given up on men, had fallen in love with him (Moss was eighteen by then, a lesser liability), or at least, she'd wanted to take care of him—it worried her how he smoked too much and ate nothing but candy bars and pizza. Despite his ratlike features—snouty face, deep lines, ferret eyes, acne scars—women, certain women, found him very attractive sexually. He was encyclopedic about music and built his own guitars (some of which he sold for good money), and had, for whatever it was worth (a lot, actually), the biggest, most well formed penis Nina had ever seen, which helped explain, she thought, his galling confidence in himself—the way he'd sit in front of his TV in his cluttered rent-controlled apartment, staring at the silent screen and noodling on his guitar while you were trying to talk to him, tuning you out, as if between his guitar and his dick he didn't need anyone else. And yet he must have felt threatened by her criticisms and ideas, because he just got meaner and meaner (that he could not dominate her, musically or intellectually, must have been a singular insult to his phallic pride, whose limitations she exposed), until one night she told him to fuck off, and he did just that, stopped calling her and refused to return her calls. When she finally got ahold of him, he apologized for his behavior and said that they would be better off as friends. It was sadder for him than it was for her (so Nina told herself), because it was clear that he would never be able to get along with any woman who wasn't emotionally damaged or not very bright. Soon afterward, Nina decided to go abroad. When she informed Sam of her plans, he became absurdly possessive, pumping her for details, as though her leaving made him feel less fortified somehow, less surrounded by the evidence of the sexual conquests by which he secretly measured his power—the audience for his music wasn't big enough for him not to feel imperiled by hints of revolt or indifference among his female admirers. Nina felt sorry for him and was tempted to stay in the city, but she knew she was only afraid of leaving Moss on his own—afraid he would fall prey to his own carelessness and start a fire, or forget to pay the bills out of the checking account she had set up for him. He had promised her he would be all right, and in fact no serious disasters had occurred. As for Sam, she'd kept in touch with him through the occasional postcard, and last year she wrote him saying she'd gotten married. She never heard back.

She walked past the bar, where the early birds were looking

around hungrily at those just arriving. Her fingers fluttered at the sight, on the bandstand, of the baby grand piano: under its heavy brown blanket it stood stiff and quiet as a sleeping racehorse. She approached it, touched the blanket, slowly pulled it back. Strange pianos still had the power to excite her, connecting her, she supposed, to her youth, when she'd nose them out in department stores, restaurants, people's homes, with the delicious anticipation of becoming, in a moment, the object of everyone's attention: she would go to them, lift their lids, feel their coolness, with a fierce conviction that the piano was *hers,* a neglected animal that had come to feed from her hands.

Sam arrived. In his studded leather jacket, guitar case at his side, he was inevitably himself, just older. Nina met him, smiling, and they embraced. "I haven't seen you since Jesus left Mount Kisco," he said. "You look incredible." When they withdrew, Sam took a pouch of tobacco from his pocket and began rolling a cigarette, which he would have to smoke outside, and for the next two minutes he bitched about the "health fascists" and how democracy breathed its last gasp the day the citizens of New York Fucking City were stripped of their right to smoke in a goddamn bar. Much of his conversation centered on his problems with intrusive government.

Nina then noticed a plain silver band on his finger.

"Are you *married?*" she said.

Sam kept his eyes on the cigarette. "It's a green-card thing."

"Wow," said Nina. She didn't know what to think. "Where's she from?"

"Latvia. The agency sent her over to clean my apartment."

"Is she here?" said Nina, looking around.

Sam shook his head. "She dances at night. She wants to learn bookkeeping." He slid his cigarette into his shirt pocket, kept his eyes averted. "So how are *you* doing?"

Before Nina could answer, the drummer and bassist came over. Sam made introductions. Both guys were young, around Moss's age, with matching goatees. They greeted Nina with a bashfulness that made her feel more old than sexually powerful. She *was* old. Still, she looked forward to playing with them; she so seldom played with anyone besides Anton.

They opened the set with a chart of Sam's that Nina knew from the old days. The audience settled. There were a dozen tables, half of which were filled, and Nina felt herself being noticed, a woman in a man's domain. She had always liked the distinction.

As the bassist and drummer rode and lashed the rhythm, Sam sat bent on a stool, cradling his guitar, just as he did when he was alone. Nina comped sparingly, wanting to stay out of his way, avoid the risk of one of his stinging sidelong looks that you could feel the next morning. She wished Moss would show up. It was still early, but his absence worried her. Where was he? Did he mean not to come? But why? He'd seemed okay on the phone last night, but today she'd missed him—she'd gone out before he got home from Danielle's, and then he went out again before she came back—and now she wondered if they were avoiding each other. Was he mad at her for some reason? What had she done?

Sam ended his solo with a nod of his head, and Nina picked it up. There was applause; Sam nodded again.

Nina looked down at her hands. How strange to think that humans had found this purpose for them, even if it did take two million years. She thought of her hands as independent creatures, the keepers of her true identity, truer than her name, truer than her face. They were smooth, slender, the veins all at the surface, gnarled and complex as a depraved mind. Away from the piano they spidered along tabletops or across her lap, scavenging for the feel of ivory. Nina believed in their secret life. Once, during a high school recital, her brain had shut down in mid-measure of a Bach sinfonia, and she'd experienced the horror of watching her hands play on without her, two headless animals scuttering through the peril of a breathless counterpoint placed before their blindness on the heights of a bluff as narrow as the width of a fingertip, any misstep meaning certain death, the continuation of life strictly dependent on the continuance of the three separate voices, one in the left hand, one in the right, the third allotted to both—so that Nina, having recovered herself enough to relate the sounds she was hearing to her memory of where the notes would lie on the page, had had to stop her mind, freeze it, knowing that all would collapse at the weight of a single thought. Who could say, then, that her hands did not possess their own intelligence? In a moment of high clarity, she had watched them save her.

The melody she'd been building had begun to stray with her thoughts; she'd gone on too long, and so wound things up with some dwindling chords and a nod, then dropped out to give the bassist space in which to announce himself. After a moment she dabbed that space with patches of obscure dissonance, wry and suggestive, but not too much, cautious even, trying to follow him, catch up with him and then anticipate him so that she could be with him when he got there, as she did with Anton. But she could not catch him—he seemed to be not listening, too absorbed in himself, his eyes closed, not deeply like Anton's, but lightly, as though he were more in a relaxed trance than any transforming pain or ecstasy. She decided to abandon him. Slowly, she withdrew her hands.

In her periphery she saw a young couple settle down at a table: it was Moss, with a woman. A striking woman. A fear flashed through Nina's heart, too fast to be known.

Danielle.

Nina took her in. Her beauty had a stately, royal quality, like that of the good princess from a fairy tale—a beauty that ennobled those around her. Moss had never looked so accomplished. Never so like a grown man. This alarmed Nina, or at least startled her; she hadn't been prepared. And there was something troubling, too, about Danielle's appearance; Nina couldn't place it at first, but after a moment she realized that she was looking at a woman who bore no likeness, none whatsoever, to *her;* practically an exact opposite. Some nights, everything felt personal.

Moss put his arm around Danielle and pressed his lips to her cheek; she closed her eyes, smiling blissfully, just the way Moss had described. Nina felt her own presence influencing them. Moss's affection toward Danielle felt excessive, too charged with his need to possess and hold on to something. He was hardly aware of it. He pressed his nose into her neck. Danielle then looked at Nina. Contact. Nina had never seen such wide, clear blue eyes. Eyes acquainted with death, Nina thought. Something to respect. A nurse. Why not a doctor? Nina looked away, thinking that she herself could potentially be this woman's patient, now or years from now. A caregiver for a daughter-in-law. A handler of crises. The thought was not entirely disagreeable.

MOSS HELD DANIELLE's leg under the table as he watched her watching his mother and extrapolating her and Moss's children from the evidence. Their child would be musical, then, and, if a girl, strong, serious, self-possessed. Moss chose not to interfere.

"She's *beautiful*," Danielle said.

"Yeah," said Moss. "She looks good for her age."

Moss felt a hand on his shoulder; he looked up and saw Boris standing beside him. "Hey," Boris said. With Boris's hand on his shoulder and his own hand on Danielle's leg, Moss felt a current run through all three of them.

Danielle gave Boris her hand. "I'm Danielle," she said, establishing hostesslike precedence. "Thanks for coming." This presumption of territory embarrassed Moss to the degree that it seemed to expose Danielle's insecurities, but Boris took it as pure hospitality, or pretended to.

"It's about time we met," Boris said, holding her hand as he spoke. "I was beginning to think you didn't exist."

Danielle laughed and withdrew her hand, so that the two

actions seemed timed. "Sometimes I wonder myself," she said, charmingly effacing, and all at once Moss was proud of her. She was glittering now; her nerves had begun to serve her.

"It's amazing you two haven't met before," said Moss, as if he had nothing to do with the phenomenon. "This is an event."

"I mean, I heard *rumors* of your existence," said Boris, who had not stopped looking at Danielle.

"It's my work schedule," Danielle said, glancing at Moss. "It makes it hard to have a social life."

"Have a seat," Moss said to Boris.

Boris sat next to Moss and looked around wolfishly for any attractive women—there were several—before resting his attention on the musicians. Boris knew that the pianist was Moss's mother, yet he did not look at her, focusing instead on the guitarist. To Moss it felt like an avoidance, a refusal. When Sam was finished with his solo, Boris was the first to clap. Then he stopped clapping—also the first—and turned his head toward Nina. At the same moment, Moss felt Danielle's hand interlock with his, under the table. Everyone was watching Nina. Moss felt that his life was on the line, that he was fully implicated in her performance. Judgment on her was judgment on him. But why should that be? They were separate people. And what could anyone say against her anyhow? Her talent was undeniable, and though some nights were better than others, most people couldn't tell the difference. Now Moss watched as she lowered her grooving head, shaking her curls, her shoulders hunched and her elbows and wrists contorted at unnatural angles:

these gestures seemed excessive to the notes she was actually pro-
ducing. She seemed to be striving too much for the inexpressible;
Moss feared she would lose her audience with her stubbornly ar-
cane phrasing and harmony, which were not without their contempt.

When she was finished, Boris, again, was the first to applaud.
"So that's your mom," he said to Moss, his eye still on her. "She's
amazing."

"You think?" said Moss, wondering if he had missed something, or if Boris had. Regardless, he had, when the night began,
envisioned accepting praise for Nina with pride and modesty;
whereas now he could only weigh it against his own lack of achieve-
ment, which suddenly seemed glaring.

When the set ended, Nina came toward their table, assessing
the two strangers as she approached. Danielle she'd heard about,
but Boris would come as a surprise. Moss held up a signaling hand
to his mother, as if she hadn't already spotted him. When she got
closer—looking more confident than she felt, Moss was sure—he
saw that the outlines of her nipples were showing through her top.

"Mom, this is Danielle," Moss said, jumping too quickly into
introductions, since his bigger fear was waiting too long and then
having the others introduce themselves and make him look bad—it
was like Boris to introduce himself before you had a chance.
"Danielle, Nina."

"It's so nice to meet you," said Danielle, beaming up at Nina. "I
couldn't have enjoyed it more."

"Thank you," Nina said, taking Danielle's hand with a masculine dominance, but also with a reverence, which suited Danielle perfectly—Danielle, who expected to be dominated and worshiped. Seeing them connected in this way, one standing and the other sitting, Moss felt like the child that he was trying so hard not to be, reduced, somehow, by their shared admiration.

Nina turned to Boris, who stood up chivalrously, nearly upending his chair, and catching it behind him with an athletic alertness. "I hesitate to shake that hand," he said, shaking it anyway. "I hope they're insured. That was great."

"Thank you."

"Mom, this is Boris. Boris, my mom."

"Nina," Nina said to Boris, in a way that made Moss feel corrected and thus again like a child.

Danielle squeezed Moss's hand in little nervous bites under the table as she watched Nina and Boris. Boris pulled out the fourth chair for Nina, which was next to his.

"What'll you have?" Boris said.

"Oh, I'm fine," said Nina as she sat. "Sam permits no alcohol. One of his rules."

"How about a Coke?" said Moss.

"Is he recovering?" said Boris.

"No," said Nina, her eyes wandering to the bar, where Sam was talking to a young woman. "He just doesn't drink. It's one of his bizarre idiosyncrasies. Like Hitler's vegetarianism."

Boris laughed.

"Did you want a Coke?" Moss said again to his mother.

"Oh, no thanks."

"So Moss tells me you live in L.A.?" said Boris. "I used to live there."

Moss sank back in his chair as Boris recounted his L.A. years, "working in restaurants and writing screenplays," after which he came back east and "started a company," his usual set-up line, followed by the kicker, "LittleEinsteins.com," which rarely failed to elicit a nod of recognition ("Oh," said Nina, "I think I read something about that"), though in this case, Moss thought, Boris was saying it more for Moss's benefit, as if meaning to show Nina that Moss, whatever his shortcomings, was nonetheless worthy of the friendship of a highly successful entrepreneur. That Boris managed to do this without any apparent condescension toward Moss was marvelous, and he went even further by confessing that his own financial independence had, on the downside, caused him to lose his direction, whereas people around him (he indicated Moss), the truly fortunate, knew just what they wanted in life.

"So—how are these kids turning out?" said Nina. "Does anyone track them?"

"They're a regular little master race," said Boris. "The company gets reports all the time. One six-year-old girl in Virginia just published a graphic novella about her cat."

"Are any of them yours?"

"You mean—am I the father?" Boris dipped into his drink. "I don't know—I don't want to know. I certainly haven't supplied any samples lately. But if anything did come to fruition, then hey, it's one way to affirm the biological imperative without having to give up your life."

As Boris spoke, Moss brought Danielle's hand from under the table and kissed it, wanting to distract her from the topic, which, as Boris must have known, would only stoke her anxieties about having her own baby—she'd even joked before about using LittleEinsteins (which she could never afford) should Moss prove an ultimate disappointment, and now Moss wondered if Boris was in fact trying to help him out by promoting an alternative, however extreme. In his uncertainty Moss kissed Danielle's cheek and neck as Nina laughed at something Boris said; then he touched her face and looked into her eyes, which shifted nervously under his scrutiny. "So, my lovely," he said, suddenly wanting to have the most absorbing conversation of his life, knowing it was impossible with her but feeling viciously entitled, "what do you think?"

"What do I think about what?" said Danielle, smiling helpfully, and Moss saw that she, too, wanted to make an impression on the others, but was relying on Moss to lead them, as she always did.

"About anything," said Moss, thinking that he should have come out with an observation instead of a broad question. He could hear the other voices—Boris was mentioning piano lessons from his childhood—and wanted to leave no gaps of silence on their end. "I always want to hear your thoughts."

"You don't think I *have* any interesting thoughts," Danielle said, with a dawning resentment that changed the quality of her smile. "Maybe that's why you don't want to marry me."

Moss knew she wouldn't make a scene in front of Boris and Nina, but by making even the smallest threat, she revealed the brittleness of the surface. It hurt Moss to think that he had ever made her feel mentally inadequate. The worst he had done was tell her that she didn't express her ideas enough. He'd never said she didn't *have* ideas.

"Don't be crazy," he said. "You know you're amazing."

"I think your mother's amazing," Danielle said, looking covetously at Nina, who could not hear them. "You're lucky."

"I'm lucky," Moss said, "because I have you," and felt a tightening-up in his throat, as often happened when such words came up from him unexpectedly; and Danielle smiled in a way that told him she was thirsty for those words, that he left her thirsting.

"Thank you," she said softly, biting her lip. "I'm lucky, too."

Moss looked at his mother to see if she was getting any of this. Her dark eyes glistened from her contact with Boris, but when she felt Moss's gaze she turned her eyes to him, and Moss knew that she'd been watching him all along: she had never seen him with a woman, and seemed to be looking at him in a different light, appraisingly, possessively. Moss shied from that—her gaze could embarrass him in the best way—and turned back to Danielle, whose eyes were lifted expectantly to him. He leaned over and kissed her nose.

Nina then excused herself to return to the bandstand, where Sam Silvestri was tuning his guitar. Boris followed her furtively with his eyes as he sipped his drink. Moss placed his arm around Danielle and watched Nina too.

Boris turned to Moss, saying, "You're mother's incredible. Someone in L.A. should make a movie about her."

"You think?" said Moss, wanting to protect Danielle from too much fuss over Nina. Danielle deserved her own acclaim.

"A film about a female jazz musician," said Boris. "I haven't seen that."

"I think it's a great idea," Danielle put in.

"I'll mention it to her," Moss said, to no one in particular.

The music started, and everyone looked in its direction with exaggerated attentiveness, as though in response to an undefined tension, which the music was quickly erasing. Halfway through Sam Silvestri's solo, Boris put his hand on Moss's shoulder and said he had to meet someone uptown. Clearly he felt like a third wheel. Yet he seemed cheerful enough. He put out his money, then shook Danielle's hand and told her again how good it was to finally meet her. If she had been a stranger at the next table, he would have said, to Moss, "I'll bet she likes it in the ass," which was what he often said about a certain type of clear-faced, well-groomed woman. He then faced Moss and put out his hand, evidently forgetting how Moss felt about handshakes. In a better world, people would bow like the Japanese, Moss often thought. Danielle's hand was the only one he wasn't afraid of. He shook Boris's hand but withdrew too quickly. To cover the awkwardness, Boris raised his hand toward himself in a continuous gesture and touched the back of his bald head. Then he turned and walked away, without looking at the bandstand. His hand was still on his head.

Moss saw that Danielle was watching him.

"He's a nice guy," Moss said, prompting her. She hardly ever offered her opinion unless asked.

"He *was* nice. I really like him." Despite Danielle's prejudices against Boris—during her fights with Moss she characterized him as a pathetic aging barfly, and Moss as his pathetic sidekick—she'd been shrewd enough to make a good impression on him, in hopes that he might speak favorably of her to Moss, whom she saw as susceptible to his opinions. "He's cuter than I imagined," she said. "Why doesn't he have a girlfriend?"

"Maybe he doesn't want one," said Moss. "Hey, it's my mother's solo." He directed his gaze purposefully at Nina, and Danielle looked over there too.

The set ended, and Sam Silvestri introduced the players. When he got to Nina, Moss clapped louder than anyone. Nina nodded at Sam, but not at the crowd; nor did she smile; evidently she was pissed off at somebody, either at one of the band members for stepping on her toes, or at the audience for not loving her enough, or, worst of all, at herself, for not being good enough. There was always some conspiracy she was fighting; always the danger that her playing would be either overlooked or overrated, always the fear that, if she were a man, she'd be considered just another serviceable piano player.

Moss took Danielle's hand and led her over to his mother, who was gathering some sheet music together. The musicians were all involved in their own small projects, the drummer lowering his snare, the bassist wiping down his strings, Sam silently noodling. Moss sensed a tension between Nina and Sam, which had spread to the others—Nina had liked Sam once: he was the last guy she was with before she went away, and only now did it occur to Moss that there was a possible connection.

"Hi," Moss said to her, cautiously.

Nina looked at him with surprise—she'd been in her own thoughts. "Hi," she said. "Are you leaving?"

"Why? Are you?"

"I was considering it."

"Going home?"

"Probably," said Nina. "You?"

"I was thinking," Danielle interjected, glancing from Moss to Nina, "that I'm kind of tired, so"—she turned to Moss somewhat urgently—"if you want to stay here, that's fine."

"It's up to you," Moss said, refusing to be pinned down. Then, to Nina: "It was fun tonight."

"Yeah?" said Nina, alert to the evasion within the generality.

"It was *good,*" said Moss, and instantly regretted that lukewarm word. Why not just say it was great, wonderful, amazing, brilliant? Why not lie, to spare her feelings, as he often did with Danielle?

"I really enjoyed it," said Danielle, looking earnestly at Nina and nodding like a social worker. "Very, very much."

If Nina saw this as an intervention by Danielle on Moss's behalf (and as a mother she might only appreciate this custodial quality in a potential daughter-in-law), she had the tact not to call her on it, as she was not always above doing when she felt she was being indulged; though of course it was entirely possible that Danielle meant every word. "Thank you," Nina said graciously.

"How was the piano?" Moss said, to avert a silence.

"I was just about to ask you," said Nina. "Could you even hear it?"

"Clear as a bell," said Moss, so eager to say something positive that by the time he realized, in a moment, that she had meant to blame the piano itself, he could only turn to Danielle in hopes that she would contradict him; but she was nodding in eager corroboration, looking to Moss for her cues.

"It sounded—*good*," Danielle hazarded, trying to help. "I could hear every note." She looked at Moss for support, but he saw the panic in her eyes. "Couldn't *you*?"

Moss turned to his mother. "I did think you were a little tentative at times," he said, to balance what he felt sounded too much like their apologies for her. "You know?"

"No," said Nina. "Explain."

"You just didn't seem comfortable," said Moss, hardly knowing what he meant to say, but sensing the truth somewhere in the murk and feeling that he must keep swimming toward it. "Like you were distracted, maybe." And that, he realized, was the most generous thing he could have said, in that it provided for the most plausible and forgiving explanation: her marital troubles.

Yet he felt Danielle's eyes burning into him.

"I guess my return wasn't exactly one for the ages, was it," Nina said. "Well. No sense crying over spilled milk. Where are you two off to?"

"You asked what I thought," Moss said.

"Of course I asked," Nina said sharply. "You're a professional critic, aren't you?"

Moss couldn't speak: he squeezed Danielle's hand, which he only now realized he'd been holding.

"I think we'll go get some food," said Danielle, answering Nina's previous question, again with the professional bedside manner with which she must have defused situations at the hospital. "You're more than welcome to join us."

Moss's skin prickled: Danielle's initiative, admirable in its own right, carried enough of the smell of condescension, however unwitting, to cause Moss to brace himself for Nina's response—the thought of her anger attaching itself to Danielle was too horrifying.

"Oh, no thanks," Nina said to Danielle, without any trace of irony. She smiled. "I'm a little tired tonight."

"Are you sure?" said Moss, so relieved by her civility that he dared to act like nothing had happened. "We'll wait for you."

"No, you two go," said Nina, still looking at Danielle. "We can do it another time."

"I hope so," Danielle said.

"Well—see you later, then," said Moss.

Nina turned to him. "Will you be home tonight?"

Moss swallowed. "Not tonight." He let go of Danielle's hand. His own was wet; he wiped it discreetly on his pants.

"When are you going to clean your room?" said Nina.

"Tomorrow." Moss felt for Danielle's hand. "Danielle'll help me."

"That's nice of her," Nina said, this time *with* irony, though it was directed more at Moss, as if he had spoken out of turn.

"I don't mind," Danielle said to Nina, catching Moss's hand in her own and placing it behind her back. "I've never been afraid to get my hands dirty."

The words seemed innocent enough—Danielle was all but incapable, temperamentally at least, of the wicked double entendre, the loaded remark—but as he and Danielle walked away, hand in hand, Moss turned the phrase over in his mind, testing it for occult meanings, wondering too if his mother detected in it any obscure recriminations, against *her*. He found nothing there himself.

Resisting his own will, he looked back at the piano: Nina, absently shuffling pages, was gazing straight at him. He quickly turned away.

7

THE NEXT DAY, MOSS AND DANIELLE RETURNED TO THE apartment to clean up after the pigeons. Danielle scrubbed while Moss put in calls to several pest-control companies, all of whom told him that the best thing to do was to cover the air shaft with a screen. But no one could guarantee that every last pigeon would be evacuated before the screen was installed—the usual technique, which involved poking and prodding with a long pole, was useless against birds that hid between cracks in the bricks, or else flew confusedly from ledge to ledge instead of up, up and away. Thus it was likely that a bird or two would be trapped and end up starving to death. Moss regretted any loss of life, but what about his own life? And what was a pigeon or two, in the scheme of things? He got an estimate and called Mrs. Bulina, who expressed a bubbly sympathy for Moss by repeating his complaints ("Ooh, the pigeons are making noises!") and then grew quiet when he suggested, off-hand, that the droppings posed a health risk to babies, the elderly and people with depressed immune systems. By raising the specter of liability, Moss knew he had fired a shot across the bow. He then added that a screen would cost anywhere between one and two thousand dollars, depending on the quality of the material, which caused Mrs. Bulina to giggle demurely, as though Moss had made a joke about the czar's underwear. "Ooh, Moss! You give me a shock." She then volunteered to personally capture the pigeons in a birdcage, one at a time, and drive them over the bridge to New Jersey. Moss respectfully noted that such a process could take a very long time, especially if new pigeons replaced the old ones. Mrs. Bulina then suggested that Moss cover his windowsills with shards of glass. "It's not nice, I know," she said, in a tone of cheerful intrigue that barely suggested cruelty, "but maybe they will say, 'It's not so nice, this glass,' and fly to somewhere else." A similar idea involving thumbtacks had crossed Moss's mind, but birdproofing his own sills was missing the point: the pigeons on other ledges were no less of a nuisance. "Or what about water gun?" said Mrs. Bulina. "This can be fun, like arcade game. Put inside gun hot water and shoot pigeons, and soon they go away to nicer place." When Moss tried to convey to his landlady that this, too, could be a time-consuming occupation, she responded with a promise to call the super, a half-wit named Woytek, and see if he had any ideas.

Moss hung up the phone, frustrated that he hadn't been firmer, yet fearing he'd already gone too far, provoked her. What if she paid Woytek five hundred dollars to contrive to turn on the gas while he was asleep? Was she capable of even having such thoughts? Outwardly she seemed so harmless, but Moss knew better. The fate of his neighbor, the Pole, was never far from his mind.

When Danielle was finished cleaning, they went to the hardware store around the corner to look for a product called Bird-B-Gone, a sticky repellent in a tube that you were supposed to squeeze onto the ledges, recommended by the pest-control guys as a stopgap. Moss's idea was to buy ten tubes and distribute them to all his neighbors on the air shaft, then subtract the difference from his rent.

As Moss and Danielle searched the shelves for Bird-B-Gone, a voice came from behind them: "Moss Messinger?"

Moss turned. Standing two feet away, wearing a thick oatmeal-colored sweater, a big leather coat and sunglasses pushed up on his oily, slicked-back hair, was none other than Nik Cattai. Moss froze like a cornered squirrel. Cattai put out his hand and smiled, showing his small sharp teeth. "Hey, how are you, man?"

Moss looked at Cattai's hand. Why did people constantly do this to him? "I'm good," he said, feeling Cattai's fingers snare his own. When Cattai let go, Moss's hand dropped lifelessly to his side.

"I'm Nik," Cattai said to Danielle. He did not put his hand out for her.

"I'm Danielle," Danielle said, smiling up at him, wondering who he was.

"I've been wanting to tell you," Cattai said, turning to Moss, "that we have a new menu. I invite you to come again as my guests."

"Nik owns a restaurant," Moss said to Danielle, giving meaningful inflection to the first and last words in hopes she would get the picture.

She didn't. "I'd love to go," she said, and her hand went involuntarily to Moss's back and scratched nervously. "It sounds like fun."

"We'll have to see," said Moss, addressing Cattai but still looking at Danielle. "Things are a little hectic right now."

"No problem," said Cattai, with an air of appreciation for the complexities of their relationship. "The offer is good anytime. Do you know Guy DeMarco? From La Ronde? This is our new chef."

"Don't know him," Moss said, wondering if the previous chef had been canned as part of any fallout from his review.

He then noticed that Cattai was holding a shopping basket filled with roach bait and several mousetraps. Cattai saw him noticing.

"Ah, these," Cattai said with an easygoing laugh, giving the basket a little shake. "I recently bought a cabin in the Catskill Mountain, very nice, but with little creatures. I don't like living with creatures in the house, except of course for my dog."

"A dog?" Danielle cried. "What kind?"

"Wait, I show you." Cattai set down his basket, pulled out his wallet and showed a snapshot to Danielle. "This is Basha."

Danielle's face lit up. "A Pyrenean! A boy or girl?"

"A boy."

"He's beautiful. My uncle had one. He always said they're the strongest breed in the world."

"Yes," said Cattai, looking at the picture with her and seeming to gain a new admiration for the animal, through Danielle's eyes.

"In the time of Louis Fourteen, these dogs were guarding the châteaux. Also, they were used in battle. But they need a lot of space, and a lot of exercise." As if sensing Moss's impatience, he retracted the photo and tucked his wallet in his jacket pocket. "I will see you, then, my friend?"

Moss wavered, noting the hint of suspense in Cattai, the raven eyes shifting between his proposed guests. "I'll call you," he said.

As soon as Cattai turned away, Moss took Danielle's arm and insisted that they leave without the Bird-B-Gone (he would pick it up later), feeling it would be awkward, having parted company, to see Cattai again in the checkout line.

Outside, Moss explained things. "That's the psychopath who's after me," he said, looking back at the store. "I was trying to get us out of there."

"He seemed nice," said Danielle.

"Well, he's not. And I'll bet you anything those mousetraps are for his restaurant. And the way he was flirting with you? Unbelievable."

"He wasn't *flirting*," said Danielle, clearly pleased by the idea.

"Of course he was," said Moss. "To get back at me."

"Oh, right, Moss—that's the only reason anyone would flirt with me."

"So you admit it—he *was* flirting."

"He was just being nice. More than nice, considering you wrote such an obnoxious review."

"Fine," said Moss, refusing on principle to defend the charge.

"Let's say, for the sake of argument, that it was obnoxious. Then why would he be 'nice' to me? Don't you think that's strange?"

"To you, maybe. But not everyone is as calculating as you are."

"What the hell does that mean?"

"You were rude to him, Moss. It was embarrassing."

"*I* was rude?"

"It's obvious," Danielle said, "that you feel threatened by him."

"Naturally, considering he threatened me."

"You know what I mean. He's got money, he's good-looking, and he's obviously a mature adult, which is more than I can say for you."

"I'm good-looking."

"And you know, you were rude last night to your mother—the way you criticized her. This is twice you've embarrassed me in less than twenty-four hours." Danielle had a phobia about being disgraced in public, suffered dreams of being naked and ashamed in the subway, or onstage in the school auditorium.

Moss laughed. "My mother? Are you really bringing her into this?"

"Laugh," Danielle said, folding her arms and slouching to affect a pitying scorn. "Since it's your only defense."

"How dare you accuse me of being rude to my mother."

"How dare you embarrass me. And you *were* rude."

"If you were so embarrassed, why didn't you say something last night?"

"Because for once we actually went out and did something—

I didn't want to totally ruin the evening, though you apparently did." Danielle shook her head. "I've had enough of this." She turned to go.

"Don't," said Moss. Her moves to leave always grabbed him in a way he didn't expect. "I'm sorry."

She stopped, faced him. "I *have* to go," she said, softening at his contrition. "I have to balance my checkbook, and do laundry." She looked straight down at her feet, which were pointed inward. "All my uniforms are dirty."

Moss wanted to offer her something, feeling that he hadn't fully earned this reprieve. "Maybe we should talk," he said, not knowing what he meant by this other than that it might give her hope that their situation was still negotiable, that he could still, under yet-to-be-imagined circumstances, make a commitment to her, which, when he thought about it, was what this argument was really about, what all their arguments were really about.

"What's the use of talking?" Danielle said. "You never say anything new."

"Sometimes I imagine things," said Moss, knowing that he was still light-years away from marriage but thinking that she should know from time to time that he was capable of at least picturing it. "I imagine what it could be like."

Danielle bit her lip. Moss put his hand on her shoulder and moved it around a little, wanting to test her mood, secure her there, at the risk of her batting him away. She stood, unsure of herself, waiting for Moss to say something, but the feel of her shoulder left him speechless. He rubbed it, searching her face for assurance. She met his gaze, then looked away, as if afraid of being discovered.

For she was, at bottom, ashamed. Ashamed of her upbringing, of where she was from, of the conclusions people might draw about her class and her intelligence. Her mother drank and "ran around," and her father, whom she'd idolized, had left when she was a teenager. Everything flowed from this. All the rotten guys. But in Moss she saw potential. She saw good in him. She saw promise. More than once she said that it was only a matter of time before he became successful, that in fact he was—if her reading of an early draft of *The Scavengers* was any indication—a "genius" (causing Moss to recount the time his teacher at college, Dan Lapidus, called him into his office and told him he was the most gifted young playwright who had ever stepped foot in his classroom, and promised to call a friend of his at the Yale School of Drama to get Moss into a program there, which gave Moss something to brag about for a few days, until the next class, when the plays were to be read aloud by the other students, and Lapidus, tall and husky, with wavy salt-and-pepper hair and wide hips, broke from his role of critical observer and cast himself as the lead in Moss's tragedy, performing the part of Mal Farrington with the intensity of a third-rate talent striving to express himself through art, making an already graceless performance seem labored and grossly egocentric, embarrassing Moss and making him wary of Lapidus, who, delivering his final line, his neck and face reddened by the strain of his effort and perhaps too by a reminder of the deeper failures of his life, looked up from the page and saw the blank faces of a dozen young people who did not share his enthusiasm for Moss's work, a consensus that, though hardly reliable, must have given him second thoughts, for he never mentioned Yale again). And though Danielle was probably not the person most qualified to determine Moss's worth as a playwright, she did have a fierce instinct about art that was uncorrupted by any cute intellectual game. She knew what she liked; she possessed a certainty in her tastes that was as pure and honest as anything about her. Moss envied her that. He felt he was always looking to others for his opinions.

"I just don't think you should have been so rude to him," Danielle was saying, as if for lack of anything else, but her tone was apologetic. "You get so paranoid sometimes. If he wanted to hurt you, he wouldn't have invited us to his restaurant."

Moss wondered why she didn't imagine that Cattai might use such an occasion to poison him. She didn't think that way. She was lucky. To her mind, Cattai only wanted a chance to redeem himself in the eyes of a critic he'd disappointed. Moss tried to see it that way, if only to bring himself to accept Cattai's invitation, to make Danielle happy and prove to her that he wasn't a total slave to his craziness, and that she wasn't either.

"We can go, then," Moss heard himself say, and he liked the feeling of sacrifice it gave him. "I'll call and make a reservation. Not that we'll need one."

"Really, Moss, it's not that important to me," Danielle said, with a new levelheadedness that suggested she had received satisfaction. "We don't have to go."

"No, no," said Moss, "I want to now. It'll be interesting. Besides, you're right: what's he going to do—poison me?"

8

NINA HAD BEEN IN NEW YORK FOR ONLY A WEEK, BUT IT had quickly become apparent to her that Moss was in far better shape than Fran had claimed in her e-mail, or than she herself had expected; if nothing else, he had made up with Danielle, who clearly adored him and would, God willing, take care of him and make him happy. From what little Nina had seen, Danielle was ideal—bright, beautiful, capable, loving; Moss could hardly do better, and that was no insult to anyone. Still, Nina wondered about the timing of their reconciliation, and thought it worth noting that while she was in town Moss had spent every night at Danielle's. After the gig with Sam, she'd barely seen him—he was either with Danielle or else locked in his room working on one of his plays, a few of which she'd read over the years when he sent them to her for her opinion. When he was younger and less susceptible to literature, he wrote really imaginative things, but when he got to college, his work became more mannered and self-conscious. Still, she felt oddly attuned to it, recognizing a part of herself in the personality of his writing, and tried to be as honest and helpful as she could, hoping he understood that when she was tough on him, it was only to make him a better playwright. And thus far he had proven himself extremely resilient, considering he'd yet to make a dime off his work. Sometimes Nina worried that by the time he was ready to give it up, he'd be too old to get a regular job; would have fallen too far behind the world. And who would take care of him then?

She'd said good-bye to him on the phone, wishing she'd had one last look at him, one last hug, but on the flight back to L.A. she told herself that an in-person farewell probably would have gone badly anyhow. There was always an undercurrent of tension between them, or rather the tension was on the surface, and everything else rushed below it. If they could only break through and talk to each other, Nina thought, maybe they could heal themselves. But she couldn't do it—the risk of words was too great, not just his words but her own; playing music had both rescued and estranged her from language, to the point where she didn't trust herself around it—there were too many hazards and temptations, too many unintended meanings to be inferred, too much danger of saying things you couldn't take back. The abuses were endless. Like when Sam told her she "sounded good"—she knew what that meant. It barely qualified as polite. Even Moss had hinted, if hinted was the word, that she had lost her touch. But what did he know about it? He'd never had an ear for music. It was one more thing he couldn't share with her, maybe the biggest thing, and he hated it.

At LAX she waited outside the terminal for Anton to pick her up. The weather was the same as when she'd left, helping her imagine that she'd been away for less time than she had, that her return was part of the same long blue day.

She heard the toot of a horn: there was the Toyota. Anton got out and walked toward her, wearing his jogging outfit and a pair of old leather sandals. As soon as they saw each other, they smiled—it was impossible not to—and her fears vanished, blown away by the force of familiarity, the recognition in each other of parts of themselves that they had missed.

She was hungry, and so they decided to go straight to a Mexican place on Pico that they liked. They barely talked during the drive; the windows were down, so that they couldn't hear the radio, let alone each other's voice.

At the restaurant Nina ordered a margarita and began drinking it quickly while Anton read the menu. Then Anton looked up and said, as if it had only just occurred to him, "So. What did you do for a week?"

Nina shrugged; there hadn't been much. Moss had gone back to his girlfriend, he was okay, and maybe, Nina admitted, she'd misjudged his condition from afar.

"He's definitely okay?" Anton said, as if he didn't fully trust her.

"I thought he needed me," Nina said, half to herself, and she realized that this was true, that it was her concern for Moss and nothing else that had sent her to New York. Only he hadn't needed her.

"So it's good, then," said Anton. "He's okay."

"Maybe I was a terrible mother," said Nina, following her own thoughts. "And so I *expect* him to be unstable."

"If you were such a bad mother, he wouldn't be so okay. Right?"

Nina sighed. "I think his girlfriend's good for him. He's extremely lucky, in fact." She remembered Danielle's noble bearing, and the way she stood beside Moss, her hand in his.

"Nina," Anton said, and there was a strange sadness in his eyes. "I've been thinking about things. While you were away. And I'm not happy."

Nina didn't move.

Anton said, "Neither of us is happy. Especially you."

Nina touched her collarbone. "What are you saying?"

"Relax," said Anton. "We're just talking."

"About what?" said Nina. "What exactly are we talking about?"

"I'm just saying that I need some time to think."

"Think about what? We just had a week apart."

"Yes. I know."

"What's that supposed to mean?"

Anton rubbed his eye, affecting weariness. "Come on, Nina. You never wanted to go to Mexico. You were looking for a way out. Moss was an excuse. Wasn't he?"

"Is that what you've been thinking?"

"Maybe you don't see it," said Anton. "But there's a pattern here. First you used me to avoid your kid; now you've used him to avoid me."

It was the worst thing he could have said. "You don't know what you're talking about," Nina told him, feeling she might lunge at his neck. He had never said anything like this before, but it was clear that he'd thought it for a long time, and this hurt her deeply. "How dare you. How dare you accuse me of such a thing."

"I'm not saying it's anything you're aware of—"

"Have you met someone?" Nina said impulsively, knowing how ridiculous it sounded, given Anton's extinct sex drive and general indifference to women, but wanting to turn things around, put *him* on the defensive.

"No," said Anton, averting his eyes, so that he looked innocent and guilty at the same time. "It has nothing to do with that."

"I've been *very* happy," Nina blurted. "I know I complain. I know we don't have the most exciting life. That's my fault too. But that doesn't mean I'm not happy. You know I've never been hung up on happiness."

Anton only shook his head. "I see the way you look at me. Sometimes I get the feeling you want to leave me, but you're afraid of hurting me. I drag you down. We both know that. You're still young." His eyes, though watery, did not plead with her; it was the face of experience in these matters. "I can stay with my sister for a while. That'll give us both some time to think."

"Why?" Nina said, feeling that she was being punished, that this had been coming to her. "Why didn't you say anything?"

"I'm saying it now."

"Bullshit, Anton. Something happened. You met someone." Nina was following her instincts and was stunned by the ensuing silence, the lack of denial. "You met someone," she said again. "Did you meet someone?" She heard the fear in her voice, the fear not so much of another woman but of her own miscalculations, her own failure to see this, to imagine it. What else didn't she see?

"If you'd have been here," Anton said quietly, "it wouldn't have happened."

Nina felt weightless. "*What* wouldn't have happened?"

A waitress heading toward them veered alertly at the last second. Anton took a breath, dug his elbows into the table and told her the story.

On the night of their anniversary, he went to the Beverly-Bonaventure, ostensibly to listen to the musicians who had been hired to fill in for them, but really to get good and sloshed in a friendly setting. At some point he was approached by a woman who recognized him; she often met with clients at that lounge and claimed to have struck several deals to the low rumble of his bass lines. That night she was in a celebratory mood, having sold a script to Paramount earlier in the day. She bought him a drink and talked about her father, who had played sax in the *Tonight Show* orchestra. When it was time for her to go, she gave him her card; two days later, having not heard from Nina since their anniversary, and feeling depressed and alone, he called the woman, and they met the next night at the hotel lounge for a friendly drink. She talked as much as she drank, which was fine with Anton, who liked to listen, and when they got outside and she invited him back to her place, he just went along, swept up in the rhythm of things, just like when he played, chugging and churning, and he knew, as he followed her car, that no matter what happened, he would have to admit all of it:

he was too old for this kind of lie, death was in him, he had nothing to fear from the truth. Of course he didn't love the woman. This wasn't about love. This was about being alive.

Nina listened with an equilibrium ominous even to herself. She had often fantasized about a separation that would spare Anton the very hurt that she was feeling now—the blow of rejection would be more dangerous to an older person, she'd thought; but this—the impact of the unforeseen—sent her reeling headlong into darkness, blind, lost, unable to speak.

But then she did speak, and the words, like her voice, reflected her essential fear.

"How old is she?" she said.

WHEN MOSS HEARD on the answering machine that Nina was leaving Anton and moving back home, his first response was to panic. Everything had changed. For one thing, he couldn't stay in the apartment. A grown man shouldn't live with his mother. Though what if she wanted him around for moral support? Unlikely; she was the most self-reliant person Moss had ever known. And besides, he wasn't good at comforting people. Fran was an example: in the weeks after her suicide attempt, Moss had spent time with her nearly every day; they took long walks all over the city, Moss pointing out buildings or people that she might find interesting, trying to involve her in Life. But her mind was always somewhere else. She hadn't *meant* to hurt herself, she kept repeating; nor did she understand why everyone was treating her like she had.

Once, Moss dreamed he was having sex with her through a hole in her stomach. Which was disturbing, because he had never been aware of any attraction to her.

These thoughts came back to him as he picked up the phone to call Fran. When she answered, he told her about his mother's return and asked her if he could stay at her apartment for a couple of weeks, until he found his own place.

"Why?" said Fran. "Did your mom say she wanted to be alone?"

"No," said Moss. "It's my idea. Why—do you think I should stay?"

"Only if you think she needs you."

Moss wasn't sure what to think. He said, "Even if she did need me, I couldn't *live* with her. What would I tell women?"

"What women?" said Fran. "You're back with Danielle, aren't you? Why don't you live with *her*? That's what I don't understand."

Moss knew that Fran disapproved of the Moss-Danielle reunion, mainly for Danielle's sake, and had told Moss more than once that if he wasted any more of her time he'd *have* to marry her, on humanitarian grounds.

"I can't move in with Danielle," Moss said. "We're not ready for that."

Fran's apartment was two blocks away, so Moss was able to walk his stuff over there—clothes, mostly. Fran had set up camp for him in a corner of the living room. The sight of the fattened pillows and fresh sheets and the carefully folded-back afghan on the sofa touched Moss deeply; he wouldn't have thought Fran capable of making up a sofa like that.

He plopped down his bags and looked around. "I've lived in the same place all my life," he said. "I guess it's time to spread my wings."

"You should move out of the city, if you ask me," said Fran, lighting a cigarette. "You need to know what it's like out there."

Moss had often thought about this. His mother had done it— had seen the world—and he assumed that someday he would too. But first he needed to get one of his plays up. He couldn't go any-where without having achieved at least that much.

Over the next few days, he paid visits to his apartment, wanting to enjoy the feel of it while it was still entirely his.

As it happened, he was on the toilet when he heard Nina's key in the front door. The bathroom door was open—Moss wasn't used to closing it—and he reached out quickly to pull it shut. He thought she was supposed to come home tomorrow, not today. He was al-ways getting his days mixed up. He wiped and flushed.

"Mom," he called through the door, "I'll be right out," and he turned on the faucet in the tub. Then he took off his pants and un-derwear, stepped into the tub, and, squatting with his back to the faucet, reached behind him and formed a warm jet with which to cleanse himself, as was his habit.

He dried off and quickly got dressed, listening for Nina. He kidded himself that it wasn't Nina out there, but a goon sent by Nik Cattai to break his legs. As happened the last time Nina was here, the threat of Cattai evaporated—he'd always felt safer with his mother around.

But he was still unsure how to act. Should he hug her consol-ingly? Make a joke?

He stepped out of the bathroom.

"I'm in here," came Nina's voice. She was in her bedroom.

Moss went to the doorway. Nina was unpacking a suitcase on her bed.

"Déjà vu," said Moss.

Nina looked up at him and smiled guiltily, but without self-pity. "Hi," she said. "Sorry for the intrusion."

"Are you okay?" Moss said. She seemed better than he'd expected, and the surprise of this made him keep his distance.

"Oh, I'm sure I'll live. How's Danielle?"

"Fine," said Moss. "So—what happened, exactly?"

Nina looked down at the clothes that she was bringing out of the suitcase with more care than seemed necessary. "What happened is, while I was here last time, visiting with you, Anton met a woman."

"What?"

"A little Hollywood agent—one of those young aggressive types who has no life outside of her work, so that when she gets a couple of drinks in her and starts talking to a stranger, and he responds in the slightest, she rolls right over him." Nina smiled again. "A guy like Anton doesn't stand a chance."

"Aren't you mad at him?" Moss said, poised for signs, like a cat watching the darkness under a refrigerator.

"Oh, it's partly my fault," Nina said. "These things don't just happen."

Moss considered that. It made him feel better, hearing her take responsibility. He could not bear to think of her as a victim.

"He's a bastard anyway," he said. "For doing this to you."

"I'm trying not to think about it."

Moss sank his hands in his pockets as she continued arranging her clothes.

He said, "Just so you know, I'll be staying with Fran until I can get my own place."

Nina looked at him. "You're leaving?"

"I think we're both too old not to have privacy, don't you?"

"Moss. I don't want you doing anything on my account."

"It's more about me. Seriously."

"Are you sure?" said Nina. "I'd hate to think I was turning your world upside down." She came from around the bed, toward him, as if with concern for his welfare.

"I'll be fine," said Moss, tensing as she approached.

"We both will," Nina said, and then she embraced him, and Moss felt, in the extra squeeze they applied to each other, an acknowledgment of her misfortune and their agreement to move beyond it. As they withdrew, Moss dared to meet her eyes, which looked straight into his, almost defiantly, and he saw too far into them and had to look away.

"So what are you going to do?" Moss said. "Like, about work?"

"I'll find something," Nina said. "Sam can probably help me out. He knows everybody. And there's other people too. I'll just have to make some calls."

"It's not so easy," said Moss. "You haven't been here in a long time. There's a whole new scene, a new generation of players. Will you get alimony?"

"Anton doesn't have any money. And who said anything about divorce?"

"But don't you want to break his balls? After what he did?"

"It's not for you to worry about, Moss."

"Then how are you going to support yourself? How are you going to live?"

"Stop attacking me!" Nina shouted, and Moss froze in terror at the anguished sound of her voice and the cold hatred in her eyes.

"I'm not attacking," Moss said, raising his hands to show that he was innocent, innocent.

"I told you, Moss, you don't have to worry about me. Worry about yourself. Okay? That's the deal."

"Jesus, what did I do?"

"Do *you* have a job?" Nina said. "How are *you* supporting yourself?"

"I told you the jobs I've worked. I scrape by."

"Do you know how high rents are?"

"Didn't you hear me? I'm living with my friend."

"For free? How long do you expect that to last?"

"Don't worry about it."

"If you're going to move out," said Nina, as if grasping for some way to impose sense on him, "then why not move in with Danielle?"

"Why should I?"

"Because it's what people do. It's what couples do."

"I'm living with Fran," said Moss. "It's my decision."

"No offense, Moss, but Fran is not exactly a model of stability. You don't need to take on her problems on top of everything else."

"You're one to talk," Moss said. "Look how *your* life turned out."

"What did you say?"

"I—"

"Get out of here," Nina said, and there was hatred in her eyes.

Moss stood there. What had he done?

"Now," said Nina.

"I'm sorry," Moss said, his throat tightening. "I'm sorry. What did I do?"

Nina closed her eyes, so that the lids fluttered. "Don't argue with me, Moss. Just *go.*"

9

TWO DAYS LATER, AS HE LAY LIMP ON FRAN'S SOFA, MOSS
dreamed that his mother was serving him dinner—she
brought him a Mason jar whose contents he was supposed to eat,
but when he held it up he saw that it was a tiny dead kitten pre-
served in formaldehyde, and he jolted awake. It took him a moment to realize where he was, and then he jumped up, thinking
he'd missed his date with Danielle at Beaujoli. But the clock on the
wall assured him that it was only one in the afternoon. He sank
back into the sofa. The dream put him off the idea of dinner,
though he hadn't exactly been looking forward to it in the first
place. He'd made the reservation over the phone with Nik Cattai
the day after their encounter at the hardware store, and they'd
agreed on a date three weeks hence, ostensibly to suit Moss's schedule but really to give Moss time to wriggle out of it if he wanted. Instead, he'd forgotten about it, and now it was too late to cancel. For
one thing, Danielle was so excited about going, and Moss didn't
want to let her down, especially since she was already mad at him

for moving in with Fran. "Great," she'd said upon hearing the news, "now you two can fuck each other like you've always wanted," and Moss had had to go through the sorry business of telling her how asinine she was being. The nature of his friendship with Fran should have been obvious, unnecessary to defend. Even when he told Danielle that Fran had stayed every night at her boyfriend's, Danielle turned it around and said that Fran was probably avoiding Moss out of fear of what might happen between them if she didn't. Moss was reasonably sure that Danielle didn't really believe this; she just wanted attention. No one in her life had ever given her enough of it. And that was what dinner tonight was about: giving her something, a special night, a romantic dinner, just the two of them. They hadn't had one of those in ages.

Moss thought to sleep for another hour or two—he'd been up till five in the morning working on the scene in *The Scavengers* in which Mal Farrington loses his erection with the last living woman in Manhattan on the observation deck of the Empire State Building—but something was bothering him. Something about his mother. In the two days since she'd ordered him out of the apartment, they'd talked once on the phone; Nina had apologized for blowing up at him, and asked him to dinner Thursday night.

Now he decided to call her, to make sure they were still on for Thursday—like him, she tended to get her days mixed up.

"Of course we're still on," she said, and Moss could tell that she'd been waiting for him to check on her. "Eight o'clock."

"Great," said Moss. "Tomorrow at eight. Where?"

"No," said Nina. "It's tonight. Today is Thursday."

"It is? Are you sure?"

"Yes, I'm sure. Why?"

Moss began pacing around Fran's coffee table. "Then I must've screwed up," he said. "I have plans for tonight, with Danielle."

"Can you change them?"

"What about tomorrow night?"

"That's not the point, Moss. We made plans."

Moss tugged at his hair. "What about Saturday?"

"Moss—never mind. Just forget it."

"I don't want to forget it," Moss said urgently. He stopped pacing. "Why not Saturday? What's the big deal?"

"You're right. No big deal at all. Just keep screwing up. Just keep making your half-assed way through life."

"Sorry," Moss said, his voice quavering. "I should have written it down." He couldn't believe she was this upset about it. Christ!

"I just wish you would get it together, Moss. I really do."

"I said I was sorry. I'm sorry, I'm sorry, I'm sorry, I'm sorry! Okay?"

DANIELLE WAS WAITING for him in front of Beaujoli. She wore her best-fitting jeans, a lightweight clinging long-sleeved pink top and the dangling silver earrings with the red stones that Moss had bought her for her last birthday. The earrings were more than Moss could afford, but seeing her wear them made him feel repaid a hundred times over. To think that he'd been ready to pick a fight with her, to punish her for having talked him into coming here, into enemy territory, and on a night when he should have been with his mother, who was apparently getting her period. Instead, he held Danielle's face in his hands, smiling as her adoring eyes produced their usual mesmeric effect on him. It was like watching sunlight rock gently on water.

"What's in the knapsack?" she said.

Moss snapped to. He had forgotten the knapsack on his shoulder. "Just a change of underwear. In case we go back to your place." It wasn't a total lie.

They went inside. The restaurant was half filled; the empty tables stood out like islands of desolation, each with a small vase holding a tense yellow rose.

A hostess in a black dress greeted them and smiled at Danielle and led them to a kidney-shaped table against the bulging cement wall, whose mosaics of broken plates, tiles, marbles, coins, glass and seashells had been described by Moss, in his review, as better than anything on the menu. He'd forgotten that particular quip, one of many cheap shots that seemed, now that he was here—and especially as he ought to have been elsewhere with his mother—utterly worthy of retaliation, likely in the form of some foreign substance in his entrée, anything from a rude bodily fluid to rat poison. But then he remembered his knapsack, and all was well again. He pulled out Danielle's chair for her, something he'd never done in his life, and she smiled with dimpled delight. Sometimes he marveled at how little it took to please her.

"I wonder if it'll fill up in here," Moss said, trying to get comfortable in his chair. He had this problem last time with the chair, and had indicated as much in print, but tonight he would let it go.

All he wanted was for Danielle to be happy. "Is the chair okay? Are you too warm?"

"I'm fine, sweetie," she said. "I'm just happy not to be in the hospital cafeteria."

Moss laughed, moved once again by her appreciation for small blessings. Where else would he find such modesty, such goodness? *I'll take a twist tie, Moss.*

Moss leaned forward and kissed her lips. "You're the most beautiful thing I've ever seen," he said.

"Flattery will get you *every*where." Danielle used that phrase a lot, but only now did Moss realize that she meant it literally, that she could be drugged with compliments, and do anything for them, so deep was her need to be valued by a man. And it was that need—as much as her beauty itself—that had inspired his words, for there was beauty in the need.

Moss then saw a new spark in her eye, brightening under the shadow of the figure coming closer. Turning, Moss saw the tall, bladelike figure of Nik Cattai, wearing a black shirt and wine-colored Prada jacket.

"I'm glad you made it," said Cattai, clasping his hands at chest level. He wore several silver rings. "It's a beautiful night, yes?"

"Yes," said Danielle, twinkling up at him. "It's a *gorgeous* night."

"It's too warm for this time of year," said Moss. "The polar ice caps are melting."

"Yes," said Cattai. "But people like it."

"How's your dog?" Danielle said.

Cattai lit up. "Yes. My dog. I showed you a picture." It was as if he were only now remembering her. "Basha is great. He's a great dog."

"I used to be a dog walker," Moss said, looking up into Cattai's dark eyes, which held your gaze in a way that made you feel you were the most important person in the room. It was the same look he'd given Danielle in the hardware store, the same look he'd given Moss at their first meeting, on opening night. "There're a lot of great dogs out there. And, to be frank, a lot of not-so-great ones. But of course it's not their fault. Thanks for having us."

"Thank *you,*" said Cattai, narrowing his eyes slightly, as if detecting something underhanded in Moss's remarks. "I hope you find improvement." And he walked away.

Danielle touched Moss's knee under the table. "Thanks for being nice to him."

"Was I being nice?" asked Moss, following Cattai with his eyes. What was he up to?

Moss then looked at his menu, as if an answer might lie there. The hare dish that he had savaged publicly was no longer available, and neither was the *pigeons au Sancerre,* although there was an entrée of crushed squab liver.

"You'd think they'd market this stuff under a better name than 'squab,'" he said. "It's so unappealing."

"Is 'pigeon' any better?"

"It's the trouble with birds. You get names like 'squab,' 'grouse,' 'snipe.'"

"Don't forget 'bushtit.'"

"'Turkey.' 'Cock.' Ugly words."

"They could say 'dove,'" said Danielle, still looking at her menu. "That's a nice word."

"Dove?"

"It's another name for a pigeon."

"Are you telling me that a pigeon and a dove are the same thing?" Moss said, unable to reconcile the squalid beasts in his air shaft with the lovely white birds they set loose at the World Series.

"A dove is a pigeon," said Danielle, charmed whenever Moss exposed his ignorance of the natural world. "Didn't you know that?"

Moss sniffed. "Well, that doesn't change my opinion about them."

"Although you can't say 'crushed dove liver,'" Danielle reasoned. "People would be offended."

"*Au contraire.*" Moss had found another dish on the menu. "Look—'Salmi of Wild Doves.'"

"Hi, I'm Gabriel," said the sandy-haired young man standing over them. "I'll be your waiter this evening. Do you have any questions?"

"Yes, I have a question," Moss said. "The Salmi of Wild Doves. What's wild about them?"

"They're captured in the wild, I'd imagine."

"Are they?" said Moss. "Or is it a breed that's bred?"

"I can ask the chef, if you'd like," said Gabriel. Then, before Moss could ask another question, Gabriel informed them that the doves were heated in pork fat and sprinkled with Armagnac, then added to a sauce of onions, shallots, garlic and red wine. The hearts and livers and brains were minced and seasoned with nutmeg and rum and spread on fresh bread fried in butter.

"Mmmm," said Danielle, who tended to moan with pleasure at waiters' descriptions, even if it was something she would never eat.

"For our specials," said Gabriel, "we have as an appetizer the grilled Treviso radicchio with smoked scamorza cheese; and a beer fondue of Gruyère cheese, with a tomato purée and a touch of kirsch, and served with French bread. For entrées, we have veal kidneys sautéed with mushrooms, in a sauce of sherry and butter-milk cream; and codfish deep-fried in a beer batter and served with green beans in a light butter sauce flavored with chives, basil, and finocchio."

"It all sounds delicious," Danielle said. "But I think I'll have the fish soup and the wild doves."

"The doves?" said Moss. "But you never eat birds."

"It's a whole new me," Danielle said, in a way that made Moss think that she was imagining that she was liberating herself from him. That was fine, but *pigeons?* They aren't *food,* he wanted to tell her. They are citizens. Denizens. I have watched them waddle on the pavement, the swaggering chesty husband and his potato-sack wife, going in circles, pecking at crumbs; I have seen their democ-racies, their tattered runts and their emblazoned heroes, have seen them assembling in peasant armies—

"And you, sir?"

Moss couldn't decide; he appealed to Gabriel for help. Gabriel recommended the fondue and the codfish, and, to drink, a Côtes du

Rhône that he claimed would go especially well with Danielle's fish-and-garlic soup.

"Red wine with fish and poultry?" said Moss, wondering if he was being taken advantage of.

"Garlic permits anything," Gabriel said. "Many people believe it should be stood up to, challenged, by a strong red."

Moss looked at Danielle. "What do you think?"

"Get it," Danielle said.

Moss nodded to Gabriel.

"Very good," Gabriel said, and disappeared.

Moss looked around. To his surprise, the tables that had been empty earlier were now filled. His first thought was that the restaurant had done well despite him, its success a verdict against his opinions and even his character. But then he wondered if the review had inspired certain key changes—in which case he'd done Cattai a service.

Gabriel returned with the wine and poured a little for Moss to taste. Moss let Danielle decide. She sipped, nodded. Wine was poured.

Moss raised his glass to Danielle. "Crazy times," he said. "My mother coming home, and all that's going on with me and you. Here's to things working out."

"If you want things to work out, why haven't you slept over since you left your apartment?"

"I said I'm sleeping over tonight. I just wanted to orient myself at Fran's, that's all."

"I'm sure Fran's not complaining."

Moss's blood went hot. Was she trying to pick a fight? "I'll ignore that," he said.

"You know it's true."

The appetizers came. Moss stared at his bowl of melted cheese.

"This smells funny," he said.

Danielle pulled his bowl toward her and sniffed it. "It smells
like cheese," she said, pushing it back. "And beer."

"There's beer in it?"

"The waiter told you that."

"What kind of beer?" Moss craned his neck for Gabriel.

"*Moss.* Just eat it."

Moss put his fork in and moved the cheese around. It was probably okay, but you never knew, and he'd decided beforehand, for
Danielle's sake, to keep his worst suspicions to himself. He discreetly pulled from his pocket the small black shopping bag of
heavy-duty plastic that was to be his first line of defense and kept it
balled in his fist below the table. His idea was to put as much of his
food as possible into the bag—he could hide forkfuls while Danielle
was looking down at her plate: she was the kind of person who con-
centrated on a task, slicing her food responsibly into bite-size pieces
with a nurse's fastidious eye—and then place the bag in the knapsack at his feet while pretending to pick up a dropped spoon or a
piece of bread.

"Here—*I'll* try it," Danielle said. "You're so dumb sometimes."

Moss thought to stop her, but she was already dipping a fluff of
bread in the cheese and putting it in her mouth in such a way as to
suggest that food was currently her chief erotic outlet: she chewed

and swallowed and glanced side to side at imaginary customers from whom she playfully wished to conceal her creamy sins.

"Everything is good?" said Nik Cattai, who had materialized above them.

"It's great," said Danielle.

"It's very good," said Moss, feeling Danielle's eyes on him.

"I'm glad you enjoy it," said Cattai, "and maybe you will tell your friends, 'Hello, there is a good restaurant, his name is Beaujoli, meet me there.'"

"I definitely will," Danielle said.

When Cattai was gone again, Moss said, "Could you make it any more obvious?"

"Make what obvious?"

"Why not just go in the back and blow him?"

"Moss. Don't be dumb."

"Whatever."

"I know what you're doing," Danielle said. "You're trying to put me on the defensive, because you feel guilty about Fran."

"Guilty over what?"

"You know what. You could have stayed at my place."

"That's bullshit and you know it. We're not ready for that."

"Not ready? After three years?"

Gabriel brought their next course, causing Danielle to drop the argument and smile.

But when she looked down at her stew of dove, the smile faded.

Seeing this, Moss cut a piece of his fish with his fork and guided it slowly toward Danielle's mouth. "Here," he said. "This is what you wanted anyway."

Danielle recoiled. "Don't."

"What's wrong?" said Moss, alarmed by her expression. She looked tormented. "What is it?"

"Please. Just stop talking for a minute."

"What?"

Danielle closed her eyes, touched her forehead. "Please."

"Please what?" said Moss. "What did I do?" Moss felt unjustly persecuted—he should have gone with his mother. Now he faced conflict in every direction. "I came here for *you,* Danielle. *You* were the one who was so goddamned excited about it."

"Just go, Moss."

"What?"

Danielle shook her head again. Her eyes were still closed, like she was concentrating on some inner pain.

"At least try your dish," said Moss.

"No. No food."

"What's wrong, then? Baby, talk to me."

"I'm not your baby."

Moss blinked. This was unprecedented.

"What do you mean?" he said.

"Please, Moss," Danielle said. Her voice was weak and defeated.

"Great," said Moss. "You think I need this? You think I need these psychotic mood swings of yours? I could have had a peaceful dinner with my mother, whom I've barely even seen. I don't need this shit. I don't need it!" He pulled out his wallet and took out money for the tip, since the meal was free, which was, he thought, the saving grace of the evening. He slapped the bills on the table and grabbed his knapsack. "You want me to leave, I'll leave." He sat there, poised for liftoff like a smoldering rocket, giving her a moment to change her mind, but she just sat there looking glum beyond all reason, and Moss found that he needed air, that if he remained in place another second he would become engulfed in his own fumes, and he stood, and the room with its crowded tables was like a city above which he rose, a crystal city steepled with bottles and flasks, a city of forked mercury rivers and stadiums strewn with gore, and there was metallic laughter in his ears as a waiter glided past balancing three bloody colosseums in his hands, and then Danielle's mouth puffed up like she was about to blow out birthday candles, her whole body heaved, and a thick rope of golden vomit flew from her mouth and lashed the full width of the table.

"What the hell!" said Moss, who had jumped back in time to avoid getting hit. He felt a fantastic terror. It was really happening! "It's poison!" he yelled, looking wildly around. He had no choice but to cry murder. The fact was there. His whole body cried out. "We've been poisoned! Someone call an ambulance!"

"*Moss,*" Danielle pleaded. She was frantically trying to wipe up the mess with her napkin, more worried about appearances than her own health. Everyone in the restaurant was looking at them, and Nik Cattai was coming their way.

"What is this?" Moss demanded of Cattai, too exhilarated by

this spectacular confirmation of his fears to be afraid of anything. "What did you do to her?"

But Cattai ignored him; he went straight to Danielle and knelt beside her. "Are you okay?" he said, obviously concerned that he had attacked the wrong person. "Can I get you something?"

"Leave her alone!" Moss said.

"Moss, just *stop* it," Danielle snapped, a mortal threat in her eyes. Her face was bright red.

Gabriel then appeared, along with a Mexican busboy, and with the military efficiency of specialists trained in quickly cleaning up the blood and glass of a particularly horrific crime, they stripped the table of all evidence of what had occurred there.

"What happened?" Cattai was saying to Danielle.

"You tell us," said Moss, emboldened not only by the presence of many witnesses, but by the perception that Cattai had done his deed, and posed no further threat. "What was it—rat poison?"

"Moss," Danielle said. She looked like she might get sick again. "Just *stop*."

"I don't think it was the food," Cattai said calmly to Moss. He turned to Danielle. "Do you want me to show you where is the bathroom?"

"I'll take her," said Moss. He moved toward her and held out his hand, and Cattai stood up and wisely yielded his space. But Danielle remained still.

"I want to go home," she said, to no one.

Moss knelt at her side, as Cattai had. "Are you okay?" he said, touching her shoulder. She was stiff as a cadaver.

"I'm fine," said Danielle, through her teeth. "Now please take your hand off of me so I can get up and walk out of here and never see you or any of these people again, because you just embarrassed me, Moss, for the *last fucking time*." And before Moss could formulate a response, Danielle got up, apologized to Cattai with the deepest, most heartfelt expression of regret that Moss had ever seen —she might have accidentally run over his beloved dog—and, as briskly as decorum permitted, walked to the exit, leaving Moss holding on stupidly to the back of her chair.

"I'm really sorry," said Nik Cattai. "She must have a virus or something."

Moss was sure Cattai was toying with him, but there was no way to prove anything at that moment, and he had to catch up with Danielle—and so without another word he turned and rushed to the door, expecting to find Danielle collapsed on the sidewalk outside.

Instead, she was getting into a cab.

"Danielle!" Moss called to her. "I'm coming with you!"

"I want to be alone," Danielle said miserably, closing the door before Moss could reach it. Her window was rolled halfway down.

"But you've got to get to the hospital!" Moss said, unable to grasp her failure to see this. "There was something in that food!"

"I told you, I'm fine," Danielle said, too weak to argue. "I just want to go home. I'll call you tomorrow. Okay?" She wanted to get rid of him. "I haven't been feeling well since this morning."

Moss didn't believe her—it was too like her to make excuses in order to avert a scandal, or to preserve her naïve worldview, in which people never took revenge upon their critics, marriage was still a relevant and meaningful institution, and happiness was as simple as a country house and a family of one's own.

"If you get sick again," Moss said, as the taxi rolled away, "you call me. Okay?" But she was beyond him now, and did not answer.

Moss turned back to the restaurant, thinking that Cattai must be watching him in the doorway. But no one was there.

10

HE AWOKE ON FRAN'S COUCH, FULLY CLOTHED. THE PHONE was ringing. It was six in the morning. Fran had not come home.

Moss looked at the phone, which was on the table beside the couch. Danielle knew the number here. Moss instantly feared the worst.

He picked up the phone. "Hello?"

"Moss."

"Dannie," Moss said. She sounded shaken, in a way he'd never heard. "Are you okay?"

"No. I'm not okay. The worst thing in the world has happened."

Moss's dread at those words was allayed by the wonder that she was speaking to him without any apparent malice.

"What is it?"

"Imagine the worst thing in the world," Danielle said. "Then imagine something even worse than that."

Moss opened his mouth; if it was something *that* horrible, she wouldn't put it so archly. Or would she?

Then it hit him: she had indeed been poisoned, and had only days to live. There were drugs that could kill you slowly like that—she'd told him a story once about a patient who OD'd on gout medicine and died after three days of massive internal bleeding.

"Please tell me," he said, "that no one is dying."

"No one is dying."

Moss released a breath. "So that's good. Isn't it?"

"Not really."

"What do you mean? Are you still sick?"

"I threw up again. A half an hour ago."

"That's it. We're going to the Emergency Room. I'm calling the cops—"

"It wasn't the food."

"It wasn't?"

"No, Moss. It wasn't."

And then he knew. Suddenly, he knew. It was in her voice. His throat went dry.

"Jesus," he said. "Are you sure?"

"Yes," said Danielle, and there was a thrill in their understanding, in their avoidance of the word. "I'm sure."

"You did a test?"

"Twice."

"Danielle"—Moss's voice softened with gratitude, for other horrors spared—"you'll excuse me—but this is not the 'worst thing in the world.'"

"For me it is. It's pretty damned bad."

"But how did it happen? When?"

"That morning. After you came to see me at the hospital."

"I can't believe it."

"Moss, I'm scared."

"No. Don't be. I'll take care of everything." As Moss spoke he had to suppress a shiver of accomplishment. "Listen," he said, with a command that seemed wired to this new validation of his manhood, "Fran went through this about a year ago. She said it was a cinch."

"You mean an abortion?"

"She has a great doctor. I'll take care of it."

"But I don't know that I want to do that," Danielle said guardedly.

"Okay," Moss said, careful not to be presumptuous in a situation like this. "Of course it's up to you. I'm here. We can talk about it." Moss was just saying these things; he did not believe them. He did not believe—regardless of this success, this passage into the kingdom of the virile—that there could be any other outcome to the pregnancy than immediate termination. "We can talk," he repeated. "Okay?"

"You want to abort it."

"That's not true," Moss said vehemently. She made it sound so inhuman that he had to deny it.

"It *is* true," said Danielle. "It's the first thing you thought of."

"Listen," Moss said, "I'm on my way. We can't talk about this over the phone."

.   .   .

SHE WAS WAITING for him at the top of the stairs, wearing red shorts and a white T-shirt with holes in it. She was carrying his child—a staggering thought—and had never seemed so beautiful. Upon reaching the landing, Moss dropped to his knees and looked up at her in awe.

"What are you doing?" she said, and laughed.

Moss laughed too. "I don't know." He wondered if she saw a similar change in him. He had achieved the defining goal of any organism, had connected himself to the universe; problems aside, he felt potent and right with nature, separated, forever, from what he had been.

Danielle helped him up, and they went inside and embraced in front of the refrigerator, rocking slowly, the way they used to.

After some minutes, they moved to the bed and sat primly on the edge of it, side by side, in silence, like newlyweds in an arranged marriage.

Danielle said, "I know you want me to get an abortion."

"That's just wrong, Danielle. Nobody *wants* that kind of thing."

"You'd prefer it."

Moss sighed. He wanted to be fair. He tried to imagine their child. He saw a little girl with golden curls, red ribbons, a dress. Tawny arms, gummy hands. Blue eyes? Brown? One of each? What if she wasn't healthy? Assuming she was. What else? A voice: *I love you, Daddy*. Moss could hear it. It was every little girl's voice. *Daddy, why do people die?* And then she'd be sucking cock and having abortions. Maybe a boy was better—the evil he knew versus the one he didn't. Or maybe not. Boys performed acts of perversion in the house. Moss squirmed at the thought of his own pubescent son, all pimples and musk, burying his hairy excitement in a warm pile of dank, stale laundry, and placing everyday objects—pencils, fruit, wooden spoons—in his ass. And who knew what Danielle's genes might contribute? What about her mother's side of the family? The drinkers, the dropouts. The arsonists. She had a cousin—a first cousin—who was in jail for torching a stable. Six horses had perished.

"We have to be realistic," Moss said. "I mean, a kid would completely change our lives." Moss then had a hunch he could appeal to her on feminist grounds. "What about your career? What about all the things you want to do?"

Danielle sat there, unmoved. "I'm not worried about my career," she said. "I'm worried about us."

Us? Moss hadn't been thinking of that. But he was quick to recognize that Danielle was prepared—even willing—to put the relationship ahead of the pregnancy; was ready to bargain, to extort a commitment from Moss that would equal the weight of that potential life. The terms, then, were negotiable.

Moss said, "The bottom line is this: we can't afford to have a baby."

"People do it all the time—they find a way."

"At what cost, Danielle?" Moss figured that she was not so much trying to convince him as hoping to be convinced. "We would tear ourselves apart."

Danielle shook her head, not, Moss thought, because of the words themselves—they were the right words, the words she wanted to hear—but because of her doubt that he really meant them, that he cared that much about their future.

"No wonder you don't want a baby," she said. "*You're* the baby. You wouldn't want the competition."

"That's ridiculous," said Moss, thinking that it was just the opposite, that she was the baby, the one who complained that he didn't love her enough, or spend enough time with her.

"Or maybe," Danielle said, looking down at her hands, "you just don't think I'm good enough."

"What?"

"To have your baby."

"Oh, Jesus."

"You don't think I'm smart enough," Danielle went on, getting bolder. "Or talented enough. You don't think I'm good enough for your genes."

"If you really think I feel that way, then why would you want to be with me?"

"*Do* you feel that way?"

"Of course not," said Moss, and he saw Danielle relent at his words, as he knew she would. "Listen to me. We're in this together. Okay?"

Eyes cast down, Danielle nodded.

Moss took heart. "I'll do whatever you want," he said. "Whatever you decide, I'm behind you."

"No, Moss," Danielle broke out. "I want us to make this decision together."

"Do you?" said Moss. "Or do you want me to make it?"

"I already know your decision."

"You don't know anything," Moss said. "You can't begin to know what's inside me. *I* don't even know. I feel so much I can't think straight. I've been alone my whole life and I've never loved anyone but you. Don't ever question that. This isn't about that. You have no idea what I go through, Danielle. Every day. Every minute. So don't tell me what I think or what I feel. You don't know. You'll never know." The words caught in his throat; his nostrils tensed and tears bloomed in his eyes. He covered his face.

"Sweetie," said Danielle, soothingly. "Moss."

Moss felt her touch him, hold him; and he shriveled in her arms and wept freely. She held him and kissed his head.

"Don't cry, baby," she said. "Don't cry."

DANIELLE WATCHED HER fingers burrow in the thickness of Moss's hair. Sometimes when he cried, the only thing she could do was hold him. He was hers then. He belonged to her then. *Mine,* she would think. My sweet broken man. She closed her stinging eyes and cradled his head, touched her lips to his hair.

She thought of the way he cried for her. He cried for himself, too, she knew, but his heart belonged to *her*. He'd told her that, many times. He loved her. But he was also afraid of love. Of course he had to battle himself. He didn't know how else to be. If she could

only show him that she was not the enemy. But he distrusted anything that posed a challenge to the reign of his anxiety—Danielle
had never known someone so comforted by that which tormented
him. He clung to fear like a kitten to a tree. And she wanted to tear
him away from it, rescue him. But if she got too close, he just went
higher. And she didn't have enough time to wait for him to come
down on his own.

Yet now she had cause for hope. She had expected that her news
would have scared him clear out of her life, or at least turned him
against her. But the opposite seemed to be true. He was here.

"It's okay, sweetie," she whispered. "We're going to work this
out."

NINA WAS A vivid dreamer, and felt that there was nothing she
could ever achieve in music that would approach the fascinating
cinema of her dream life. The visual detail alone astounded; back-
grounds remained static and consistent against the action, sustained
by some ingenious photographic mechanism, while the foreground
changed with her own motion, so that when she flew, say, above the
streets of the city (streets of her mind's design, unlike any found in
life), the buildings, ornately gargoyled, spangled with windows, appeared from around corners with a certain inevitability, as if they
had been there all along. Other times, a musical rival would stun
her by playing a figure that she could have never thought of herself,
so that upon waking she felt shaken, wounded, until she realized
that the brilliance had been supplied by *her;* proof, she felt, that a

deposit of magic ore lay deep in the pit of her imagination. Still, she found it impossible to mine it; the closest she came was in the first fog of morning, when, eyes closed, brain hot, her mind was flooded with melodies: it was then that she was touched by her highest potential; and if she was lucky, she might capture those vapors and rush them to the keyboard before they disappeared.

She was in the middle of one of these delicate, semiconscious musical moments when she was awakened by a voice. She opened her eyes—the music was obliterated—and saw, in the doorway of her room, Moss, chewing his lip like he did when faced with her authority, as if he'd been summoned; he came into sharper focus, fiddling with a button on his shirt.

"What's new?" he said.

"I was just getting up," Nina said, swallowing a yawn. "Are you okay?"

"I have some interesting news."

Nina didn't like the sound of that. "Good news?"

Moss grinned. "Well, sort of. It appears I'm not sterile."

Nina's grasp was so swift that she must have known it beforehand: that dance in his eyes of triumph and terror. "Uh-huh," she said, guardedly. She had no idea what she felt, beyond a general alarm. "Danielle?"

"We did it once without protection," Moss said. *"Once."* He held out his hands, a victim of dumb odds.

"Once?" said Nina. "How do you think *you* got here?" She couldn't hide her anger. "What were you thinking?"

"What about you? You weren't so careful yourself."

"I was a kid. There's a big difference." Nina stopped; Moss hadn't come here for a lecture. Or had he? What *did* he want? And what had she done, to deserve this, on top of everything else? She never claimed to be perfect, but she'd tried her best, alone, for him, and how often did he call her? Once a month? When she first left home, *she* was the one who'd made the effort to stay in touch. More than once she'd invited him to come to Europe, offering to pay his airfare, but he always had some excuse, some job he couldn't get away from, some premonition of disaster in the skies. In any case, she'd refused to play the part of the needy, forsaken mother, which was why, after years of being put off, she'd finally stopped troubling herself. And so it was with a comforting sense of her own martyrdom that she could be there for him when he needed her most; for she saw that beneath everything he was scared as a little boy. "So what happens now?" she said softly.

Moss placed his hands together and brought them to his lips. "She wants to have it."

Nina tried to translate this. Did he want her to intercede on his behalf? "Has she made up her mind?" she said. "I mean, is she ready? Are *you* ready?"

"*I'm* not. But it's her decision. It's her body."

Nina discerned her own imprint on this opinion, but the respect for a woman's "right to choose" that she'd inculcated in Moss hadn't occurred to her as a defense for *keeping* a baby. "Does she intend to raise it herself?"

"She wants us to get married. She hasn't said it in those words, but I know it's what she wants."

"It's what she's always wanted," said Nina, with a tinge of contempt for Moss's failure to heed the signs. Maybe it was her fault. She'd never taught him about women.

"She might move back home," Moss was saying. "Her family would help her out. Help her raise it."

Nina laughed bitterly at that. "If she has it, Moss, believe me, *you* will be raising it, too."

"I've been trying to reason with her. I keep telling her, 'What about your career? What about your freedom? If you have a baby, all that'll change.'" Moss looked knowingly at his mother. "You know the argument."

Nina's skin tingled. "What argument?"

"When you were pregnant. You wanted to abort me, didn't you?"

"What gives you that idea?"

"You were so young. Why didn't you do it?"

"I chose not to," Nina said, flustered, "but if I had, it wouldn't have been you that was aborted; it would have been this—*thing*. I hope you understand the difference."

"Why did you choose not to?"

Nina considered for a moment. She had never told him this before. "When I was three months pregnant—maybe it was earlier—the doctor examined me and found your heartbeat, and he let me hear it, too. It was incredibly strong; it boomed. And that's what settled it for me. I knew you had to get here." As she said this, Nina saw Moss thinking perhaps of Danielle's reaction to such a heartbeat, and it pleased her to be able to attest to her own humanity while warning Moss against Danielle's.

"And what about after I was born?" Moss said, like a detective gathering the facts. "You must have had *some* regrets."

Nina grew cautious. Was he looking for a testimonial, she wondered, with which to build a case against a child, or was he getting personal?

"No, Moss, I never *regretted* it," Nina said, as if that were the most absurd thing in the world. It wasn't, of course—naturally she'd had her doubts (who didn't?)—but what else could she say?

"But what about your life?" said Moss. "All the time you had to spend on me? All the energy and resources? What about the effect on your career?"

Nina saw that at bottom he wanted honesty; she felt she owed him at least that much; and if, when he was younger, she had said things that might have given him the idea that she wished she'd done things differently, it was also true that Moss, the fact of him, and the feelings and actions that grew from having him and raising him, had made her what she was. And when she thought of all she had accomplished in her career, it was impossible to say that Moss hadn't been part of that, just as it was impossible to say, with absolute certainty, that she might have gone further without him.

But she could not convey this, she felt, without making too strong an argument for childbirth. "I told you—I have no regrets," she said, in an effort to remain as neutral as possible while assuring him that he hadn't screwed up her life. "But every situation is different. The point is, you can't just sit back and let her make a decision without at least giving your opinion. You should tell her how you feel. Tell her what *you* want."

"What do *you* think I should do?" said Moss, anxiety in his eyes.

Nina saw that it wasn't advice he wanted, but orders. He wanted her to take care of things. Despite herself, Nina was moved. She remembered when he was small, and she'd wake up to find him curled next to her under the blanket—he must have come to her with a bad dream, seeking her through black space, guided by child's radar, reaching the shore of her bed. The innocence! And here he was again. In general, Nina did not believe in "childlike innocence," since she could not remember having ever had it herself—by the age of three she'd known just how to get what she wanted out of people. But she had long since given up on trying to understand Moss; how could she, when her own mind was a mystery? Her deepest self-inquiries turned up glaring contradictions of taste, opinions, beliefs, dredged up barrelfuls of recycled ideas and plagiarizations, from whose sludge, if she was lucky, there dropped a buff gold coin, an original idea that showed her who she was. But giving birth, nearly thirty years ago, to a sovereign mind—a reflection of her but also reflective of itself—had landed her in a hall of mirrors; looking at Moss, trying to know him, she was blinded by her own limitations of self-knowledge.

But the solution was clear to her. An abortion was, she knew, the best answer, the only answer. No, she could not be neutral. She was his mother, and this was her chance to save him, to give him the word he needed, the confidence to do what was right. She was about to speak—to state her opinion—but her tongue froze: coming from her, such advice might seem loaded, she thought. To argue for an abortion could be seen as an attack on his existence, a sequel to the abortion that she wished she'd gotten herself twenty-seven years ago: she would appear too eager to erase him all over again. This was crazy—she knew that—but she had to think of his perspective. Was the fetus not partly *his*? How would he feel, then, being told by his mother that she'd prefer that he got rid of it? Beware of his imagination, Nina warned herself; he'll think you're trying to kill him.

"All I know," she said, aiming somewhere for the middle, "is that I can't tell you what to do. But"—and here she veered to one side, thinking she must balance her inner conviction—"if you and Danielle do decide to have this baby, I'd be—I'd be thrilled." And she realized this wasn't altogether untrue: the idea of a grandchild enlivened her, it touched a primal nerve.

"You mean—you *want* her to have it?" said Moss.

"Honey, it's not up to me. It's not my life or my baby. It's a decision that you and Danielle have to reach together."

"What if we can't?"

"You will," said Nina. It was as if she'd turned over his card.

Moss was quiet, absorbing a prophecy that it was now up to him to fulfill. He nodded, stood. "I guess it's that simple," he said. He shoved his hands in his pockets and looked at the floor, unrescued. He'd wanted his mother to snap her fingers, wave a wand. By creating such unreasonable expectations, he could now feel angry at her for letting him down, and in turn (Nina hoped) would use that anger to negotiate more forcefully with Danielle.

"Are you okay?" Nina said, knowing that he wasn't.

Moss gave a small assurance with a smile and a nod; and it wasn't until he walked away—leaving her there on the bed, to wonder— that Nina realized that they hadn't touched.

11

IT HAD BEEN A LONG TIME SINCE NINA PLAYED SOLO PIANO, and her left hand was weak—she stumbled over her walking bass lines, and her stride figures had her grabbing sloppily at wrong chunks of keys. No one noticed. Part of the charm of playing in a restaurant—in this case a Czech joint in midtown with Christmas lights running along the ceiling of the bar, a junk-shop chandelier, and small tables with floral print cloths—was that you were relegated to the background, less a performer than a glorified servant. She'd played worse places. Sleazy owners wanting her to show off her tits. Derelicts on the bar stools. Meals that made her ill. Late nights, early mornings, Sunday afternoons. Drinks. Broken keys. All those pianos in her past, like bodies. She'd hoped to relax another week before looking for work, but things changed with Moss's big news, with its latent threat of huge expenses he'd never be able to cover. And so she'd called Sam Silvestri, who, sounding distant and preoccupied, expressed regret for her failed marriage and gave her the numbers of people who might be able to help her, while making no mention of the chance of her playing with *him*. Nina tried not to read into this—Sam did have a regular piano player—but these days it was hard not to see conspiracies. There was Anton's duplicity, of course, and Moss, with his mean-spirited remarks ("Look how *your* life turned out"), had been *intent* on hurting her, whereas *she* had wanted only to shield him, speaking so casually about her split with Anton, not wanting Moss to be sad for her, hiding her own sadness. Not that she'd ever expected the marriage to last. Anton was right. Getting married had been, in part, an act of self-defense. She had feared the sight of Moss—a man now, grown, immeasurably changed; feared having to resume responsibility for him; feared, more than anything, his anger at her for leaving him. Marriage provided a buffer; Anton was between them now.

Looking up, Nina spotted her one admirer of the evening, wearing jeans and a dark T-shirt and posing seductively by the bar, watching her. There was always one. Where had she seen him before?

And then she knew. It was Moss's friend. Boris. (Nina counted it in her favor that she remembered the name; it indicated her interest in Moss's life.) Had Moss told him she was here? She hadn't noticed his build the night she'd met him: he was shorter than she would have thought, in the surprising way that movie actors are shorter in real life. She remembered his shaved head, and the way he monopolized her attention, diverting it from Moss and Danielle with a peculiar neediness, as though he'd been waiting to meet her, been imagining her. Nina had been more interested in Danielle, but Boris was too strong, the dominant child at a table of children, the precocious one.

When her set was over, Nina went to the bar to collect her lowly wage (Sam had said take what you can get), pretending not to notice Boris, who was a few feet away from her, still leaning, his pelvis thrust out a little, thumb in his belt loop, a whiskey glass twirling idly in his hand. But when she turned to look at him, he was standing right beside her.

"Hi," he said. "We met a month or so ago. Boris."

"I remember." Nina smiled, but made no move to shake hands, and neither did he. "What brings you here?"

"Moss mentioned that you were playing, so I asked him where." Boris smiled. "I'm a fan."

"Thanks," said Nina, wondering what he wanted.

"Do you have time for a drink?"

"A drink?" Nina hesitated. She felt exposed: Moss would have explained to Boris why she was back in New York. "What's this about?" she said, thinking it must have to do with Moss. Had Danielle decided to have the baby?

"What'll you drink?" Boris said, already pulling out his wallet.

"Bourbon and soda, since you insist."

Boris ordered two from the bartender, handed one to Nina, then led her to a corner table that had other people's empty bottles on it. A barback took the bottles and wiped away the rings.

Nina lifted her glass and took a long sip through the skinny red straw. The effect was instant—she felt both comforted and fortified. Since her return from Europe she'd been drinking more, but not too much. Just enough to feel a little happier. She never had more than two drinks in a night.

"You and Moss really look alike," Boris said. "You could be brother and sister."

"Occasionally people mistake us for a couple," Nina said.

"Same here," said Boris. "I'm bald, and he's got that hair. We get some funny looks." He drained half his glass.

"I wish he'd get it cut," said Nina. "When he was a kid I used to cut his hair. He never liked it, but it saved money."

"I'd let you cut mine, if I had any."

Nina pulled one of her curls, let it spring back. "I've considered shaving my head before. It's too much responsibility. Hair." But she loved the compliments she got for it; she kept her hair for others to admire.

"How long have you been playing piano?" said Boris.

"Longer than you've been alive," said Nina. "Thirty-seven years."

"Did you teach Moss?"

"I tried, when he was little. He never took to it." Nina pointed to her ear and frowned, to indicate Moss's tone deafness. "How long have you known him?"

"About two years."

"Do you know his girlfriend?"

"Barely," Boris said, as if this injustice was never far from his mind. "I met her for the first time the night I met you."

"That's a little odd."

"Moss likes to compartmentalize."

"What did you think of her?"

Boris shrugged. "She seems good for him," he said, betraying,

Nina thought, a trace of jealousy. "He probably needs someone like that. A nurturing type."

Nina stiffened. "What do you mean?"

"I mean he needs someone to take care of him," Boris said. "Don't we all?"

"Not necessarily."

Boris drank. "What do *you* think of her?"

"Danielle?" said Nina, having nearly forgotten the name. "I liked her." She looked at her drink. "Did Moss tell you about their little problem?"

Boris arched an eyebrow. "He told you?"

"Is that surprising?"

"Sort of," said Boris. He rubbed his head. "It's not anything I'd share with *my* mother."

"I'm glad he came to me. It means he feels he can. He's always been able to come to me."

"You're lucky, then," Boris said solicitously, as if he felt he'd offended her. "You're both lucky."

"I doubt Moss would say that," said Nina, to compensate for any undue sanctimony. "I'm sure he has his complaints."

Boris laughed. "Are you kidding? Moss worships you. He idolizes you. Which is why Danielle doesn't have a chance. No woman does."

Nina looked away, not because she believed it was true (she didn't), but because the praise in it was undeserved. "I'm sure he hates me."

"Why?"

"I did horrible things." Nina sighed: evidently the decision to talk had been made. She drank some more. "I cut him down."

"How?"

"I told him things like I wish I'd never had him," said Nina, aware that something of this confession might be transmitted to Moss, in a way favorable to herself. "Maybe he doesn't even remember, it was so long ago. I can only hope."

"You were young," said Boris, subdued and compassionate. "I'm sure you did the best you could."

Nina shook her head. "I just had so much to do. For both of us. Sometimes I lost my patience."

"Everybody does."

"No. It's no excuse. There are some things you should never say. As a parent you have to control yourself. I don't care how young or old you are. Otherwise, you become this complete agent of destruction. One word can scar a kid for life."

"Nina," Boris said, and the sound of her name, spoken by Boris for the first time—a man's voice, assuring, gentle—was a buzz in the flower of her heart's open ear. "I think you're being too hard on yourself." He smiled. "You're just like Moss."

"What do you mean?"

"The way he talks about his girlfriend. He thinks he single-handedly ruined her life by not wanting to marry her. Everyone thinks they're either destroying someone or being destroyed. But the truth is, very few people destroy anyone."

"I never said I *destroyed* him," said Nina, wondering if she'd given that impression. "And anyway, what's going on between him and his girlfriend is totally different from what I'm talking about."

"Of course it's different," Boris said. "I just notice a similarity in your personalities. You both worry about people. The people you love."

"I hardly think we're exceptional that way."

"It's a matter of degree. You both take on a lot of psychic responsibility."

"And yet we're both so selfish. Go figure."

"Everyone says I take after *my* mother," Boris said, as if this mitigated his assessment of the Messingers.

"How so?"

"Our restlessness. Never sticking with one thing. The fear of failure." Boris looked over at the piano. "More like a lack of confidence, I guess."

"My mother and I were nothing alike," Nina said. "She was good to me when I was young, very attentive, very nurturing. But everything changed when I got pregnant. She was scandalized. And then out of nowhere she told me about an affair she'd been having, which I hadn't known about, not consciously anyway, and which had obviously burdened her with a lot of guilt. Anyway, she confessed it to me, to show me that she wasn't perfect either, trying to gain my trust, so I would listen to her and get an abortion, and save the family from disgrace."

"Wow," Boris said.

"Tell me about it. I mean, we'd had our fights, but nothing like when I told her I was going to have the baby. She said it would ruin my life, that I'd be 'tainted.' Maybe at that point I wanted to be. Or figured I already was. But it was my baby, not hers. She tried to bargain with me. She tried everything. She even arranged to put the baby up for adoption. I think her main fear was that she would have to raise it herself."

"So what happened?"

"I had Moss. And I knew I couldn't give him up. Holding him, the way he smelled, the way he looked at me with those big eyes; I just couldn't. Which was just more selfishness, in a way. He might have had a better life if I'd been strong enough to give him to someone else."

"What did your parents do?"

"They managed. My mother ended her affair. And she and my dad pretty much raised Moss the first two years of his life. In a way, it brought them closer together."

"That's not too bad."

"I eventually left Moss anyway, of course. When he was nineteen."

"You think that's too young?"

"Not necessarily. Lots of people have been on their own at that age, including me. The thing with Moss was that he wasn't going to grow up as long as I was there to take care of him. How can you grow up when you live with your mother? Answer me that, and I'll buy you a drink."

"My mother died when I was thirteen," said Boris. "But you can buy me a drink anyway."

"Thirteen," Nina said. "That's tough." She rested her head on her hand. How had they gotten here? "Was there something else you wanted to discuss?"

Boris folded his arms on the table and leaned toward her. "Yes. There is. I wanted to know if you could teach me piano."

Nina laughed. Was he kidding? But she saw that he wasn't.

"I don't do much teaching," she said, the change of subject making her even more conscious of having talked too much. "I mean, are you a beginner? Have you ever played?"

"I took lessons as a kid. But I stopped when my mother died. And lately I've been thinking I want to pick it up again. Does a hundred an hour seem fair?"

Nina did not blink. "I think so," she said, knowing there were more qualified teachers out there who charged half that. She had never taught; she didn't have the patience.

But then it occurred to her that Moss had maybe voiced concerns to Boris about her job prospects, and that Boris was doing her a favor—or doing Moss one. *We need the money.*

"You'd have to come over and audition," Nina said coolly.

"When?"

Nina looked at his hands, which lay on the table, the pink-yellow fingers curled in repose. Nina had an urge to touch them.

She said, "Why not now? Since neither of us is busy."

"Now? But—I don't have anything prepared."

"I'll take that into consideration."

"But—what about Moss?"

"What about him?"

"What if he's there?"

"He won't be," said Nina. "But what if?"

12

HAVING SPENT A QUIET NIGHT AT DANIELLE'S, MOSS DE-
cided to stop by the apartment in hopes of getting further
advice from his mother. She owed him more than she'd given, he
felt. He had expected her to take a firm stand against the pregnancy.
With her blessing, Moss would have gone confidently to Danielle
and persuaded her to abort. But Nina acted as if supporting him
no matter what was the fairest, most responsible thing she could do,
and it made him think that somewhere in the back of her mind she
wanted him to be saddled with a child, just as she had been saddled;
wanted him to sacrifice his life—his time and his resources—to the
needs, just as she had, of another living being.

The apartment was quiet. "Hello?" Moss called, closing the
door gently behind him. "Mom?"

There was no answer. Moss noticed that the piano bench was at
an angle. A pair of her shoes were scattered on the floor; in a corner
of the sofa was a crumpled dress. Moss remembered other mornings like this. At the very least it meant she'd gotten drunk. She

wasn't a big drinker, but given the collapse of her marriage—and Moss assumed she was far more upset over it than her pride allowed her to admit—she had good reason to want to escape. As did he. Danielle was still pregnant, and each day, each hour, was crucial; the longer they waited, the more convinced Danielle would become that the thing inside her was *their baby*. True, she'd implied that she would get an abortion in exchange for a "deeper commitment," but Moss wasn't comfortable with those terms—not just because he knew he couldn't honor them, but because it seemed wrong to barter so freely with what was arguably a human life. As Danielle's nursing textbooks pointed out, the fetus would, by now, after a month's gestation, have a bulging, pulsating heart, a tucked head, the faint beginnings of eyes. Where the arms and legs would be, little buds had sprouted. The thing was now the size of a lima bean. In another week there would be fingers, toes, extruding genitalia. Moss tried not to dwell on it. Last night, he opened his eyes from sleep to see Danielle sitting up beside him, placing her stethoscope on her belly. He thought it was a dream at the time, but now he wasn't sure.

He went into the hall and saw that Nina's door was closed. He stood by the door and listened. Silence. He turned the knob, opened the door an inch, and peeked through the crack. She was lying on the bed, her back to him, covered from the waist down in a sheet, so still and quiet that Moss dared not make a sound. He saw the dark diamond-shaped mole on her right shoulder blade: the mark of her, recalled from earliest memory. After a moment, he withdrew.

He turned and opened the door to his bedroom, to see if Nina had already begun converting it into an office. But she hadn't touched it. Through the closed windows came the bleating of the pigeons. Their ranks had grown with the mild weather. They were building a kingdom. Moss raised a blind to look onto the air shaft. Stout birds squatted on the window ledges and atop the industrial bulk of air conditioners. Moss took some pennies from a jar on his dresser and opened the window wide enough so that he could poke out his head and arm to get a shot at them. But as he was about to throw the first coin, there appeared, below, a human figure, short and stocky, wearing a plaid wool coat and a blue baseball cap. It was Woytek, the super. He was looking up at the windows. Moss drew back and watched as Woytek began making loud sounds meant to either frighten or beguile the pigeons from their aeries. "Wa-*yow*!" he called, waving his arms. Then he took off his cap and tossed it high in the air, but it came back down without result, and when he went to pick it up he lost his balance and nearly fell over.

Moss left the apartment and walked to Fran's. It was the middle of the day and here he was, homeless, jobless, uninsured, with no prospects and possibly a child on the way. The only good news was that in his involvement with the life cycle he had lost his fear of Nik Cattai, if for no other reason than a Cattai ambush, at this point, seemed preferable to unwanted fatherhood. And even if he *was* ready to have a baby, the world would still be a frightening and violent place, and maybe it was a mercy, in the end, to prevent a child from entering it. *A mercy*. Moss had yet to play that angle to Danielle, but if pushed, he could paint a highly upsetting picture of their own innocent offspring coming of age on a hot, dying planet wracked by war and floods and human clones. "And how do we *know* God would disapprove of an abortion?" he might add, speaking to her deeper concern. "The Bible is filled with killing." And not just the Bible. What about the horror show at the hospital? Children with cancer? Did she not wonder about God then?

And what about money?

Moss walked up the four flights to Fran's apartment. As soon as he entered, he heard a sound coming from behind Fran's bedroom door. A box spring working, a mattress bumping the wall. Moss froze. This was not responsible behavior. Why wasn't she at school? Had she taken the day off? Quit? Forgotten? Her voice dripped into his ear: a moan, a squeal, a sob, a laugh.

He moved closer to the door. An excitement gripped him, painfully familiar, as if it knew him as well as he knew it. He reached for the doorknob, feeling as though he were revisiting a beautiful and terrifying dream. But as the knob turned in his hand, he got weak in his arms and legs, his heart sank, a despair cried out within him. He heard guttural noises, male, swinish, the slap and suck of flesh. And then a woman's cry, full of theft and betrayal.

The door opened an inch, two inches, and he saw the serpent thrashing green and orange on the naked back of the transgressor as he dipped and rippled above her, her white feet clamping him tight from behind, and her white arm, bruised inside the elbow, dangling placidly over the bed's swaying edge. On the night table were two syringes, a metal spoon, a bottle of rubbing alcohol, two white pills and several bloated cotton balls. Moss forgot himself and pushed the door wide open. "Hey!" he shouted, causing the man—

Zak—to collapse briefly onto Fran before rolling, slit-eyed, off the bed, exposing Fran brutally to Moss's vision, her inflamed cunt still gasping, her flaccid breasts sliding from either side of her, her eyes half open, seeing nothing. Moss rushed to her and took her wrist in his hand and felt for her pulse, the way Danielle had showed him once. "I was almost there," she said weakly, and Moss let go of her arm and in one motion overturned the night table so that the para- phernalia spilled onto the floor, and then he began stomping on it, and Zak rose unsteadily from the other side of the bed, still hard, saying, "Please, don't kill us," and Moss picked up the ceramic ash- tray that had also been on the night table and fired it at the wall above Zak's head, where it shattered and took off a nice chunk of paint, causing Zak to raise his hands in befuddled surrender. Moss then grabbed the crumpled orange comforter from the foot of the bed and pulled it slowly and tenderly over Fran's ghostly flesh, up to her neck. "Good-bye," Fran mumbled, and Moss turned and saw that Zak was looking down incredulously at his dick as it pointed up at him. "At least use a condom, you idiot," Moss said, and then he bent down and carefully gathered the smashed syringes and the spoon from the floor and dropped them in the small trash can be- side the dresser.

INCREDIBLY, SHE WASN'T too hung over, though it was past noon and she was still in bed, with no recollection of how she got there. Had he brought her in? And when did he leave, and on what terms? Most of what she remembered occurred in the living room—when they came in, she had placed him at the piano and lit the vanilla-scented candle that she'd bought the day before, and stood over him as he interlocked his fingers and stretched them out in a burlesque of pianistic bravado. When he placed his hands on the keys, with a long pause that was not for comic effect but from nerves—this was an audition, after all—she leaned over behind him so that her breasts brushed his back and reached her hands around him and arranged his bare arms. "Begin," she said, and he began playing the Turkish rondo—it was the only piece he knew, he'd said in the cab, a piece he'd been working on all his life. He played it atrociously. A hundred dollars wasn't nearly enough, Nina thought. The idea of actually teaching this man filled her with exhaustion. "To be frank, Boris," Nina said, after he banged out the climactic chords, "I don't think there's much I can do for you"— feeling, in this rejection of him and his money, that she had some- how avenged herself, but for what? "You weren't serious about lessons anyway," she told him, and he said, "You're right," and then he stood and faced her, and before she knew what was happening he kissed her while moving forward. Her impulse was to resist, but she knew she had roused something in him stronger than herself, and she did not try to fight it.

Now, the morning after, she was flushed from the physical sat- isfaction of it, the rude thoroughness. She had a fuzzy sense of being soothed afterward in her bed, her hair stroked, her breasts kissed, some final tenderness that had already lost its meaning. Or had it? She pulled the sheet more tightly around herself, not ready to be naked in the daylight. She would have to notice herself now.

She wanted to know that Boris didn't regret what had happened, and that he would never, ever breathe a word of it to Moss, though that had seemed implicit enough last night. Only now did she consider that Boris's true loyalties might lie with Moss, and that by sleeping with Boris she had betrayed her son. Last night she had accomplished the mental trick of separating Boris from Moss, but the distinction was less convincing in the sober light of day. She had to talk to Boris. What was his last name? She didn't know. Nor was she about to finagle any information from Moss. Boris knew the number here, and if he had any decency, he'd use it. Certainly if he had even a shred of it he would keep his mouth shut. What would Moss do if he found out? How would he react? Nina felt guilty of *something,* but she wasn't sure what crime she had committed, if any. At worst, she'd used poor judgment, and there was plenty of that to go around.

THEY WENT TO a revival of a Vietnam War movie that neither of them had seen. Danielle loved going to the movies, and always made Moss stay through the credits—she loved to read the names. "What do you think of 'Lila,'" she'd say, her eyes on the screen, "or how about 'Caleb'?" Usually she paid for his ticket, and so Moss would sit there and read the credits too, playing games with himself, thinking that if the names Moss or Danielle came up he would have to get married, or would win a million dollars, or would die that night, or else he'd pretend that any of the last names could be that of his father, and then try them on for himself. But under present circumstances he thought it wise to get out of the theater before the credits rolled. For three hours the sound of helicopters and explosions had pounded their eardrums. Bombs fell balletically from the sky, hootches burned like flame-haired faces, people were slaughtered, blown apart, men, women, children, babies. It wasn't Danielle's kind of movie, and when it was over, they got up wordlessly, as couples do after a film, when the opinions aired will likely expose a weakness in the relationship.

"So," Moss said easily when they got outside, "what did you think?"

"I don't know, Moss. I was thinking about other things."

Moss bowed his head. She was in a mood and there was nothing he could do. He wished he hadn't called her, but events had driven him to it: after his raid on Fran's bedroom, which ended in Zak agreeing, as Moss stood over him brandishing a woman's shoe, to enter rehab, and to use a condom, Moss had let them sleep it off; and as he often did when he was anxious or upset about something other than his relationship, he called Danielle and suggested they see a movie. But it was only when they met in front of the theater that the reality of her condition came back to him. She was luminous, charged with sugars, proteins, frantic cells. Moss thought again about the thing growing inside her, remote and fateful as a tumor, and he approached her with reverence. They went inside, watched the movie, and now, afterward, on the street, had gone silent, standing at aloof angles.

Danielle put on her knapsack, which contained her scrubs for work. Her shift started at eight, in less than an hour; she'd planned to go straight to the hospital.

She said, "I thought you might like to know—I saw a doctor today."

Moss looked at her: she was not being malicious. "A doctor?" He felt the promise of deliverance but didn't dare think of it.

"I had some tests done." Danielle lowered her eyes. "Just in case we decide."

"Decide what?" said Moss, wanting to hear it from her. As often happened when coming out of a movie, Moss had the sensation that the action outside, the people and the lights, was a filmic continuation, and things seemed less than real.

"She can see me tomorrow morning. If I want."

"You mean for an abortion?"

"I hate that word."

Moss was overjoyed—he was home free—but he refused to let it show.

He said, "Everyone hates that word."

"Then I don't know how you can say it so casually."

"You think I'm being casual about this?"

"Face it, Moss. It's just not as real to you as it is to me."

"How could it be?" said Moss. "I can't begin to imagine what it's like. No man can."

Danielle glared at him. "Am I supposed to feel sorry for you now, because you're a man? Because you're so inferior?"

"I never said inferior."

"Am I supposed to consider you a *victim*, then," Danielle went on, "because you've been robbed of the amazing experience of childbearing? Like feeling sick all the time and not knowing what to do, because the self-absorbed jerk who got you into this can't give you a straight answer about what he wants or what he feels?"

Moss shook his head. He never knew what to do when she got like this. She was always in the right. He was no match for her.

"Do you love me?" Danielle said. "Or don't you?"

Moss gave her the look he often gave, which said that the answer was either so obvious or so irrelevant that the question was meaningless.

"It's incredible," Danielle said. "You can't answer a simple question."

Simple? She was wrong on that one. It wasn't simple. What if he said yes?

"I'm waiting, Moss." Danielle's face was hard. "Do you love me or not?"

She looked old and stern; her anger aged her. Moss knew that it was her love for him that made her angry, but it was impossible to return that love, to feel it, when she looked so full of hate.

"Well?" she said.

"Forget it!" Moss shouted, thinking, I'm no longer responsible, she *wants* me to snap, wants to force the issue. "Just forget it!" He was trembling, hating her for killing them with her dependency on him. She was too much for him, for his conscience, his heart, everything. Why couldn't she stop? Why couldn't she leave him alone? Didn't she know that he would come for her? That he would rather pursue her than be beaten down?

"You're right, Moss," Danielle said, rising supremely to his call, as if she'd only been waiting for the chance: "Let's just forget the *whole thing*." Her face then broke into a tense public smile that was more like a grimace—her last defense against tears—and she turned and walked off, caught up in her own raging storm.

"Of course I love you!" Moss yelled, but she didn't stop. "Dannie!" He could chase her down, but what would he say to her? Better to let her go and cool off. She never stayed mad for too long. He followed her with his eyes: she was far away now, dark and featureless, an ambiguous figure in the distance, walking in place, either coming or going. She would go to work, and then, when the morning bell rang at eight, would change her clothes and take herself to a clinic (a nice one, Moss hoped) and undergo the procedure. A clot of blood, a cat's claw of a skeleton, head and tail, ticking in its tiny sac. General anesthetic. A vacuum tube inserted into the vagina.

"Danielle!" Moss called. But she had already disappeared.

13

THE PHONE HAD BEEN QUIET ALL DAY, AND BY EVENING
Nina could no longer wait. She had to know how Boris felt
about last night, had to make him swear not to blab about it, to anyone. Or should she be preemptive, sit Moss down and tell him? No,
that would attach too much importance to the event. What she
should have done was gotten an explicit promise from Boris, that he
would keep his mouth shut. Why hadn't he called?

She went into Moss's room for the first time since her return, to
try to find Boris's number. The room was dark and airless. When
she was younger, she had resisted much temptation to go in there
and snoop around. She was afraid of what she might find. She suspected porn, maybe pot, nothing too unnatural. Still, she was afraid.

She turned on the overhead light. The bumpy bed, the dresser,
the small wooden desk, the blank walls; the effect was instantly depressing. The bed had been stripped after the pigeon incident and
sloppily remade with what was probably his only spare set of sheets.
All Moss's carelessness and difficulty with life could be discerned in

those whorls and furrows and uneven folds. A bed captured a person, like a pair of shoes. He'd had it since he was five. It was a boy's bed, and had the disturbing smallness of a child's wheelchair. Nina went over and placed her hand on the mattress. The springs were pressing at the surface, almost poking through. How did he sleep on it? Now he was sleeping on Fran's couch. Years on a bed like this and he could sleep anywhere.

She turned to his desk, which was the most likely place to find phone numbers. There were stacks of paper, old drafts of his plays. Nina recognized her own handwriting in the margins. She did not wish to revisit any of it. All his stories involved some horrendous disaster, and he had an alarming tendency to kill off his female characters.

Next to the stack of plays was a magazine, facedown. Nina picked it up. It was a copy of *Eat New York,* with a cover photo of a topless woman holding, in front of her breasts, two bowls of ice cream with unusual toppings—black pepper, corn niblets, cherry tomatoes, scallions—and, below, the words NEVER ON A SUNDAE? Nina turned to the table of contents, wondering if Moss had left the magazine for her to discover. She hadn't asked to read his review, knowing that it was a sore spot with him. Now she flipped through the pages until she found, at the back, a column called "The Layman's Lunch," next to which was a stamp-size photo of Moss.

I am duty-bound to report, comrades, that despite Beaujoli's promisingly fruity appellation, which is a coupling of the names of owner Nik Cattai's dogs, Joli and Beau, who were

annihilated, as Mr. Cattai informed me, in a NATO airstrike
some years ago in his native land; despite, my fellow inhabitants, the wondrous tile mosaics that grace the interior of what
was once a Salvation Army outlet that served the less fortunate
of our community; despite, friends and neighbors, the fantasti-
cally sexy waitresses, my dining experience at Beaujoli was a
brute endurance test in which my companion and I had to slog
through five courses of food so poorly executed that even the
large roach we observed scuttling across the wall seemed to be
in full retreat. One wonders if it had encountered the loin of
hare or just seen the prices.

Nina couldn't bring herself to read on, feeling that something
in the hostility of the attack was aimed, obscurely, at her, or that she
herself was somehow the cause of it. She focused on the picture.
Moss. Nina had so few pictures of him. She was struck by the lost
look in his eyes, the depths of sadness that only a mother could see.
A faint, joyless smile was all he could manage. Nina remembered
how he used to throw his arms around her neck, with a smile that
could light up the world, and how it saved her again and again.
That was gone now. "Baby," she murmured. She pressed her lips to
the picture, the way she used to kiss his head to see if he had a fever.
Why couldn't he be small again?

She heard a key turn in the front door. Moss! She dropped the
magazine, wiped her eyes and rushed to meet him.

She figured he was dropping in for a visit, but as he closed the
door she saw that he was carrying his suitcase, which she'd shipped

to him for his twenty-first birthday in hopes that he would use it to visit her.

"Moss? Are you okay?"

"I'm fine," Moss said. He stood there, suitcase in hand, his head down.

"What is it, baby?" Nina said. Obviously something had happened. "Moss? Sweetie?" And before she knew what she was doing, she threw her arms around him, wanting to save him. But he was unresponsive, and when she tried to bring his head to her shoulder, he resisted, and when her hands moved to his face, to hold it so that she could see him, see into his eyes, he grabbed her wrists hard and threw them down away from him, and his eyes were wide with disgust, and he looked like he might hit her, but instead he moved past her, the suitcase banging the walls as he turned the corner toward his room.

Nina wanted to follow him, grab him—she looked at her hands, the hands he hated, and she remembered a time when he was six months old and he wouldn't stop crying, and she hadn't slept in days, and her nipples ached and her head hurt, and she had held him in front of her eyes and screamed into his hot red face that she would kill him if he didn't stop, and it was in her, at that moment, to throw him against the wall, or squeeze his neck so that the shit would squirt out of him for the last fucking time. God, what was it that had stopped her?

MOSS LAY ON his bed, listening to the slam of the front door and Nina's footfalls on the stairs. Why had she grabbed him? Couldn't she see that he wanted to be alone? When he was small she'd come to him like that, grab him and hold him when the rest of the world had failed her. He was the one thing she always had, no matter what—the thing she took most easily for granted. And he made himself dependent, to keep her from leaving him. He became too dependent. Too helpless. And then she left him.

He wished he'd followed Danielle; he might be in a better place now. Instead he had gone back to Fran's to pack his clothes. Fran had been asleep, snoring like an old man. Zak was gone—forever, Moss hoped. Still, he had to leave the place. Clearly he had overstayed his welcome.

He was tired, so tired. He did not know how Danielle would make it through a twelve-hour shift. He wondered if she'd told any of her colleagues about the pregnancy, if she was seeking advice. But she had made her decision. She'd gotten the tests. That was why she was so upset. In her mind, she had already committed the act, was already condemned. Moss decided to meet her after work in the morning and offer to go with her. She would want an accomplice. And even if she accused him of showing up just to make sure she went through with it, it was better, he thought, than not showing up at all.

Where to sleep, then? He didn't want to stay in the apartment.

He grabbed a pillow and two blankets from his closet; only then did he know where he was going.

He left the apartment and climbed the stairs. At the very top was a latched door. He lifted the latch, pushed the door open and stepped out onto the roof, imagining, as he always did, that he was exiting the hatch of a spaceship that had landed atop one of the rocks that shot up from the ground in all directions—glowing stalagmites of varying height, spiking the terrain. Moss spread out his blanket. The skyscrapers of midtown to his right, the shimmering towers of downtown to his left, the squat lunar capsules of water towers, silhouetted, dotting the rooftops in between. The Empire State Building was bathed in red light, a syringe plunged into a gauze of fog. The world below was meaningless.

Moss dropped the pillow and lay down on his back. On the edge of his vision an occasional star, hard and bright, moved slowly across the heavens, becoming, as it passed overhead, an airplane, its crucifix outlined on its belly with tiny stars of its own. Moss thought of the cosmic journey of sperm, the galactic dimensions. Sperm as manifold as the stars. Of the half-billion sperm in an ejaculation, only a few thousand live long enough to swim against the milky current to the outer limits of the Fallopian tube, and only a hundred make it to the egg itself. They approach the giant orb, confront its surface, beyond which lies the jelly of immortality; in their bid to survive they release an enzyme to break down the cells of the wall, only to meet another barrier, the zona pellucida, through which a single sperm is permitted to enter. This anonymous traveler, one of millions, now squiggles on the cusp of fame: it reaches the plasma membrane, making the egg impermeable to all else. The capsule is sealed; the nuclei of egg and sperm are fused.

Moss closed his eyes and drifted off. In the old days, his mother would get an occasional urge to go up on the roof and watch the sun set, and she always took Moss with her. There were certain things she needed to share. God knew she couldn't share music with him—the few times she'd tried to teach him how to play the stupid piano he got so frustrated that he banged the keys and kicked the trunk so that it echoed. And then she'd smack his hands and tell him he was tone deaf. Once, he spit at the instrument, when she wasn't looking. He had fantasies of taking a hammer to it. But he loved listening to her play. It relaxed him. And so did coming with her to the roof. She would always sing "Up on the Roof" by The Drifters. She taught him the words, or maybe he just got them in his head from hearing them so often. She had a pretty singing voice. It was Moss's belief that she secretly wanted to be a singer. At least he got that impression, from the way she sang to him—it was like she was auditioning for him, wanting to seduce him, test her effect on him, to see if she had the gift. "Do you think I have a nice voice?" she once asked him as they sat on the low ledge that separated their roof from the one next door, watching the sun slowly crash and burn and bleed across the sky. Everything was so still.

"Yes," Moss told her, "you have a very nice voice." He was a teenager by then. "Why don't you sing in a club?"

"Oh, no," she said, waving her hand, as if that were the last thing on her mind. And Moss understood that he had given her what she needed. They fell silent. The ambient wash of distant traffic and air conditioners was like the sound of waves, so that it was almost like being on the beach at sunset. There was a breeze, and wafts of cooking smells. With his eyes, Moss followed the flight of a pigeon, amazed by the speed with which a pigeon could travel from one side of town to the other—nothing in the whole city moved more swiftly than a bird skimming the rooftops. Yes, it was good just to be up high in the open air, away from the rat race and the noise in the streets—just like the song said. But when he asked his mother if he could sleep on the roof, she said it was too dangerous. What if he started sleepwalking and went off the edge? Or what if some psychopath—a favorite word of hers—came across him as he slept? The rooftops were full of them. Peeping Toms, mostly, but also burglars and rapists and serial killers. Once, when Moss was five or six, he saw, in a window across the street, a naked woman eating at a table. His mother saw this too, and had used the phrase "in the nude," which struck Moss like poetry. Back then, you could still shoot fireworks on the Fourth of July, and everyone would come up to the rooftops to see the big fireworks show, and the whole city looked and sounded like it was under attack, with rockets flying and flares exploding and M80s going off like crazy, rattling windows and triggering car alarms. And Moss would hold his mother's hand, afraid that some errant homemade missile would whiz horizontally from a neighboring building and strike him down.

WHEN HE WOKE up, it was morning, hazy and warm. He scrambled to his feet: what time was it? He looked at a clock tower in the distance: seven-thirty.

Leaving the blanket and pillow on the roof, he went back into the building and took the stairs in leaps. He burst through the front door and ran to the avenue to catch a bus or a cab, but he realized he had no money, and so kept running, stopping every few blocks to catch his breath, until he reached the hospital with minutes to spare.

He waited at the corner, keeping his eye on the doors. At ten past eight, Danielle came out, dressed in the clothes she'd worn last night at the movie, her knapsack on her shoulder. Normally she left work in her scrubs. She put on her sunglasses and began walking uptown. Moss followed her at a distance. He thought to catch up to her and talk to her, but she was so clearly on a mission that he held himself back: she was beyond him now. He could not reach her where she was. He felt powerless, invisible, a mere ghost. It was *her* life, not his. He could not intrude. She didn't need him. She was stronger on her own. He felt it. He kept her from living. He was useless to both of them. He ought to disappear. But he couldn't; he couldn't save her from himself. Only she could do that.

She crossed the street, heading west. Moss followed close behind, knowing she would never turn around. She was forever oblivious to her surroundings, lost in thought, daydreaming about how her life should be.

Moss could not imagine what she was thinking now.

She stopped in the middle of the block and pulled out a piece of paper, which she checked against the numbers on the buildings. Moss, frozen on the corner, watched as she entered through an unmarked door.

14

NINA LAY AWAKE ON THE COUCH, WHERE SHE'D FALLEN asleep waiting up for Moss. When she walked out last night, he was in his room, and though she didn't necessarily expect him to be there when she got back, she didn't think he'd be out all night. He was an adult, and had been taking care of himself for a long time, but that didn't mean she shouldn't worry, and she thought of how easy it had been when she was far away; she hadn't worried so much then. Where was he? Chances were that he'd spent the night at Danielle's, but something told her he hadn't. And she knew for a fact he hadn't stayed with Fran. Her fear was that he was with Boris.

She should never have gone out. She'd walked around for twenty minutes, or maybe it was an hour, trying to calm down. In her anger, which surprised her in its intensity, she felt that she never needed to see Moss again, that they were better off without each other. Why should they remain in this struggle? What did he want from her? Why did he hate her? She didn't deserve his hatred. He could go to hell, the ungrateful little shit. Let his girlfriend deal with him. Or better, let him have a kid of his own, and feel what it's like to be despised.

She must have been the oldest person on the street. So many new faces. Kids. Babies, really. Had she really left Moss alone at their age? But they, too, were on their own. On her way back home she stopped at a liquor store.

When she reached her building, she saw, slumped on the stoop, a young girl wearing black fishnets, a red plaid skirt and a white long-sleeved shirt unbuttoned to the cups of her black push-up bra. Her face was pale and streaked with mascara, as though she'd been crying, or maybe she'd painted it that way on purpose. In the old days there'd always be people washed up on the stoop. Occasionally Nina would give them some change, or some food, and then nicely ask them to go somewhere else, so that Moss wouldn't have to step over a body in the morning on his way to school, but every so often a person got belligerent and she had to call the cops.

Nina tapped the girl's shoulder. The eyes opened.

"Hi," the girl said groggily. "You're Moss's mom."

"Fran?" It had been a long time, but Nina saw her now. "Are you okay?"

Fran blinked slowly. "I was looking for Moss."

"He should be upstairs. Did you want to come in?"

Nina took Fran's hand and helped her to her feet, thinking that Fran would be useful as an offset. She would rather not face Moss alone.

Inside, Nina settled Fran in the kitchen and went to Moss's room to tell him he had company, but to her surprise, he wasn't there. He must have left between the time Nina went out and Fran landed on the stoop. Nina went back to the kitchen and invited Fran to stay for a few minutes, should Moss turn up. In his absence, she no longer felt mad at him.

"Is that a bottle?" Fran said, eyeing the bag in Nina's hand.

Nina poured two glasses of Maker's Mark and added ice and some flat Coke from the refrigerator. Fran drank hers quickly, and then began to cry. It seemed that her boyfriend had disappeared. They were together earlier in the day, took a nap together, and when she woke up, he was gone, and she hadn't heard from him since. It was Fran's recollection that Moss was in her apartment around the same time and might have some information. "Moss never liked Zak," she said. "He thinks he's bad for me."

"Why is that?"

Fran shrugged. "Everyone's bad for me. Have you met Boris?"

"I have," said Nina, startled by the name.

"What did you think?"

"What do you mean?"

Fran crossed her arms over her chest. "Just wondering."

"You sound like you have an opinion."

"I always have an opinion."

"What is it?"

Fran gave an imploring look. "Promise you won't say anything? To Moss?"

"Okay." Nina didn't like how this was building.

"Well," said Fran, "we sort of had a thing. Back when Moss first introduced us."

"A thing?"

"Sexual, mainly."

"Really."

"It didn't last very long. The first time we did it, I got pregnant." Fran poured herself more booze. "It happened in his Jacuzzi. He has this amazing loft in Tribeca. And a house in Maine, too. He's got a picture of it in his bedroom. A big picture. Framed. No people. Just the house. Do you see the problem?"

"You got pregnant?"

"Don't tell Moss—he thinks it was someone else. Oh, and in his medicine cabinet? Three kinds of antidepressants and a whole shit-load of Viagra. And this hair-growth stuff. I just thought, Poor Boris, man. I stole some Viagra—have you ever tried it? For yourself?"

"No."

"You should see his kitchen. You could go bowling on his counter space. Needless to say, he paid for it. The abortion, I mean."

Nina hardly knew what to think. She wasn't exactly jealous; creeped out was more like it.

She said, "Did he at least call you afterward?"

"After the abortion? Maybe once or twice. He went with me, though, to the clinic. I wanted Moss to come with me, but Boris insisted on being there, so I had to keep Moss out of it. Do you think he's depressed?"

"Who?"

"Moss. That's why I e-mailed you that time."

"Right," Nina said, straightening her spine at this reference to Moss's mental state.

"He needs a new woman," said Fran, stirring her drink with her finger.

"What about things between *you* and Moss?" Nina said, still reeling from the Boris revelations but determined to remain focused on her son. "He came back here tonight with his suitcase and said it was a long story."

Fran shrugged one shoulder. "I have no idea. When I saw his stuff was gone, I figured he went to live with his girlfriend, or whatever she is." She threw back the rest of her drink and turned to Nina with a woozy smile. "You know what I think? I think we should do a song together."

Nina recalled that Fran was a vocalist of some sort. "What do you sing?"

"Everything. I'm eclectic. It's my downfall."

If only to take her mind off both Moss and Boris, Nina led Fran to the living room; and for the second time in as many nights, she sat tipsily at the keyboard with one of Moss's friends. Fran leaned against the piano, looking down mistily at Nina, exuding a boozy, battered sexuality. Nina played a slow blues turnaround, and Fran closed her eyes and tapped her fingers on her hip, and then she started to sing. She had a sweet, girlish voice, almost virginal, but there was a roughness too, an injury, a genuine pain etched deep in her throat. "My man done left me; left me all alone. Yeah, my man, he done left me; left me cryin' all alone. So if you see my man on the street, cousin, tell him to please come home." There were tears in her eyes and she was swaying her hips slowly. "My man ain't got no mercy; he just walks on down the line. Said my man ain't got no mercy; he just walks on down the line. But Lord, have mercy on my daddy, 'cause you know he's still all mine." Fran subsided, but the words lingered. Nina dropped her head so that her hair fell over her hands. She was feeling the mood that Fran had generated, and wondered how much of it was coming from herself. Some people thought a piano couldn't cry, but Nina felt the anguish in the tips of her fingers as she hit her notes, and the sound was like a voice, a female voice. Fran bent her knees and hunched over and clutched at the thighs of her fishnets, touched by an unexpected phrase. When it was over the women looked at each other and laughed, half in embarrassment, for the emotions revealed, and half for how good it felt, how wonderfully good.

Nina said, "Do you play around town?"

"Not right now," said Fran. "I need to figure out what kind of stuff I want to do, then I have to find the right people to do it with."

"Well," said Nina, "you sound great."

"You really think so?"

"Absolutely."

Fran smiled, and then she began to cry again. But she was still smiling. "I've been fucking up," she said. "I know that. I have to get it together. I have to cut out all the shit." The smile crumbled and she covered her face with her hands.

Nina got up and touched Fran's arm, held it, as she had tried to hold Moss's arm earlier. Fran slackened in her grip. "You'll be okay," Nina told her softly. "I know you will."

Fran fell into her arms and hugged her. Nina hugged her back, thinking for a moment what it would be like to hold Moss this way, but it seemed so impossible, and that saddened her and made her embrace Fran harder, and she felt Fran's hands start to massage her back, as though she were embracing herself, soothing herself, but the lines were fuzzy right now, and Nina managed to slip away; and after a few more minutes of consoling and agreeing to stay in touch, Fran gathered herself and went to the door. "If you see Moss," she said, "tell him to call me."

And so when the phone rang again in the morning, bringing Nina out of this recollection and off the couch, her first thought was that it was Fran, in trouble somewhere and latching on to her; and was surprised when the voice on the other end was male. "Hey," it said. "Hi."

"Moss?" Nina said, filling with hope.

"It's Boris."

"Boris." Nina thrust her hand in her hair. "Hi."

"I need to see you."

"What is it?"

"I'm sorry," Boris said, "but I'd rather not talk over the phone."

AS DANIELLE WENT under, she saw her father standing in the woods in his camouflage and his orange hunting cap, his rifle against his shoulder. He looked at her, called her name, motioning with his head for her to follow him. She was ten years old, and this was her first hunting trip. Normally she liked going into the woods, but the echoing blasts of gunfire frightened her, and she kept one hand on the door of her uncle's sky-blue pickup. Her uncle and grandfather were still inside the truck (Danielle and her father had ridden in the back, with the weapons), eating ham-and-cheese sandwiches and drinking blackberry brandy from a flask. Her father then raised his gun and shot at something that had caught his eye. Danielle looked, and saw that it was a raccoon—it lay twitching in some brush, twenty feet away. Her father went over to it, saying, in his loud, instructive voice, so that Danielle would learn something, that you should never let a wounded creature suffer. He then picked the raccoon up by its bushy tail and smashed its head against a tree, killing it. This made Danielle cry, and as a result she was ordered to stay behind in the truck with her grandfather while her father and her uncle went deep into the woods with their guns, only to return later, carrying, on their beefy shoulders, the biggest animal she had ever seen (her absence had been necessary to their success, she sensed), antlers like trees, dead black eyes, oozing tongue; and it did not bother her, later, to watch the men take their knives to it (she'd always liked cutting dead things open and seeing what was inside), nor did the sight of blood and intestines spoil her enjoyment of the meat when it was cooked. Her father was a superb cook—his venison, marinated in peppercorns, cloves, parsley, thyme, rosemary, bay leaf, salt, red wine and brandy, was famous back home, the recipe having been published in the local paper. But he had other kids now, other daughters. Danielle tried not to think about it. He never called, not even on her birthday. Whenever she drank too much, which was seldom enough, she dared herself to call him and ask him straight out why he had forsaken her (she didn't buy the excuse that it was her mother who'd driven him away—that was too easy); or, if he didn't answer, to leave a cryptic message in a disguised voice—a way to get inside his head, his life, without revealing herself. She'd done it to Moss once, after their original breakup—had drunkenly recited a line from a poem by Keats about a dead dove. A dead love. She was sure he would know it was her, especially if he had bothered to read the poem in the collection she had given him (a doctor had given her the same book, trying to woo her, but it was Keats who had won her over, and she'd wanted to share him with Moss), but instead he thought, in his crazy way, that it was a threat from Nik Cattai, the same Nik Cattai who had tried to help her the night she got sick at his restaurant. Her father, of course, knew nothing. He had no idea about her life. He had no idea that she was lying here with a needle in her arm, dreaming of him.

WHAT WAS TAKING so long? It had been two hours. For two hours he'd been pacing the sidewalk. He began to worry. What if the doctor had botched it? But no, there'd be an ambulance. She must be sleeping off the drugs.

And then she appeared. Whatever had happened, had happened. She was there; the world continued. But it was no longer the same.

From his stakeout on the other side of the street, Moss tried to gauge her mood. This was difficult on account of her sunglasses. She walked west, with style and purpose, as if, like anyone else, she was on her way to an office. I am unscathed, her chin declared.

When she reached the corner, Moss hurried across the street toward her.

She stopped when she saw him; she looked caught—there was an attempt, behind the glasses, at a smile, which Moss read as an appeal for understanding: seeing him had put her on the defensive, yes, had revived a doubt about her actions, that *she* might be in the wrong, for having acted rashly, hastily, on her own, without him— Moss sniffed a chance to gain a footing.

She said, "How did you find me?" Her voice, though tense, contained a leniency that snared Moss's heart.

"I followed you," Moss confessed, wanting desperately to hold her. "I'm sorry. I didn't know what else to do."

"I know," said Danielle, calmly, reasonably. "I know you didn't." A counselor at the clinic must have talked sense into her, Moss thought.

"So—how do you feel?"

"I feel good. The nausea's gone. It's amazing."

Moss swallowed. Was she forgiving him? "That's *great*."

Danielle looked away, as if there were something improper in his enthusiasm. "And how are *you*?" she said. She faced him again.

Moss tried to find her eyes through the dark lenses. "That depends."

"On what?"

Moss shoved his hands in his pockets. "If you're mad at me."

"No. I'm not mad."

"What, then?"

"Nothing," Danielle said. "I just feel—nothing."

"What do you mean, nothing?"

"When I woke up—it was gone. The nausea, everything."

"Everything?"

"I'm tired, Moss. I just want to go home and sleep."

"I don't understand," Moss said. He wanted to say, What about us? But that was impossible now. "Dannie."

"I've got to go."

"Why?"

"I told you. I'm tired."

"Okay. You're mad at me. Fine. Be mad at me. Blame me. But don't hate me. Don't hate me, Danielle. Do you hear me?"

"To be honest, Moss," Danielle said wearily, "I'm not even thinking about you. I'm just moving on with my life."

"I think we should talk."

"About *what*?" Danielle broke out. "About what, Moss? You have no intentions for me. No plans. And even if you did, I wouldn't want to be with you. Not now. I used to think we were meant for each other. I was sure of it."

"Don't do this."

"But these past few days showed me who you are. You're the most selfish person I've ever known."

"Don't say that word."

"Selfish. Selfish! If I'd had this baby, you wouldn't want any part of me. *Or* the baby."

"You're crazy."

"And just so you know, I quit work this morning."

"What?"

"I'm moving back home." Danielle surveyed the tree-lined block, jaw clenched. "This isn't the place for me."

"You *quit*?"

"I'm sorry, Moss. I've got to go now."

Moss felt weightless. This wasn't like the other times. No. This felt real. He'd done it. He'd finally done it. Had destroyed the indestructible. "Danielle," he said, his voice breaking. "Please."

"Please what, Moss? Please *what*? Stand here and waste my time in a stupid, meaningless conversation?"

"I'm sorry," Moss blurted, not knowing what he was sorry for, but sorry, sorry.

"It's too late, Moss. I mean it. I don't want you following me, or calling me, or writing to me, or anything." Danielle's arm went up; a taxi bore down on them.

"Don't do this," Moss warned. "I love you. Do you hear me?"

The taxi stopped. Danielle opened the door and got in without looking at him.

Moss stood there. Everything was spinning. "I love you. Don't do this, Danielle. I love you!"

The door closed; the report was like a shot. Moss dropped to his knee. The taxi pulled away.

"Marry me," Moss murmured, watching the back of Danielle's head through the window. "Come back to me. Danielle!" People on the street were noticing him now.

She was gone. She loved him no longer. He had failed, he had killed them, and she would always remember him for that.

Minutes passed before he was able to pull himself from the sidewalk and limp away. The limp was necessary; he was a hobbled animal, defenseless. The world was a jungle. He'd been bitten, gored. Left for dead. But this was crazy. They could straighten this out. Sure they could. She would calm down, come to her senses. Love couldn't die just like that.

A block away he found a pub that was already open. Inside it was dark and woodsy, with Tiffany lamps and a chalkboard on the wall with the specials written on it. Moss took a seat at the bar. The bottles on the shelves shone gold and emerald and ruby. Hennessy, Frangelico, Cinzano, Cuervo: they were like the names of saints. It was eleven in the morning. Above the bar hung framed portraits of Jack and Bobby Kennedy.

The bartender, a big middle-aged Irishman in a white shirt and bow tie, set a coaster in front of Moss.

"What can I get for ya?"

"My girlfriend just left me," said Moss.

"She left you, did she?" said the bartender. This drew the attention of the other customers: firemen, Con Ed guys, off duty. A big guy in a suit reading the *Times*.

"She's a nurse," Moss said. "She tells me about people."

"She does."

"People who are dying. Some of these people will die alone. They have no one. My girlfriend sees this every day. It's taught her things. That's why she left me." Moss took a breath against the threat of tears. "No one," he said, looking down at his hands, "should have to die alone."

15

NINA HAD AGREED TO MEET BORIS FOR DINNER THE FOL-
lowing night, after securing a guarantee that he hadn't
leaked a word of their adventures to Moss, and wouldn't do so in
the future, though he still refused to tell her what he wanted to talk
to her about, saying it would have to wait until he saw her; and
when Moss came home a short while later, looking pale and shaken,
and shut himself up in his room, Nina was tempted to make a connection. Through his door she heard him crying—a low lamenta-
tion, a rhythmic cooing, as peculiar to him as his voice or his laugh,
but even more personal, as if pain were his true identity, and like a
superhero he returned to it every so often in profound secrecy. It
tore at her heart; she had never heard him cry as a man. She
knocked on his door, asking if she could come in, but he wouldn't
let her, and then finally he did, and she entered and sat beside him
where he lay limp and bloodshot on his spiny bed, and he told her
his story, how Danielle had had the abortion and how she'd killed
him too. His back was turned to her, but he didn't flinch when she

touched his shoulder, and she had to be strong not to cry herself. My baby, she thought. Who will take care of him now? As much as she hated his suffering, she could not blame Danielle. Danielle was brave. And now Moss would have to be brave. This was the hardest part of living, and Nina vowed that she would see him through it.

On the night she was to meet Boris, she fixed Moss a light dinner (tuna sandwich, a pickle, a bowl of tomato soup) and brought it to his room, his bed, where he floated lethargically under a wreath of crumpled tissues. She had told him earlier that she had a gig, adding that she could cancel if he wanted her to, but he insisted that she go, that he'd be okay, and she believed him, and turned her thoughts to Boris, thinking that if nothing else, a dinner would close out their account on a dignified note. She dressed as she would for a gig—a sleeveless black dress, red lipstick—and tied back her hair.

They met at Beaujoli, which had been Nina's choice (she was curious, and Boris, though skeptical, said he believed in giving things a second chance). Boris was waiting for her at a corner table; he stood up, with his arms at his sides, like a soldier.

"Thanks for coming," he said.

"Sorry I'm late." Nina was about to explain that she'd had to make dinner for Moss, but decided, for now, to keep any Moss stories to herself.

They sat. Boris folded his hands on the table and looked at her expectantly.

"Are you okay?" said Nina.

"I'm fine," said Boris. He quickly picked up his menu.

Nina did the same. They hid their faces until the waiter came. When the waiter took their menus, they were left undefended.

"So—have you talked to Moss?" Nina ventured.

"Moss?" said Boris, as if recollecting a name from his distant past. "No, I haven't. Why?"

Nina was confused. Didn't Boris know? "His girlfriend left him," she said. "He's in pretty bad shape." She checked her watch. Should she call him?

"I think he's better off," Boris said decisively. "He always said she wasn't right for him."

"He's no judge."

"And you are?"

"I see things. He needs someone to take care of him."

"That's not what it should be about. It should be about an equal partnership. Two people who understand each other, who see the world in similar ways, who appreciate the same things, who know how to communicate honestly and openly. That's how people take care of each other." Boris was looking meaningfully at her. "The fact is, Nina, I haven't stopped thinking about you since the other night." He held up his hand to check any objections. "I know it's a little awkward, because of Moss, but if you wouldn't mind, I'd like very much to keep seeing you." His chest sank, but his eyes remained intent on her.

"Wow," said Nina. "This is a surprise." What else could she say? Two days ago she might have been intrigued—flattered at the least, tempted at the most—but given Moss's condition, this was the last thing any of them needed. In the past it had always been the man not wanting to get serious with her because she had a kid; now, *she* was the one citing Moss. She couldn't do this to him. It felt downright predatory—on Boris's part as well as hers. And besides, there were other reasons not to get involved with Boris—his youth, his inexperience, her own lack of readiness, and, not least, his past affair with Fran, which she saw no point in bringing up, but which suggested that Boris was working his way pathologically through the women in Moss's life—Danielle might be next.

"I'm sorry," Nina said. "It's just not a good idea."

Boris sighed; his hands sucked themselves into fists on either side of his plate. "I guess I should make myself a little clearer, then." He bowed his head, took a breath; and when he looked at her again, his eyes shone with feeling. "You may not believe this, Nina, but I'll say it anyway. You're the person I've been waiting to meet. You're it. I mean, you've been in my dreams. My whole life."

"Boris," Nina said gently, because she was now the slightest bit afraid of him, "I can't get involved with my son's best friend. You're a reasonable person and I'm sure you can understand."

"Forget Moss for a minute."

"I can't forget him."

"Try. Just so you can see how you really feel. Give yourself that luxury. For once."

"*Stop it,*" said Nina, in a severe parental tone that struck cold fear in both of them.

"Okay," said Boris. "Okay. We don't have to talk about it now."

The food arrived, and Boris spent the next half hour elucidating the merits of his herb-encrusted salmon (Nina had ordered the lamb, though she wasn't hungry), saying that a new chef must have been hired, and then he talked about the kind of restaurant he himself would like to open one day, in a space with clean lines and blank walls, instead of these swirling mosaics, which he found no aid to digestion. He was lashing out desperately against silence. Nina persisted in saying nothing. The whole thing was a mistake.

"I didn't mean to upset you before," Boris said. "I was just telling the truth."

"I'm sorry," said Nina. She looked at the door, half expecting to see Moss there. "I should probably get home."

"Fucking great." Boris abruptly signaled the waiter.

"I'll pay," Nina said, reaching into her bag for her own wallet, feeling she needed to offer something, even if she couldn't afford it, and at the same time place more distance between them; but Boris's determination to not allow her this advantage seemed to draw the waiter quickly to him, and he handed over his charge card (he didn't even ask for the check) before Nina could find hers, so that it was Nina who felt undermined. She spent the next minute fumbling for cash with which to redeem herself. She came up with twenty-three dollars, barely enough to cover her entrée.

"Thanks," Boris said in a hollow voice, taking the money before Nina had fully reached out her hand: he calmly placed the bills in his wallet, and in the next moment the waiter returned with his card. Nina felt as though something more than money had been taken from her; a notion of dispossession, physical, irrevocable.

Outside, Boris went to the curb for a taxi.

"Look," said Nina, keeping back several paces. "Let's not be enemies. It's a crazy time for me. Okay?" She was surprised by the plea in her voice. "Boris."

He didn't move. A taxi appeared in front of him as if conjured by his humiliation: without a word, he opened the door and got in, leaving Nina standing there with deep regrets, and the queasy fear that Boris, in retaliation (for what? what had she done?), would now go to Moss with their secret.

TWO DAYS AFTER the abortion, Moss, from the grave of his bed, called Danielle's apartment. The number had been disconnected. Moss pulled the blanket over his head and cried into his pillow. How could she cut him off like this? Where did she find the strength? And what had he done to deserve it? He tried to think of a way to kill himself that would haunt her the rest of her life. It would have to be something dramatic that would make the news and reach her wherever she was. The George Washington Bridge? During rush hour? He started to write a letter to her, telling her how much he loved her and how he couldn't live without her, and that he didn't deserve her (he saw no contradiction in the question of what he did and didn't deserve), but nothing was right; he kept changing and correcting, until the words were sapped of their meaning. Not knowing what else to do, he began outlining a new play, which would have nothing to do with Danielle. A true distraction. But every hour or so his bereavement came back to him, and he would resume the fetal position and weep. He saw her face, her smile, the love in her eyes, heard her call his name.

At first, his mother took care of him. She brought him deviled eggs and carrot sticks with peanut butter and sat at the edge of his bed, the way she used to when he was a boy.

"It's all for the best," she kept saying. "Danielle deserves a chance to be happy. And so do you."

"I *was* happy," Moss said.

He hadn't known it, but now he did. Meanwhile Nina brought him pizza, cupcakes, ice cream, falafel. He requested these things but often left them uneaten. The days sank and drowned, one by one. And then, when he was nearly beyond the point of noticing, there was a change in the air: upon waking one day, he realized that the pigeons hadn't bothered him all morning. Curious, he got up and stuck his head out the window. No pigeons. He looked up. Spread across the top of the air shaft was a black netting. Was he dreaming? Had Mrs. Bulina really done it? But why? Was it his veiled threat of lawsuits? He told his mother about it and learned, to his surprise, that it was *she* who had called the landlady, she who had demanded action. "I knew they were bothering you," she said almost guiltily, as if afraid he'd think she was meddling, "and so I told Mrs. Bulina, 'Listen—you have a responsibility to your tenants, and if you don't do something about this problem, I'm calling the city.'" Ah, the city! Moss thought. God bless the bureaucrats. And God bless my mother. And God bless Danielle, wherever she is.

And so he slept in peace; and when he had the strength, he filled his notebook with what was becoming, he suspected, his finest work to date: *The Passion of Bobby Boxcar*. The eponymous character was a twenty-year-old drifter who rides the rails in search of his unknown father, and after a series of quasi-philosophical adven-

tures with thieves and folksingers, ends up in the town of Amaryl-
lis, Idaho, where his father is the spiritual leader of an apocalyptic
sex cult that, as Bobby eventually learns, has been awaiting the arrival of a healthy young male, much like Bobby himself, to be used
in a human sacrifice meant to bring about the end of days. Meanwhile, Bobby commences a fateful romance with his father's favorite "wife," a sixteen-year-old girl named Nutricia.

Upon finishing the play, he wrote a brief letter to Anton:

I know we've never met, nor do we know each other very well,
but you are—despite your crimes—still my mother's husband,
and, as such, morally obligated to assist the two thirds of our
little family left reeling in the wake of your iniquities (yes, kind
sir, I am speaking of your adultery, which, aside from wound-
ing my mother, sets a poor example for me, your devoted step-
son). Assist how, you say? Easy. Take the enclosed manuscript
and give it to your concubine, the Hollywood agent, and lean
on her to get me a deal. Believe me, you'll feel much better.

The next day, he mailed the package to California. It was one of
his few ventures out of doors since the abortion. Waiting in line at
the post office, he began to second-guess the climactic scene, in
which Bobby, bound and gagged and being carried to the altar by
chanting cult members, is saved at the last possible moment by a
providential swarm of locusts. Moss watched the clerk stamp the
large yellow envelope and toss it in a pile. Oh, well. What was the
worst that could happen? That the agent hated it? So what? She

could love it and make him rich. He walked out of the post office, and no sooner had his foot hit the sidewalk than he felt a fat raindrop land on his head. He stopped. It wasn't raining, and there were no dripping air conditioners above him. He felt a liquid matter creeping through his hair. He didn't dare touch it. Looking down at the pavement, he saw the signs all around, tiny splashes of white and green. Whose joke was this? Christ! He should never have left his bedroom. The universe was speaking to him, singling him out, mocking him. He rushed home, went to the bathroom and looked in the mirror. Smack in the middle of the nest of his hair lay a walnut-size chunk of white birdshit. What were the chances? He shook his head over the bathtub and the turd fell out, light and brittle as a biscuit, landing silently near the drain.

ONE AFTERNOON, MOSS awoke to find, on his night table, an envelope, addressed to him in a chillingly familiar hand. The postmark was from Michigan, Danielle's home state. There was no return address. Moss was afraid to open it. He didn't know why. Maybe it was because he'd been praying for it.

He sniffed it, touched his lips to it, then opened it slowly. A letter. His skin tingled. He had no idea what to expect.

He unfolded the paper and read the words.

Dear Moss,

I hope you're okay. I'm back home, staying at my mom's. It's so boring here. But it's not all bad. It's definitely a change of scenery. And change can be a good thing. I'll bet you've never seen so many trees in your life. And the sky is so wide. You'd love it, actually.

I do miss you, Moss. After the abortion I was so mad at you, as I'm sure you could tell. I really felt that you let me down, in so many ways. And all I could do was to cut myself off from you, because otherwise I would have just tried to hurt you, and I don't want to do that.

Leaving you was the hardest thing I've ever done. Even harder than killing our baby. And yet I can't even say for sure that the abortion was the wrong decision. I honestly don't know if it was or not. Sometimes I regret it, sometimes I don't. Which is kind of how I feel about us.

I know everything wasn't your fault. I made my share of mistakes. I expected too much from you. I was too demanding. I put all my dreams onto you, and that wasn't fair. It's a bad habit of mine, and I never seem to learn the lesson, which is that I can't depend on other people to make a life for me. I think that's why I always wanted a baby so badly—I thought it would give meaning to my life. But for now, I need to focus on me. I'm looking into doing travel nursing, maybe for a year or two. I don't know where yet. Or maybe I'll go back to school and get an advanced degree. I don't want to be wiping asses for the rest of my life.

I am still mad at you, Moss. I can't deny that. You should have never let me go into that clinic alone. I don't think I'll ever understand it.

But I don't hate you. I honestly want you to be happy. And

I think the only way for either of us to be happy is if we both move on with our lives.

You won't be hearing from me again, or at least not for a long time, until I am over this. I'm sorry if this letter is in any way confusing or upsetting. I don't want it to be. And it shouldn't be. We just both need to be strong. I guess that's what I'm really trying to say.

Danielle

Moss read the letter several times. It cut him. She was right: his behavior had been unconscionable. There could be no excuse. Or rather, none that she would ever accept. He supposed he would have to live with his mistakes, just as she would have to live with the guilt of "killing our baby." She probably thought she was going to hell for that. Oh, Danielle, he thought. I wish things could have been different.

HE LAY IN bed staring at the stray cobwebs on the ceiling when someone knocked on his door.

"Come in."

The door opened. It was Fran, wearing a green tank top and a red leather miniskirt. Moss hadn't seen her since his raid on her bedroom, an act she had obviously held against him, considering she hadn't talked to him since. Yet here she was.

"What are you doing?" she said, grabbing his foot through the sheet and shaking it. She was always forgetting her grudges.

"I'm recovering," said Moss. "What about you?"

"I came to rehearse with your mom. We bumped into each other one night—I don't know if she told you—and we decided to play together."

"No one told me anything," Moss said. He would question Nina about this later. "Are you still seeing what's-his-name?"

"Who, Zak?" Fran let go of Moss's foot. "No. Not anymore." She gave the tough smile that always made her seem so young.

"You weren't in love," Moss said.

"*You* obviously were."

"I guess my mother filled you in."

"I'm so sorry, Moss. I know how hard it is. I want you to get better."

"I'll be okay," Moss said. "It just takes time." He didn't believe that, but just saying it gave him a small amount of strength.

"Have you heard from Boris?" Fran said, with an air of rescuing them from an unpleasant subject.

"He's been up at his house," said Moss. "He said he needed to get out of the city. But I had a feeling there was a reason."

"Maybe he just needed a change of scenery."

"Maybe."

"You should visit him," said Fran. "Get out of here for a few days."

Moss didn't want to discuss it—it upset him that people thought he was such a hermit, that he had no experience of the outer world. Wasn't it enough to have an imagination?

"So why didn't my mother tell me she was playing with you?" he said, to change the subject. "When did this happen?"

"I asked her not to say anything. We're playing Wednesday night. I've been so nervous I didn't want anyone to come. But then today I thought, Why not tell Moss? At least it'll get him out of bed." Fran lowered her eyes. "Anyway, I want someone there who would cheer for me even if I bomb."

"Of course I would," said Moss. "But you won't bomb."

"You never know."

"I know," said Moss, who was accustomed to saying supportive things to Fran, mainly to keep her from killing herself (not literally, but that's what it came down to, when he thought about it), only this time he felt he was simply speaking the truth, as if his pain and heartache had aged him into wisdom. Fran would be okay.

A few minutes after she left, Moss heard the piano in the other room, followed by Fran's voice. Some soulful, haunting pop ballad of yesteryear. Moss closed his eyes and let the sound crawl over him; he felt himself sinking into a dark, soft place, with sweet vibrations all around.

NINA WAS SURPRISED to see Moss appear in the kitchen, where she was drinking coffee and nursing faint regrets about Fran, who kept screwing up the lyrics to standards everyone knew.

"You two sounded great," Moss said. He dropped himself into the chair, wearing only a pair of gray sweatpants. His chest was bony and hairless, like a boy's. "I never imagined you guys would get together. I kind of feel responsible."

"Why?"

"Because you know each other through me."

"Well, you're not responsible. Don't worry."

"Why would I worry?"

"Fran is very talented," Nina offered, thinking that Moss might take any criticism against her personally. "She drops a lyric now and then, but—"

"I've got to make a change," said Moss, forgetting Fran. He fidgeted in his chair. "I've been cooped up for too long." He looked at Nina. "*You* did it. You went around the world."

"Where do you want to go?"

"Someplace quiet. Where I can see the sky."

Nina agreed about the sky, but she didn't like the idea of his going off to travel. He couldn't afford it, for one thing. And how would he support himself?

"I'd miss you," she heard herself say. She wanted to discourage him, but instead she smiled, letting those words stand by themselves.

"Why would you miss me?" Moss said, with faint suspicion. "You got along without me before."

"That doesn't mean I didn't miss you. Anyway, those were different times."

"You mean you're lonely now? Afraid of being alone?"

"That might be part of it," said Nina, recognizing that he was asking these questions out of concern rather than anger. "I think maybe I made a mistake eight years ago. When I left."

"What do you mean?"

"I mean I shouldn't have gone away." Nina bit her lip. This was it, apparently: she was finally saying what she needed to say, what she had rehearsed in her head a thousand times, and which was now occurring of itself, and it wasn't nearly as frightening or difficult as she had imagined. "I was running away. From a lot of things."

"From me?"

"From my responsibility to you."

"I was an adult," said Moss, defending her.

"No. You weren't. Neither of us was." Nina shook her head, not meeting his eyes. "And I'm so sorry, Moss. I made mistakes."

"Mom. Please. I was fine. I had a good time. I took care of myself."

Nina saw that he was worried she might cry. They were not at ease with each other's emotions, even after so many years.

"You did your best," Moss went on. "And who knows what your life would've been like without me? Maybe you would've been happier. I'm the one who should be thankful. You gave me life." He was telling her he loved her, the best way he knew how. But he had forgiven nothing.

"I wanted you to come to Europe in the worst way," Nina said, searching for a deeper connection. "I'd be somewhere, in some city, and I'd think, Moss would love this. He'd get such a kick out of it."

"I know," said Moss. "You tried to get me to come. It was my fault. I was afraid to fly."

"I should have insisted," said Nina. "It's a huge regret." She had an urge to touch him. She worried for him. She wished she could give him everything.

"Maybe I'll end up over there," said Moss, absently, drawing a circle around his nipple with his finger, "and you can visit me."

"What would you do over there?" said Nina, taking him seriously.

"Nothing, of course."

"Moss."

"What?" said Moss, coy and mischievous.

"You know what. You can't just do nothing."

"I'll meet a girl."

Nina laughed. He was trying to get to her. "I'm sure the girls would go crazy for you, baby."

She realized that she was speaking her fear—women were a danger to him, she felt. They would hurt him. The Danielle episode was just the beginning. Nina did not trust anyone to take care of Moss the way he needed to be taken care of. He was a great person, but he was still a child. It was probably her own fault. Mothers always got the blame, whether they deserved it or not. But at least she hadn't smothered him, by being controlling, overbearing, domineering—words used by the most severe neurotics to describe their mothers. At least she would never be accused of *those* things.

"So," she said, reaching out to pluck a piece of lint from his hair. "Are you coming Wednesday night? To hear us play?"

Moss shrugged. "Fran wants me to," he said. "So I guess I will."

16

THURSDAY MORNING, NINA WOKE UP AND VOMITED ON
her sheets. This made no sense—she'd had only two drinks
the night before. Or was it three? Regardless, she never got sick like
this. Fran must be even worse off—she'd downed three shots of
tequila minutes before the performance to fend off an attack of
stage fright, and another when it became clear that her parents had
failed to show up. And yet she nailed every tune—words and everything—and at the end of the set, the audience, about twenty people,
mobbed her with praise, all but ignoring Nina, who sought Moss
out with her eyes, wanting him beside her, but Moss, too, was fighting to get to Fran, and Nina watched from a short distance as Moss
and Fran embraced. When Moss finally greeted Nina, he was far
more complimentary than he'd been the last time he saw her play,
but it was nothing like the attention he had given Fran.

Nina got out of bed and went to the bathroom, where she
puked again, in the toilet. What was this? A virus? Something she
ate? There was another possibility, far-fetched, hardly worth enter-

taining. But a physical memory returned to her; her body tingled with a witchy foreknowledge. The toilet water sizzled. She flushed it, then stood and locked the door. "No," she murmured. "Can't be." Already she felt a twitch, a pinprick of hope within the panic, a promise of change, as of an irreversible circumstance whose demands must be obeyed: that, too, was freedom—the peace of mind of the condemned. She put her fist to her mouth. What would she do? Maybe it was nothing, a scare, the body's rumor. She rinsed her mouth, studied her face in the mirror. It wasn't impossible. "To the drugstore, then," she said gamely into the glass. But the eyes staring back at her looked terrified.

"MOSS. THERE'S SOMETHING I need to discuss with you."

They were in the kitchen. Moss had just sat down to a breakfast of bagels and cream cheese. Nina sat across from him, peeling a banana. Moss couldn't remember her ever eating a banana.

"You're leaving again?" Moss said, recalling her demeanor the night before, at the piano, where she seemed to fade willfully into the background as Fran stole the spotlight. "You're going back to California?" He heard the fear in his voice, the accusation.

"No," said Nina, stuffing half the banana in her mouth. She chewed. "I'm not going anywhere." She was looking at Moss like she wanted him to make another guess.

"Is something wrong?" Moss said suddenly. He couldn't imagine what.

"No, nothing's wrong," said Nina. She blinked. "In fact, it's good news. Very good news. For all of us."

All of us? "You and Anton made up," Moss said, as if it were plain as day. "He's moving here. Into this apartment." The sour pleasure he took in spoiling whatever happy surprise Nina had deluded herself into imagining he might get from this news was hardly enough to negate the sickening prospect of his being driven, finally, from the only home he'd ever known, of virtually being replaced. No one would expect him to stay—the apartment wasn't big enough for three—and now he understood that the "good news," as Nina saw it, was that her shiftless son would now have to strike out on his own and become an adult.

"I'm pregnant," Nina said.

"What?" said Moss. Nina was wearing a simpering, apologetic smile, such as Moss had never seen. He thought there must be a mistake.

"It's a shock to me too," Nina said, as if Moss had just said something humorous and reassuring. "But I've been thinking about it—"

"Did you say you were pregnant?"

"I know. Amazing, isn't it?"

"Are you saying you're having a baby?" said Moss. He slid his bagel away. "Is that what you're telling me?"

"Yes," said Nina, and there was a whiff of maternal protectiveness in that, for her other child.

"But you're forty-four!" Moss gripped his hair with both hands. "Are you sure about this?"

"Moss."

"Who's the father?"

"If you'll just let me talk."

"Are you definitely decided on this?"

"I'm talking to you, Moss, because I want to be able to trust you. I want to be able to trust that I can say anything to you and that you'll listen with at least a little understanding."

"Who's the father?"

Nina hesitated. "It's not important," she said. "What's important is us. You and me."

"It can't be Anton. Can it?"

"As a matter of fact, this has nothing to do with Anton. It's no one you know."

"Is it anyone *you* know?"

"What does that mean?"

"Think about it," said Moss, sensing her weakness, and his own power, which had moral underpinnings. "Both of your kids"—the phrase brought his unborn sibling to life for him in an unexpected way—"have unknown fathers. Unless this guy, whoever he is, plans to take an active role. Is it Sam Silvestri?"

"To think that I was expecting you to be happy," Nina said, her voice breaking.

"I *am*," Moss said fervently, afraid she might cry. But he wasn't happy, not for her, not for anyone.

"I want you," said Nina, wiping her eye with the back of her wrist, "to be a brother to this baby."

Moss gazed at her. A brother? What did it mean to be a brother?

"We'll be three of us," Nina said, emboldened by his silence. "A family. We never had a third person. We never had that balance. This could be good for us, Moss."

Moss hung his head, disappointed that she felt she must appeal to him in this way; it suggested her guilt, her knowledge that this would hurt him. And how could it possibly be "good" for them? In what sense? She would be focused entirely on the baby. But why should he care? He was a grown man. He didn't need her. And yet she seemed to need him. Or was she just trying to involve him, include him, make him feel wanted? Because there was no disputing that she had already formed that special bond with the fetus. Another fetus! Christ. Did she talk to the thing? Sing to it? Maybe it was too early for that. She didn't look any more pregnant than Danielle had. And while *she* was obviously more determined to give birth than Danielle had been, Moss figured that if he really wanted to talk her out of it he could, although to do so would require a degree of selfishness that even he found repellent. He couldn't ask her to abort it, especially after she talked about it like it was already a person. Nor could he deny, in himself, an odd pang of excitement. He'd always wanted a sibling. A girl, though: a sister. Not a boy.

It then occurred to Moss that Nina *would* need him—need him to help her raise it. She needed him, all right.

"Who's the father?" he demanded.

"I told you, it's not important," said Nina. She seemed frightened. "It's a part of my life that belongs to *me*. It's personal."

"I think I deserve to know the name of the father of my half-sibling."

"Not *half*," Nina said, with a passion for equality and the preservation of her embattled family that Moss felt was being exploited to subdue him. "No one is half an anything. I don't want to hear that word."

Moss resisted this plea. "And the kid deserves to know too," he said, with his own righteousness. "And the father deserves to know about the kid."

"Moss. Just stop."

"Is it a secret?"

"No, it's not a secret."

"Then who the fuck is he?"

"Don't talk to me like that!"

"Like what?"

"Did you hear me?" Nina banged her fists on the table.

"What?" Moss said, frightened by her anger, by what the strain of it might be doing to her, and hating her for that advantage, that she could attack him from the shadows of her mysterious and delicate condition.

"Show some respect!" she said. "I'm your mother, goddamn it!"

"I just asked a simple question. Why are you getting hysterical?"

"You bastard. You selfish, ungrateful little shit. You *disgust* me!"

"And you disgust me, you whore!" Moss yelled. He could not stop himself; walls were falling. "I hope you have a miscarriage. I hope the baby's retarded. There's every chance, at your age—"

The next thing he knew, his face had been slapped incredibly hard, so hard that he didn't feel it, and then the blows came at his head and he had to cover up with his arms, thinking that he must defend himself, grab her arms and stop her, but he couldn't face her, did not want to see her, and so he backed away, toppling his chair behind him, and then he saw her coming at him from around the table, and with an animal squeal, a yelp for survival, he escaped, spinning blindly from the kitchen and down the hall into his room. She was crazy. He slammed his door, gasping. "You're crazy!" he yelled. "You're fucking crazy!"

There was no answer. After a moment, Moss heard the front door open and close. His teeth chattered.

"That's right!" he shouted. "Walk it off. Get some air. Buy some Pampers. But don't blame me for getting yourself knocked up. It's not my fault!"

He knew he had to get out. Permanently this time. They were finished.

He looked at the phone. He wanted to call Danielle, tell her everything. But she was no longer available to him. He didn't even know where she was.

Instead, he called Boris in Maine—they hadn't talked in weeks —and claimed that he was still grieving over Danielle and needed to get away for a while. He was too embarrassed to explain that Nina was pregnant by an unknown party, someone other than her husband, though there was a part of him that wanted to erupt with the news: he was going to be a brother.

Boris, sounding starved for human contact, assured Moss that Danielle would eventually come back to him ("Hasn't she al- ways?"), and that in the meantime he could stay as long as he wanted.

17

BORIS WAS WAITING FOR HIM AT THE BUS DEPOT, WEAR-
ing jeans, sneakers and a Red Sox sweatshirt. For the first
time in their friendship, they embraced and slapped each other's
backs. Boris took Moss's bag and led him to his Jeep.

"So how's it going?" Moss said, looking around. Trees and sky.
Fresh air. Droning insects. He watched as a flock of dark birds burst
from a budding treetop: they fell and rose, the flashes of wing and
netherwing creating a flicker like confetti, and then they swerved to
one side and curved around, fluttering, into the arms of another tree.

"I'm writing a screenplay, man," said Boris, like an alcoholic
announcing that he was one month sober.

"Great. What's it about?"

They got into the Jeep. Moss couldn't remember the last time
he had been in a car. Probably with Danielle.

"It's about a gambler," said Boris, grappling with the gearshift
and the wheel. His physical mastery of the vehicle translated to
Moss as dominion over the surrounding wilderness, its nameless

twisting roads. "I call him Van Edsel. He's known as the best poker player in the world, but he becomes addicted to losing. In the Freudian sense. Meaning he derives sexual pleasure from it. He has orgasms, like Dostoyevsky. And he loses everything—his house, his wife, even his kid; he loses them in a poker game. But the thing is, the people he loses to are really terrorists, who've been watching him for a long time and need him for a doomsday operation in which he can use his skills at cards."

"To do what?"

"To gain secret information," Boris said impatiently. "The head of the CIA is also addicted to gambling—it's a secret addiction that even the president doesn't know about. So obviously, Van Edsel's job is to get him to play poker for a top government secret. And if Van Edsel wins, the terrorists will give him back his family. On the downside, of course, the information he gets could lead to the final destruction of the country." Boris was perspiring visibly. "This is the conflict."

Moss had gotten lost somewhere. "Sounds interesting," he said encouragingly.

Boris glanced at Moss, needing to believe him. "Of course, in the end," he said, with revived enthusiasm, as if he were no longer alone in this, "in his showdown with the CIA guy, which is being watched by the terrorists—unbeknownst to the CIA guy, obviously—Van Edsel tips the CIA guy off by sending a code through the cards he keeps turning up."

"Where's the ocean?" said Moss. He thought he could smell it, but all you could see were trees and fields.

"I know it sounds complicated," said Boris, his face darkening, "but I have it all figured out."

"No," said Moss, "it sounds good."

Boris honked his horn irritably at a squirrel that crossed their path. "So what's going on with *you?*" he said. "Still depressed?"

"I'll be okay."

"Of course you'll be okay." Boris gave Moss a punch on the shoulder, which hurt. "You're young."

Moss rubbed the pain. "I'll be twenty-eight."

"Twenty-eight." Boris laughed with derision. "You're a kid."

Moss wasn't sure how to take that. Even as an insult, it conceded something. They drove in silence for a while.

"So," said Boris, adjusting the rearview mirror. "How's your mom? Still playing?"

"Why wouldn't she be?"

"You never know."

Boris turned left onto a wooded, winding road, then braked at a hidden driveway that he nearly overshot, and turned onto that. The fat tires crackled over the gravel as the house came into view beyond a light fortress of tall thin trees. It was a long house with gray cedar shingles, bent slightly in the middle, like an arm, like California, bookended by low gables. A Mexican in a white tank top pushed a wheelbarrow along a dirt path on the side of the house and disappeared down a slope. The house alone had to be worth millions. There was a silver Lexus, too, parked behind the trees on a patch of dirt. This display of Boris's wealth filled Moss with wonder. He was lucky to know Boris. He would never have anything like this for himself, but to know someone who did was one of the real accomplishments of his life.

Inside, Moss was surprised to find the place nearly empty, the wooden banisters unfinished, the walls bare and only half painted in a pale lichenous green. The living and dining areas had minimal furnishings: a long oak table, a cream-colored leather couch. There were several large boxes on the hardwood floor, presumably containing furniture. Moss hadn't expected the place to be so desolate. He hugged his shoulders.

From the windows you could see onto the back of the property: at the end of a stone path that wound downhill amid spindles of trees there lay the blue, ribbed corpus of a long swimming pool, surrounded by mounds of black dirt. The water shone like some live, waiting thing, rolling slowly in its pit.

"You didn't tell me you had a pool," Moss said, moving closer to the window.

"We'll take a swim," said Boris, "when it's a little warmer."

"I don't swim," said Moss. "Where's the ocean?"

"A few miles away. We'll go sometime."

They cooked dinner in the eat-in kitchen, which was the size of Moss's entire apartment. Wooden trusses crisscrossed the high, yeast-yellow slatted ceiling, and light fixtures with stems ten feet long hung motionlessly from the cornice. Boris was extremely proud of the room. "The counters are flamed limestone," he said. "That's a laminated bamboo floor. My architect suggested vinyl, since it's cheap and easy to clean. But I always wanted a kitchen with a floor like this." It gave Moss no small pleasure to hear the phrase "my architect" roll off the tongue of a close personal friend. Boris had an architect, a lawyer, an accountant, a doctor, a dentist, a dermatologist, a podiatrist, an internist, an agent, a personal trainer, and those were just the ones he talked about. Sometimes Moss wondered if he himself was just another hired specialist, since Boris always bought his drinks. A paid friend. Boris didn't seem to mind, and God knew he could afford it. But the effect on Moss was wearying. Would it always be like this?

They made pasta with olives and capers and roasted Italian sea bass topped with olive oil and a squeeze of blood orange. Then they sat down to eat.

As the sun went down, and Moss's brain grew heavy with food and wine, Boris became a dim figure across the table. Moss had never felt such stillness or heard such silence. It was them and no one else.

Darkness had come. The windows were black mirrors. The world had disappeared. Moss wished he were home, where there was light. He hadn't counted on nighttime and the bare fact of Boris. The house seemed to expand with its own darkness. How was he supposed to sleep?

"You want to hear something crazy?" he said, thinking that he had something of his own, equal to Boris, equal to this house, equal to the night, that he could raise against all of it. "My mother's pregnant."

"Huh?"

Moss felt adrenaline, obscure danger.

"She's *pregnant*?" said Boris.

"So she claims."

Boris narrowed his eyes. "What are you talking about?"

"What do you mean?"

"What do *you* mean?"

"I mean, she's pregnant."

"Are you shitting me?" said Boris.

"Why would I?"

Boris put his finger against the side of his nose. "So who's the father?"

"I don't know," said Moss, confused by the tone of the question, a reasonable enough question, but delivered with the same insinuating challenge that Moss had used, when he'd asked the same of Nina.

"What do you mean, you don't know? She didn't tell you?"

"Maybe she doesn't know."

This was hardly plausible, yet Boris seemed willing to entertain it: "How could she not know?" he said, watching Moss carefully.

"She knows," Moss said, because it was the only thing that made sense.

"If this is a joke," said Boris, "I'm not sure I get it."

"It's no joke," said Moss. "Someone got her pregnant. Someone not her husband."

"Don't fuck with me, Moss." Boris gripped the edge of the table with both hands. "Is that why you're here?"

"What are you talking about?" said Moss, and when he saw

Boris look more closely at him, trying to read him, it struck him that Boris knew something about Nina, and that he suspected Moss knew this.

"Look," said Boris, holding up his hands. "We're all adults."

"Did you fuck my mother?" Moss blurted. He heard how wild and stupid it sounded, and wanted to laugh, but instead his face froze in a bewildered smile.

"What did she tell you?" Boris said nervously, shying from Moss's smile, which he seemed to interpret as crazed.

Moss couldn't speak.

"Listen to me, Moss. I don't know what she told you. But we were together for one night. That's it." Boris saw Moss not believing him. "But—you knew about this."

Moss said nothing. He could not be entirely sure that Boris wasn't joking. It did not make sense to him that any of this could have happened without his knowledge.

"I guess you figured you'd come up here and give me a scare," said Boris, assuming a casual tone. "Pregnant." He laughed, as if only now seeing what was funny. "Fine, Moss. I should have told you. Not that it's any of your business. Okay?"

"She never told me anything about you," Moss said softly. "All she said was that she was going to have a baby."

Boris drew back slowly in his chair.

Moss stared at him. "She's pregnant, asshole."

Boris opened his mouth. "How do you know it's me?"

"It's you." Moss refused to allow any other possibility.

"Did she *tell* you it was me?"

"How was she?" said Moss, feeling entitled to everything. "Repulsive? Sublime? Something in between?"

"Wait a minute, Moss—"

"Did she make a lot of noise? What position did you use? Do you realize how unbelievably wrong this is?"

"If you'd just calm down—"

"When did this happen? *Why* did this happen?"

"Just shut up for a minute and I'll tell you. Okay?" Boris took a breath. "I went to see her play one night. And afterwards we started talking. We had some drinks. Then we went back to her place. Your place. She was going to audition me for piano lessons. You were staying at Fran's."

"Piano lessons?" Moss laughed—he had no idea what to believe. "And then what? She just attacked you? Against your will?"

Boris shook his head—he looked like he really didn't know.

"And where did this event take place?" said Moss. "On the fucking piano bench?"

"On the floor. And then in her bed. Okay? You happy?"

"Without a condom?" said Moss.

Boris's eyes got wide. "She's forty-four! What are the chances?"

Moss wanted to tell him that the world record for oldest mother was sixty-five, a fact he had held in reserve for Danielle, for when she got worried that her eggs were disappearing. But it hardly mattered now. "How drunk was she?" he said.

Boris didn't hear him. "Are you telling me," he said, "that she's planning to have it?"

"Call her and ask."

"But if it is mine," Boris said, seizing on the idea, "she would've called me."

"Why? It'd be more important for her to keep me from knowing the truth. She couldn't even tell me who it was. That proves it's you."

"I want to talk to her," said Boris, as if calling Moss's bluff.

"Go ahead."

Moss thought about the note he'd left for Nina, telling her that he was going to see Boris. Angry as he'd been, he'd left a note—he hadn't wanted her to worry, given her condition. But now she must be worried sick, wondering what would happen between the two men.

Boris eyed the phone, which lay between them on the table like a weapon. He was completely white.

"She's forty-four," said Moss, watching Boris impassively. "There could be complications." His lip then curled into a snarl. "You might have ended up killing her."

NINA LAY IN bed, reading Moss's note over and over. She'd discovered it an hour before, under the kitchen table, where a breeze must have sent it drifting from the counter. So instead of her having had a chance to call Boris and warn him of Moss's arrival, it was left to Nature. The whole question rested on Boris's reaction to Moss's news of her pregnancy; if Boris played dumb, Moss wouldn't be the wiser. But odds were that Boris would confess everything. And then what? That she'd yet to hear from either of them was an ambiguous sign at best. She could only hope that Boris, as the more mature of the two, and as the father in question, would figure out a way to guide Moss through it. Of course, it was just as likely that he was already scheming, with or without Moss's help, to convince her to abort. But he'd be wasting his time. If it was medically feasible, she would have this baby; at the first sign she had recognized her fate, had poured her booze down the drain before she even took the test. It made a harsh sense to her, induced a harsh obedience. Only then did she realize that it was something she might have wanted all along, without knowing it. Or at least, some undefined longing inside her had been exposed, which the pregnancy seemed to address with bitter logic. Even now, she could feel the nearness, like an object in the dark, of some obscure promise of absolution. She did not explore it further.

It then occurred to her that Moss might have been too ashamed to share the news with Boris, lest Boris judge him against his mother's habit of getting pregnant by strangers. That seemed likely, in fact. Moss would be ashamed. And it was to this depressing idea, which really would explain the quiet phone, that Nina fell asleep. In her dream she was at the house in L.A., except that it was her childhood house, and she was telling Anton about the pregnancy, which she had yet to do in real life. (She was still not convinced that there wasn't a way to avoid telling him.) In the dream, though, Anton took the news well enough. He wanted to be the baby's godfather. Nina cried at this, for how good he was, and how she had hurt him. And then they were riding in a horse-drawn chariot, in Russia, and people were throwing rice at them, and Anton said, "Without money, you'll have to sell lawn fertilizer," and Nina was about to ask him if he meant "lawn furniture"—for some reason the answer was of vital importance—when the phone rang. Nina opened her eyes. Her light was on. The phone lay on the pillow beside her. Moss? Boris? She looked at the clock. Ten till midnight. The phone rang again. Don't be afraid, Nina told herself. If *she* wasn't entirely innocent, her baby was, so that any defense of herself might appear synonymous with the unimpeachable defense of the child.

She picked up the phone. "Hello?"

"Nina. It's Boris." He knew. Nina heard it.

She sat up. "Is Moss with you?" she said. "Is he okay?"

"He stepped outside."

Nina steeled herself.

"So is it true?" Boris said.

"There's no need to be mad or afraid," Nina said calmly. "I'm not asking anything from you."

"Is it definitely mine?"

"Yes," said Nina, wincing at his "mine"—she could think of it only as her own. "I haven't been with anyone else."

"And Moss tells me you're going to have it?" said Boris, as if nothing could be more reckless. "Have you really thought about this? All the risks? To your health?"

"I appreciate your concern," Nina said. She knew what he wanted. And though she'd recently seen his predicament through Moss's scared eyes, and been sympathetic, she now felt how selfish this attitude was, how arrogant.

"I think we should talk about this," said Boris.

"If you'd like to talk about how you might want to participate in raising it, then yes, we can do that."

"What do you expect me to say?"

"I don't expect anything, Boris. You can do what you want."

"I suppose I'll have to call my lawyer. I suppose money comes into this."

"I don't care about money. I don't want your money." This wasn't exactly true, but it was how she felt in that moment. She just wanted him to take an interest. "Do what you think is best," she said, thinking too that by encouraging him to be an involved parent she was risking a lifelong entanglement with him. What if he became a controlling, jealous, abusive father? He had that obsessiveness. What conflicts was she inviting?

"I'm sorry," said Boris. "I'm in shock here."

"I'm not trying to scare you, Boris. I don't want you to feel bad about this. That's not the idea."

"First you tell me you can't see me, and now you're going to have my baby? You're full of surprises."

Nina saw no point in telling him that she didn't think of it so much as *his* baby. And yet the designation was interesting: he was already claiming the child for himself. There could be worse reactions, Nina thought.

She said, "What does Moss think about it? What did he say?"

"What does Moss have to do with it? It's not his kid."

"No, but Moss is *my* kid," said Nina, thinking how much more important it was to her that Moss, rather than Boris, should want this baby.

"Maybe it'll take all of us," said Boris, cautiously, as if guarding against Moss playing too prominent a role, challenging his authority. "All three of us, pitching in. Me and you and Moss. We can talk about this."

Nina decided, having gained that much, to leave him balanced there, and asked to speak to Moss. She wanted to hear his voice, get some sign that he didn't hate her. But now, through the muffle and static of the connection, she heard him refusing to talk to her, saying, to Boris, "I want to be alone right now," after which Boris got back on the line and told her that Moss was busy stargazing—"He's never seen a sky like this," Boris declared, sounding alarmingly like a father arguing for custody of a child based on his ability to provide better things. "I'll have him call you later."

STANDING BAREFOOT UNDER a night sky streaked with stars, the fertile hatcheries, the milky mists, and the young grass cool and hairy between his wiggling toes, Moss experienced a momentary reprieve from his earthly troubles, feeling wonderfully meaningless to the universe, and yet necessary to the spectacle, as its sole observer; so that when Boris came outside, waving the phone, saying that Nina wanted to talk to him, Moss's anger against both of them was inflamed even more, by their stupid unawareness of their own insignificance, and by their total insensitivity to *his*—for a precious moment he had been beyond them, just a man standing on his planet, looking up. But they would not let him be. They would be after him now, wanting him between them. Moss glared at Boris, saw the terror in his eyes: he would never be free now, immune even to the insect freedom conferred on him by a billion cold stars. Real responsibility had come. Moss could empathize, having escaped that fate himself, narrowly enough to feel a twinge of his own panic come back to him at the sight of Boris's. But he remained rigid. Boris went back inside, badly rebuffed, one hand on his head. Moss sniffed a moral advantage that would insure him against anything he might do; but his impulse was to punish Boris not violently, but with kindness, some shaming act of generosity. He pursued Boris into the house, full of a raging beneficence by which he would draw blood. Boris was standing behind his chair, gripping the back of it for support, his head bowed—it struck Moss as dramatic, a bid for sympathy. And yet when he crept up behind Boris and touched his shoulder, Boris didn't move: in his distress it took him a moment to register the contact, and when he turned around, his eyes were black with resentment. Yet Moss kept going, initiating an embrace, his momentum leading him; and Boris, unprepared, blindsided by life, yielded softly, helpless against Moss's decisiveness, which he craved. "Don't worry," Moss told him. "Things are going to work out." Boris then drew away, as if doubtful of Moss's sincerity; or maybe he was just wary of the optimism, afraid to believe in it. Moss smiled supportively. Boris's cooperation was crucial, and Moss, apart from any loyalty to his mother, or any pleasure of self-righteousness, sought to unite the parties, to create as healthy an environment as possible for the child who was coming. Any baby deserved that much, even this one. And though Moss still felt betrayed by both Nina and Boris, he recognized that the blood of all three of them would be commingled in this baby, and that he and Boris were as family now, for whatever it was worth. But he had no plans to return to New York. He did not want to see his mother, or witness her changing body. And Boris, chastened, wanted him to stay—he even offered to pay Moss to help him fix up the house, whose empty rooms now saw some hope of being filled. Moss accepted the offer, perceiving its implications, the meanings ricocheting between them, unspoken; and this activity, which they pretended to ignore, energized them in their work, so that all their industry—the sanding, the hammering, the painting, the weeding, the landscaping (Boris was a real do-it-yourselfer, clearly a man who had grown up with a father), the hanging of fixtures and the smoothing of rough edges—all their worker-bee enterprise hummed with a spirit of service, church devotion, of preparing the way for an arrival. At first, Moss couldn't even use a screwdriver without having it slip and gouge a surface, but once he learned to do a thing halfway decently, he took pleasure in the controlled violence of it, and it was good to hear, across the house, the icy ping of Boris's hammer, or the warped sputter of a drill boring through drywall. Day by day, as small improvements were made, Boris's attitude toward the new occupation in his life seemed also to improve; it was through just this sort of tinkering that he seemed to be building his inner resolve. Moss, too, felt mysteriously fortified: cheerfully he called Nina once or twice a week to "check on your progress," and though she seemed to want more from him than he could give—his unqualified blessing—she was grateful that he and Boris had made their peace, knowing, as she must have, that Boris's growing acceptance of his coming fatherhood could be attributed in no small measure to Moss's influence. But in denying her his physical presence, Moss knew he was hurting her, knew that the life inside her only increased her desire for the life she had already given. He would leave her with that irony.

Boris meanwhile made several trips to New York in the Lexus, acting in part as Moss's emissary to Nina, but mainly as the father-to-be, negotiating over money and responsibility (Boris insisted that these meetings occur face-to-face rather than on the phone, as if by inconveniencing himself he was proving himself in advance of the birth, that he would be a conscientious, serious partner, willing to go out of his way), an arrangement that precluded any rekindling of the Boris-Nina romance; they had established a business arrangement more than anything, a point they were both diligent to stress to Moss. And Moss didn't doubt them: they were both afraid of him, he sensed. Especially Boris. Everything he did—whether it was paying Moss an astonishing three thousand dollars in cash for his work on the house (Moss had never held that much money in his hand in his life), or preparing elaborate and seductive meals (scallop ceviche with cilantro salsa, spaghetti with lobster and mint) from recipes in cookbooks that he pulled down from the shelf—felt calculated to pacify what he feared was Moss's suppressed anger. But this anger, in fact most of Moss's attention, was being absorbed by the pages of Boris's cookbooks, which Moss found even more satisfying than the meals themselves: here were secrets revealed, magic potions, explicit directions that even he might follow, and which could lead, with any luck, to a carved little moment of success, the pleasures going out to others as well as to himself. He memorized the formulae of twenty different sauces (browns and whites, hots and colds), the seasons and habitat of fish, the regions and classifications of cheeses; read how to truss a duck, bone a rabbit, trim a rack of lamb; studied beef charts and lamb charts, both American and French, compared the *charcuterie* of Corsica to that of Alsace, dreamed of the perfect bouillabaisse, with the freshest rascasse, the finest saffron. He would lean against the counter, watching Boris chop and dice and sprinkle and splash, the thick hands wet and bloody with food. Moss wanted to help, but the knives—high-end stainless-steel F. Dick cutlery that hung with weight and perfection on the wall, absurdly and temptingly within reach—daunted him in a way that a power drill couldn't; something in their silence, their potential. But as with the other tools that Boris had taught him to use, the knives, when he took them up at Boris's beckoning (what made Boris trust him with such an obvious weapon?), felt sure and precise in his grip, as did the long black handles of the frying pans, heavy as dumbbells, which he guided over the fire, watching the ingredients jump and sputter as he shook them. Under Boris's eye he made sautéed sole in lemon and oil, oyster bisque, eggplant fritters, cold summer borscht. He even enjoyed cleaning up afterward, with a snifter of Cognac to warm his full belly, while Boris dozed off on the couch.

But if Boris was showing enthusiasm in his renovating and cooking, a more destructive side began to reveal itself: at least twice in the summer he had gone swimming during a thunderstorm, and when he went to the grocery store in town, he insisted on buying the most expensive items, just when he ought to have been cutting back. And now, as the air got colder and the days shorter, and the leaves turned yellow and orange, and the night gave a sweet, burning smell, Boris had begun making after-dinner trips to the Clanking Pot, ten miles away, where guys on motorcycles gathered with fisherfolk and a smattering of yuppies to eat chowder and drink. Moss had gone there once, but some big redneck at the bar had called him "Tumbleweed," referring, apparently, to his hair, causing his drunk buddies to laugh, and say, "Hey, Tumbleweed, why don't you blow on outta here," and though Moss managed to escape to the other end of the bar, his night was ruined and he vowed never to return. Boris had been shooting pool at the time with a fat sunburned guy with a tattoo of a mermaid on his arm, and Moss decided against mentioning the incident, thinking that Boris, in his volatility, might attempt to defend Moss's honor. He seemed to be waiting for a chance to go berserk in public, and Moss fully expected, on any given night, to get a call from the hospital saying that Boris had been beaten unconscious. In fact, Boris had, on several occasions, failed to come home, having spent the night if not in the hospital then in the bed of a willing piece of divorced bar trash whom he was, by his own admission, too ashamed to parade in front of Moss, who he suggested would be offended by the idea of his spending the night with women other than the one bearing his child. Moss was not aware of such a feeling in himself—Boris was free to do as he liked—but he thought he saw in Boris more profound levels of despair. In any case, no further details of these sad conquests were discussed; there were some conversations they simply couldn't have anymore. It was just as well. Moss would rather not be reminded of women, any women, and conveniently they were not in abundance in that part of the world. He would rather sit home and read his cookbooks. Boris could disappear forever for all he cared, even though, alone in the house, he still felt vulnerable, if not to human intruders then to hungry bears, crashing deer, scorpions, wildfires: the slightest noise could make him jump. But if he ever got really scared, he figured, he could always call his mother. She had a way of minimizing his fears by belittling them: "Get a grip, Moss," she might say. "A bear isn't going to attack *you*." It almost always worked.

But he was wary of her. Each time they talked, he could hear her need for him in her voice, and especially in her avoidance of an explicit plea, which she strained to hold back. She did not want to pressure him, or reveal too much of herself. But she made it clear that it was a tough time to be alone. Moss did not want to hear any of it. He refused to give her what she didn't deserve. He said he would come home soon, but he knew he wouldn't. Unless, of course, there was an emergency.

Which wasn't out of the question.

And what if? What if she died? It happened. He'd read all about it.

He would be sorry, then. For how he'd treated her since her pregnancy. He hated her, and she knew it. He let her know it.

But he loved her. She must know that too. She knew everything. Unless she didn't; unless she really feared that she had lost him. But Christ! How could she? How could she have another kid?

One day in the early fall, he got Boris to drive him to the beach. It was his first time there—the ocean had been far enough away to be out of mind. But now he wanted to go. Boris had brought Moss's winter clothes back from the city on his last trip, and as Moss bundled up, he recalled an earlier excursion to the sea. It had been hot then. His mother had borrowed a friend's car and packed Moss up along with a basket of towels and food and taken them early in the morning on a ride that seemed to go on for hours. Finally she parked the car on a road that ended at an uncrowded beach. She wore a blue and green bikini top and cut-off jeans, which she eventually removed, revealing what seemed like her underwear. Moss held her hand—he must have been around four years old—and took slow, tricky steps across the hilly sand, stumbling toward the thrashing edge of a wild, unknown element: dark water gathered and swelled like the drama of an object stared at in a dream, changing shape, then rising up in violence. But since she held his hand, it was fun to jump over the foam that broke charging from the toppled waves, and when she pulled him in a little deeper, it was okay, it was safe, because he now knew that his mother was bigger than the waves, and that they could not take her away from him. She lifted him, and he clung to her neck; she lowered her shoulder and surged them through watery walls as she bounced along the floor. He heard laughter, hers and his own, and each time they conquered a wave, she kissed his ear or his cheek, and when she said, "Ready?" he knew that the next one might swell up and smash them, and he closed his eyes and turned his head and pressed his mouth against her shoulder that dazzled in the sunlight like a wet rubber ball, and tasted her skin. They bobbed and pitched to the careless rhythms of the sea, which had become warm as bathwater, so that the air was now what was cold. And when it was time to go back, she pointed out how far they had drifted from their original spot, which was marked far down the beach by a burning white towel. The mystery of their displacement seemed bound up in the progress of joy; and it was a cold, bittersweet walk along the spongy sand, which sucked their plunging feet and left their footprints, which then disappeared behind them.

BORIS PARKED THE Jeep behind a grassy dune. The beach strongly resembled the one from Moss's memory, though of course it wasn't the same. Moss and Boris got out of the vehicle, fully clothed except for their shoes and socks. The sky was blotted with low clouds, and the sand was cold under their feet. But it was good to stand there and watch the waves. Nina actually knew how to swim—the summer before Moss's birth she'd worked as a lifeguard at a community pool in White Plains. And then she got pregnant. The catastrophic event of her life. Moss hated that she would always remember her pregnancy with him as such a low point. Of course, she'd be the first to say that you can't let your past get you down. That was how she tried to get him to forgive her for loving her music more than she'd loved him—by suggesting that to hold grudges and dwell on misfortunes, real or imagined, was not only self-defeating, but weak and unmanly. Only a coward blamed others for his troubles. *Coward:* how easy it was for her to use that word to discredit his every fear. *Don't be a coward, Moss. Planes are the safest form of transportation there is.* Danielle, too, had called him a coward, but only because he wouldn't commit to her, which was, to the contrary, he felt, a sign of strength. He hadn't *wanted* to get married and have a kid.

"Can I borrow your phone?" he said to Boris. "I have to call my mother."

"Why?" said Boris. The word was like a reflex; he made no other move.

"Because," Moss said, "I haven't called her in over a week." He remembered the way she put the lotion on his back, that day at the beach; the summery smell, the warmth of her hand. "When she went away to Europe, I never called her; she always called me. Even when she went to California, I never called. For one thing, it cost money. For another, I didn't care. It was her decision to leave. It's not like she *needed* me. You know?"

"Here's the phone," said Boris.

Moss took the phone and dialed. The waves made him feel, as the stars had, reassuringly insignificant, above earthly conflicts.

"Hello?" Nina said.

"Mom. It's me."

"Moss. Where are you?"

"Boris and I are at the beach. How are you feeling?"

Boris began walking toward the water, as if to give them privacy.

"How do *think* I'm feeling?" Nina said wearily. "This pregnancy is killing me."

"Don't say that," said Moss, not wanting to hear any regrets—it wasn't fair. She had made her choice. "It's not going to kill you."

"We'll see about that. In the meantime, I could really use some help around here."

Moss stiffened. "Maybe you should have thought of that before."

"Excuse me?"

Moss felt tricked. He hadn't been looking for a fight. But he knew what was killing her. She couldn't stand that he'd done what *she* had done—that he had gone away. Her desire was to stop him.

"Boris is the one who should be helping you," Moss said. "I mean, I'd come down if I could, but I've got work to do here—we're painting the house this week. Boris is paying me."

"I'm sure he'll let you take a couple of days off," Nina said, implying, in her tone, that Moss's employment was less than legitimate.

"You should be happy for me," said Moss, sounding hurt, to get to her, but feeling it too, more than he'd expected. "I'm living on my own, and I'm earning my keep. I'm surviving. Anyway, I didn't call to have an argument."

"Good, because I don't have the strength to argue," Nina said, and Moss could hear what the baby was taking from her, which encouraged him—*he* hadn't worn her down like this, young as she'd been, and maybe she would remember that, and favor him for it. "Do you at least plan to be here for the birth?"

"Why?" said Moss, who had no plans for anything at all. "I'm sure Boris'll be there."

"I'm not worried about Boris. Boris is not my son. You are."

"So?"

"Don't fight with me, Moss. I'm still your mother."

"Who said you weren't?"

"Then you could at least show some consideration."

"Consideration?" Moss said with a bitter laugh. "You're telling me about consideration?" He was referring to her having slept with his friend, but he could have meant any number of things, including the fact that she was turning everyone's life completely upside down.

"Listen to me, Moss. I know I've disappointed you. You have every right to be mad at me—and we can talk about that, when you come down."

"I'm not mad at you," Moss said, refusing to give her even that. He was sure she was putting on an act for herself, as the needy, forsaken mother, to make herself feel less guilty, and thus put Moss on the defensive. That, or she was having a true breakdown. Either way, Moss wanted no part of it.

"Of course you're mad at me," she said. "Don't you remember? You called me a whore, and then you left."

"I was mad then. I'm not mad now. But I will be, if you keep badgering me."

"When will I see you?"

"Soon."

"When?"

"I don't know!" Moss shouted, loud enough to make Boris turn from where he stood by the shoreline. "Leave me alone!"

"I'm sorry—Moss, baby, I'm sorry—"

"You're a lunatic! Just stay away from me!"

"No," Nina moaned. "Moss. Don't do this. I need you." She hadn't sounded this desperate and miserable since guys dumped her when Moss was a boy. "I'm sorry, baby. Don't hate me."

"You must be hormonal," said Moss, needing an explanation that would mitigate the drama for both of them. Certainly she had notorious PMS, so why shouldn't a pregnancy make her just as crazy? Did she really expect him to come to her, so that she could yell at him, and hug him, and cling to him, and then toss him aside when she felt better?

"I have to go," Nina said meekly. She sounded thoroughly defeated. "I don't have the strength for this." And then she hung up on him.

Moss stood there. This was absolutely nuts. What right did she have to demand things of him? She just wanted him to share in her misery. Fuck that. That was practically child abuse. She was right: parents and their children must separate at some point. What was the point of carrying on an insane, infantilizing relationship? It was stupid and offensive.

He closed the phone and started walking toward the water, where Boris was. Boris's back was to him. Moss gripped the phone tightly in his hand as he approached.

When Moss was just a few feet away from Boris, he said, "She's a fucking psychopath."

Boris turned to him. "What'd she say?"

Moss hesitated, remembering Boris's bad faith. He said, "I

think she's extremely lonely," establishing his role as interpreter of her moods, while implying blame against Boris for causing this one. "She's alone. She's exhausted. And I'm sure she's a little confused as to why we're both still out here."

"I'm here," said Boris, "because I live here."

"But the summer's over. People usually go back to the city."

"Why don't *you* go?"

"Why should I? It's not *my* kid she's pregnant with."

Boris sensed danger. "I've been visiting her every two weeks," he said righteously. "Sometimes more. I'm going the day after to-morrow, as a matter of fact. She's having a test."

"What test?"

"I think it's her amniocentesis."

"What's that?"

"I think it's to see if the baby has Down syndrome."

"Jesus Christ. That's a major test."

"There's a definite risk, at her age."

"So what happens if it comes out positive?"

"Then she'll abort it," said Boris, and it was hard to tell if this was his hope or his fear. He looked off at the water. "Anyway, she has an appointment, and I told her I'd go with her."

There was no disputing that Boris had the better record when it came to seeing Nina. Then again, it was his job; Boris could hardly claim the moral high ground simply by doing the very least that was expected of him, whereas Moss's behavior was, under the circumstances, pretty damned good. Especially considering that he had begun to grow jealous over the putatively nonsexual bond that was developing between his friend and his mother—they were sharing something that Moss could never share with either of them. Maybe there were worse options than an abortion.

"I tried to tell her," said Boris, "that she was playing with fire, having this baby."

Moss didn't like that attitude. "She's healthy," he said. "I'm sure everything'll be okay." He wanted to punch Boris in the face. Be a man, asshole, he wanted to say. Love your kid. Don't be afraid of it.

"It's funny, isn't it?" said Boris, still gazing out. "If we didn't have sperm, we'd be of no use to them."

"That's not true," said Moss, thinking that Danielle had needed him regardless—his words, his kisses. Then, for the first time, he wondered if Boris had ever been in love with Nina. Was she the reason he left the city? Had she hurt him in some way? Both Boris and Nina had insisted that their night together was an alcohol-fueled anomaly, and that had seemed plausible enough. But it seemed that Boris was weighed down by something more than the baby.

Moss was then startled by a noise: it was the phone, ringing in his hand. He looked at the incoming number.

"It's her," said Moss. He had no intention of answering. "You want to take it?"

Boris held out his hand. Moss gave him the phone. Boris looked at it, and then, raising his arm, took a hop and a step and threw the phone high and far into the air: it turned black against the white sky, tumbling, then landed silently beyond the breakers and disappeared.

Moss was silent: the act struck him as heroic, but he couldn't help from feeling it as a personal attack.

"It's not her fault," he managed to say, not knowing quite what he meant.

"I've always wanted to do that," said Boris, staring at the waves. He did seem to feel a little better.

18

"THANKS FOR COMING," NINA SAID, AS SHE ALWAYS DID when Boris arrived. They were in a café on Nina's street— one of the old kitschy places, full of beads and red lampshades, that had been there before she'd left the city, and which, many years ago, had had an old upright piano that she would play on Monday nights.

Boris looked around as he took a seat, as if to make sure there was no one there to recognize him—he hadn't mentioned the baby to anyone, as far as Nina knew, not even his family. Nevertheless, he'd been coming to the city twice a month to meet with Nina, trying to appear responsible, no deadbeat. He wanted credit for his effort, and Nina gave it to him, but not too much. Driving hundreds of miles in order to buy her lunch and express his concerns did not a father make. He tried to assure her about the future by confessing his current doubts, as if candor alone were proof of his character. He felt he was doing her a favor by participating at all. He liked to talk about how screwed up he was because of his mother's death;

how he was afraid to attach himself to anything that could die. Thus the house, the permanence of property. Thus the hobbies and pastimes, none of which he ever pursued seriously enough for it to betray him. Nina could feel sorry for him, but she didn't let on—it was too much what he was after.

"What time's the appointment again?" Boris said, shyly facing her. "For the amnio."

"The amnio?" said Nina. "I had that months ago. You mean the ultrasound. That was this morning."

"You mean you *had* the amnio? You didn't tell me that."

"It came out fine, so there was nothing to tell." Nina saw his anger. By excluding him, she denied him things he didn't even want, which made him want them.

"So—what happened? What did they say this morning?"

"Everything's fine. The baby's fine." She watched for his reaction—a part of her expected to see a flicker of disappointment, as if he still held out hope that the pregnancy would go away.

"That's great," Boris said, and Nina saw that he meant it, even if he wasn't convinced of it himself. He was more invested than he knew; he might not even be able to explain why he felt relieved.

"I've been so sick, though," Nina said, resenting him for not suffering enough. "It's ten times worse than when I was pregnant with Moss." Back then she'd been too young to understand what was happening to her, but at least she'd had energy. Now she could hardly get out of bed. Her legs cramped, her skin itched, spiderlike veins had broken out on her thighs and in the crooks of her knees. She was being disfigured. She'd gained twenty pounds. (And yet when she sat at the piano, her belly throbbing in front of her, she could feel the exchange of energy between herself and the piano and the baby, imagining that she was reaching deeper than ever into the jaws of the instrument, pulling things out from it, golden eggs, blood up to her elbows, and her belly a glowing ball, a source, absorbing the nutrients that she was extracting, and giving her, in return, a profound center of gravity.) "The doctor told me to sleep on my left side, so the baby would slide off my bladder."

"Sounds like good advice," Boris said.

"Well, I won't sit here and complain."

"You can complain. Complain all you want."

It was a tempting offer. But Nina saw that Boris was inviting her anger (all her complaints contained her anger against him, for the ways in which his life was easier), seeking to endure it in order to feel better about whatever failings he anticipated in himself.

"Actually," said Nina, "I'm more interested in what's going on with Moss."

"What about him?"

"I wouldn't know," said Nina, faintly accusatory. "He doesn't tell me a thing."

"Maybe you're not listening."

"Tell me, then. What does he say?"

"About what?"

"Anything. The baby."

Boris had to think for a moment. "He wanted me to ask you if it's going to be a boy or girl."

"He knows the deal," said Nina, thinking that Boris was asking the question more for himself. "I want it to be a surprise. It's more natural that way." But she had better reasons for wanting to preserve the mystery. Not least, an answer might rob both men of some incentive to attend the birth, whose main appeal lay in the element of surprise; and that by declining to obtain the information, she was somehow maintaining an advantage.

"That's not exactly fair," Boris said. "To Moss or to me."

"Please don't talk about what's fair. You have no idea."

"What's that supposed to mean?"

"Look, Boris. I don't think I've asked too much from you."

"What do you want from me, exactly? I've never understood. You say it's not about money, yet when I come here, you keep me at a distance."

"What I want," said Nina, in the low tones of controlled argument, "is for you to be happy about this, or if not happy, then at least not depressed. I mean, I'm having this baby, and all you want to talk about is how difficult it is for you, with all your unresolved issues. What crap, Boris. Take it up with a shrink."

"Why? Because I'm not overcome with joy? Well, guess what? Neither are you. And neither is Moss. But you expect *me* to keep everyone's spirits up."

"No—just your own."

"Even that's too much."

"You could at least pretend. It's not happening to *you*."

"You make it sound like torture. Why are you having this baby, exactly?"

"To torture myself," Nina said. "To punish myself. Why else?"

"Maybe it's true."

"No. It's really to torture you."

"I wouldn't be surprised."

"Why do you *think* I'm having it, Boris? For my health?"

"I'm asking."

"Believe it or not, it's what I've wanted for a long time. I just never realized it until it happened."

"And you never tried to get pregnant since Moss?"

"No. I was always careful. And when I wasn't careful, I was lucky."

"So now you're *un*lucky?" said Boris, his face an exaggerated mask of confusion. "I thought you just said you wanted it."

"It's a figure of speech. You know what I meant."

"No, I don't. And I don't think you do either."

The waitress, who had been observing the argument from a short distance, detected an opening and went over to take their order. Both indicated that they needed more time.

When the waitress was gone, Nina looked hard at Boris. "You know what I want from you?" she said. "Beyond anything?"

"I'm listening."

Nina softened her features, but felt the pressure behind her eyes. "Bring Moss home to me," she said. "I want him here when this baby is born."

Boris was silent. He seemed to understand.

He said, "You realize I can't force him to do anything."

"Try," said Nina, wiping a tear away with her pinkie. "I need him here." For years she had denied that she needed anyone, much less Moss. She, who had been needed all her life—first by her parents, then by Moss, then by Anton, and now by her baby. What had made her think she could be alone? Was it pride? Spite? Rage? Grief? She couldn't say, but the suddenness with which the structure crumbled told her how tenuous it had been, and maybe the clue lay there. "I need your help with him, Boris," she went on, trying desperately not to break down. "I can't do it alone."

She needed Moss, needed his forgiveness, not just to relieve her conscience, but to have a chance at the moral and emotional support that he, better than anyone, was able to provide (she could taste his compassion, so pure, so beyond his years—the way, as a boy, he touched her hair as she lay crying—where was that person now?). More than that, she wanted to know—and a display of his sympathy would go a long way to verify it—that he was, despite everything, still reasonably stable. One of the few advantages to being pregnant at a young age, she realized, was that her anxieties were limited by her experience; when she was pregnant with Moss she never worried that her child would have emotional problems, since her own neuroses had yet to fully develop and she was not aware of them. But now, in middle age, her biggest fear for her baby was that it would grow up to be a complete mess.

Not that she was any crazier than other people she knew. She'd always thought Anton was the real wack job between them. And yet—though on reflection it wasn't surprising, given his temperament, and his connection, or lack thereof, to the baby itself—Anton was handling things better than anyone. Years of marijuana had softened his judgments, spawned mercies and sluggish surrenders. Naturally, the news came as a blow, but he insisted that he was okay, that he was "happy" for her. They could discuss a divorce later, he'd said, when she felt up to it. His advice in the meantime— for she had told him everything—was that she set things right with Moss.

"Please," she said to Boris. "Bring him home."

"I want you."

"Excuse me?"

"I want you. In bed. Right now."

Nina laughed, but she saw that he was serious. She recalled his intensity the night he confessed his love.

"We can go back to your place," said Boris. He placed his hand over hers, on the table.

"Boris—"

"You think you can just demand things from people, without giving anything in return?"

Nina was stunned. "Are you fucking blackmailing me?" she said, yanking her hand away. It was too monstrous to bear. It made her sick for her baby, that it had this person's blood.

"I'm not *blackmailing* you," Boris said, as if *she* were suspect for even thinking such a thing. She welcomed that possibility.

"Then what *did* you mean?" she said. But she knew. She knew he didn't come all the way to New York every two weeks just to prove what a good guy he was. He wanted to take something from her, unable to accept her seemingly illogical decision to have his baby while refusing to love him.

"We should be together," Boris said, his bald head darkening. "It's the only way I can do this. I want it all. Me, you, the baby, the house—a real family. Why don't you just give me a chance?"

Nina closed her eyes, opened them. "That's just not possible right now," she said, and she saw that this really was a form of blackmail. There was the hint of extreme behavior, should she not comply. And she wouldn't. She couldn't. He was too young, too intense, and he was Moss's friend, and she was tired.

And yet he wanted her. Deformed and sexless as she was, he wanted her. Or rather, he wanted to immerse himself physically in her and the baby, in his need to connect to certain facts, believe in them, *feel* them, gain some truth. He must have contact, that submerging of self, the sinking, sickening burial. He wanted it like nothing else, and Nina could begin to feel, where she least expected to feel anything, the buzzing urgency of his wish.

"Come on, Nina," he said softly, coaxing her with his voice, his warm eyes. "Let's forget everything else. Let's just see how it feels."

"I'm ugly," Nina said. She couldn't face him. "My whole body."

"You're wrong."

"I don't want you to see me."

"It was me who did this to you," Boris said. "I'm not some stranger."

It was all happening too quickly. Nina didn't have the strength to fight. Many times, she had tried to muster feelings of guilt over

Boris, for her treatment of him, tempting herself to submit to him. But it never worked. He was not part of the Trinity: Moss, the baby, herself. He was not part of that. There was no room. But the Trinity existed only in her mind. Moss was far away, and he hated her. And here was Boris, offering communion. Or at least pleasure. He had given it to her once. And she had always wanted more. She was filled up with her pregnancy, but there was still an emptiness inside, which she felt more acutely now, as if her womb were pressing on it. Maybe a little pleasure was what she needed. They left the café, and she was on the street, under a heartbreakingly blue sky, walking behind Boris, her child's father, whom she didn't love, and whom she had never given a chance. She could not deny that her decision to have the baby was made easier by her instinctive approval of the father, whose better qualities were not lost on her. She wondered, as she opened the front door of her building, if she would have been interested in him had he not been connected to her son; and as she led him slowly up the stairs, a new idea struck her: what if *she* weren't connected to Moss? Maybe Moss had already cut her off. What if? What if Moss no longer existed? Wouldn't her life be easier, no longer having to bear her Moss guilt, her Moss resentment, her Moss worries, her Moss failures? Couldn't she at least pretend?

She lay on her back, in the dim curtained light of her bedroom, watching as Boris, on his knees, raised her dress over the smooth hill of her belly and gazed down at her black lace panties, her sexiest pair, which she had put on this morning only because everything else was in the wash. She thought to tell him this, to let him know that this was really the last thing she'd planned to do today, but she didn't want to distract him toward the veins in her flabby legs, or the live, kicking baby just inches from both their noses. Boris unbuttoned his pants. Already he was hard—Anton he wasn't. Excited, Nina reached out for him, but he brushed her away. He had his own ideas. He started to peel the panties away from her, and without thinking she moved to stop him, but he kept going, and the panties slipped off her ankles at the edge of the bed, where Boris had fallen from view. When he reappeared between her legs he was naked. He parted her swollen knees. Nina put her hands on her belly, wanting him. She had forgotten Moss. Eyes closed, she grabbed again for Boris, and this time she caught him, and tried to bring him closer. But something was wrong. The life was going out of him; she felt the retreat of his blood, the shrinking weight. He grabbed her wrist and squeezed it until she let go. Nina felt a chill, as if she had done something, had repulsed him. "What's wrong?" she said.

"This is stupid," said Boris.

"What is?"

"I'm too old for this." Boris shook his head intently, as though trying to rid himself of a voice, a vision. "This isn't what I want."

"What do you mean?"

Boris stopped shaking his head. "I want a real partner. Not this. This is a waste. It's a joke. You don't want me."

"That's not true," Nina said, feeling strangely threatened by the charge. "It's not true!"

"But it is," Boris said. "You got what you wanted from me, and that was all you wanted. Why don't you tell the truth?"

"If it wasn't for Moss—" Nina stopped herself. She didn't know the truth anymore.

"Don't talk to me about Moss," Boris said. "I live with him. I'm the one at risk."

"At risk? For what?"

"What do you think?"

"I have no idea," said Nina. She was afraid of the answer.

Boris looked meaningfully at her. "Sometimes," he said, "in the kitchen, while we're making dinner, I'll see him with that knife in his hand. And I'll think: He's capable." There was a strange excitement in Boris's voice. "The feeling that at any second he could snap and come after me. For what we did."

"Moss would never hurt anyone," Nina said with conviction. There were some things she knew.

"The other night I had a dream that he came into my room with a steak knife, ready to cut out my balls. I escaped by breaking my window and crawling out."

"Then what are you doing here?" said Nina. "Hoping to get caught?"

"Very funny." Boris got off the bed and started putting on his clothes.

Nina lay there in the position he'd left her, on her back, with her knees apart, her dress hiked over her breasts. She was too lazy to move, or cover her body, whose veins and wrinkles made her feel vicious. She wondered if she herself wanted to take risks with Moss, as a way to explode things between them.

She closed her knees and pulled her dress back down.

"I think we shouldn't see each other for a while," said Boris, putting on his shoes. "I'll come down when the baby's born. This is getting too weird."

"It's true," said Nina, as if she knew specifically what he meant. It would be better to blame the whole malfunction of their relationship on their shared desire to protect themselves from Moss, so that no one would be personally offended. On the other hand, by hurting Boris—by confirming that she could never love him, Moss aside—Nina would short-circuit any blame that Boris might level at Moss for destroying his chances; and from what Nina had heard, anything she could do to ease the tension between the two men would be advisable.

But looking at him, she couldn't do it. She did not want to hurt his feelings any more than she already had, and alienate him further from the baby. She just couldn't afford to do it.

She said, "Moss complicates things. I think we can both agree."

Boris stood there, nodding slowly. But as he turned and walked out of the room, without saying good-bye, Nina felt she had made a grave mistake, had somehow placed her son in danger.

MOSS AND BORIS were just sitting down to a dinner of baked halibut and leeks in a tangerine glaze—Moss's own recipe—when the phone rang. At this late date, a ringing phone held consequences. Nina was one month away, and Boris had already made it clear that in the event of early labor they were to drop everything and jump into the Lexus; evidently the three thousand bucks that Moss had earned for *his* labor included prepayment for the honor of accompanying Boris to the city for the Big Event. "It's all I ask," Boris had said, as if he had a right to ask for anything. In point of fact, Moss saw Boris as being in his debt—the money, while nothing to sneeze at, was thin restitution for Boris's crime against their friendship, a crime whose degree would be raised immeasurably should the unthinkable occur. There were various contingencies. Premature separation of placenta from uterine wall, resulting in fatal hemorrhaging. Renal failure due to shock, vascular spasm, intravascular clotting. Hemorrhaging due to uterine atony, or retained placental fragments, or lacerations of the cervix or vagina. And then there were the risks to the fetus, resulting from preterm labor, anemia, hypoxia. Moss had looked it all up on Boris's computer. A "boggy uterus" was how one symptom was described.

Now both men looked at the phone.

Maybe she'd had it already. Maybe there were complications.

Boris picked up without checking the number. "Hello," he said, and then appeared surprised. "Moss Messinger? Sure, he's right here." He handed Moss the phone with a wry, insinuating look, which meant it was a girl.

Moss's throat dried up. Could it be? Danielle? After all this time? But who else? Moss wasn't sure what to think. Did she miss him? Was she worried about him? He had tried his best to forget her, and had come a long way, but now he felt the slightest pull in his heart. He wanted to feel it—the yawn of the pit. The falling in. He wanted it more than he felt it, and even then, part of him was on guard against it, and another part of him suspected that he was manufacturing it out of a need to feel something at all.

He took the phone, placed it to his ear.

"Hello?" he said softly.

"Is this Moss?" The voice was female, but it wasn't Danielle's.

Moss strayed into the living room, out of earshot, and stood near the windows, through which he could see the bare trees shining in the moonlight; and ten minutes later, he returned to the table, where Boris was looking at him, his food untouched, as if he sensed that the call might take Moss away from him, leave him alone in the big cedar house. He was right, but it wasn't what either of them could have imagined.

"What's going on?" he said, scanning Moss's expression.

Moss took a seat at the table and looked down at his plate, unable to face Boris.

"It's weird," he said.

"What's weird?"

"They want me for a meeting."

"Who? What meeting?"

Moss raised his helplessly sparkling eyes to Boris. "I didn't tell you," he said, "but I wrote a script and sent it to an agent in L.A., and she read it and called my number in New York, and my mother gave her this number." Moss wished he could call Danielle to tell her the news. She was the only one who had ever predicted something like this for him.

"What's this agent's name?" said Boris, with some annoyance, as if he should have been told about this.

"Suzie Wolf. She's with IBM, or CIT, something like that—"

"ICM?"

"Yeah. ICM. She said she showed my script to a friend of hers at Paramount, you know, unofficially, just to see what he thought, and it turns out he liked it, and he wants to meet with me."

"Who is he?" Boris said. "Is he an exec, or just a reader?" There was an assumption, in his tone, that he was Moss's advocate, looking out for his interests. "Did they make an offer?"

The questions irritated Moss. "She just said they want to meet me," he said, his knees knocking together.

"Are they flying you in?" said Boris. He looked petrified.

"No," said Moss, and he saw Boris's shoulders relax. "But they want to meet me."

Boris took his fork to his halibut. "How did you find this agent?"

"Through my mother's husband," Moss said. "Get some glaze with that."

"Must be a good fucking script," said Boris, eating the bite on his fork, without the glaze. "What's it about?"

Moss sensed that Boris was ready to rip it apart. "Maybe they'll change their minds," he said, ignoring the question. "Maybe they're full of shit."

"It's possible," said Boris. He chewed the fish without seeming to taste it. "When are you going?"

"As soon as I can, I guess. Maybe this week."

"Shouldn't you wait until after the baby's born? It could happen any day, you know."

"I don't have to be there, necessarily. I think my mother would understand. This could be a break."

Boris set down his fork, then picked it up again. "So—who's this guy at Paramount?"

"Josh Levitt."

"Levitt." Boris thought for a moment. "Doesn't ring a bell. Not that that means anything."

"Maybe I'll have to move out there," Moss said, more to himself.

"Don't even think about it," Boris said, and laughed to make light of that.

Moss looked at him. "What do you mean?"

Boris touched the back of his head. "We could use your help. You know?"

Moss tensed up. "You mean you want me to stay around to be your babysitter? How much does it pay?"

"You're the brother," said Boris. "It's your job."

"My *job*? I don't think so, Boris. I certainly didn't tell you to fuck my mother."

Boris stared at Moss in disbelief. "Excuse me?"

Moss felt a thrilling release. "You think *I'd* fuck *your* mother," he said, "even if she wasn't fucking dead?"

In a flash Boris came around the table: he grabbed Moss's T-shirt and lifted him from his chair. He was even stronger than be looked.

"Get off of me, Boris," Moss said, his eyes darting fearfully.

"Yes," Boris hissed into Moss's face. "I fucked your mom. And she loved it. She couldn't get enough. How's that for news?"

"Get off of me, Boris."

"She loved it. But she couldn't admit it, for the simple reason that she couldn't be with me. And you know why she couldn't be with me? Because of *you,* you infantile little creep. She didn't want to hurt you. Isn't that nice?"

"Get off of me, Boris."

"She'd do anything for you—she would have had an abortion if you'd've begged her."

"But I didn't, did I."

"Why didn't you?" said Boris. "I've been meaning to ask."

"Because," said Moss, and the answer came to him like a magic coin in his hand, "I'd rather see you stuck with a kid."

With brutal quickness, Boris threw Moss to the floor and stood heaving over him with his fists.

Moss lay on his side, motionless. He wasn't hurt, just shaken.

"That wasn't necessary," he said.

Boris's fists were opening and closing at his sides. "Get up."

"Fuck you."

"I'm not going to hurt you," said Boris, who seemed to be getting an idea of what his actions might cost him down the line. "I shouldn't have done that."

Moss was silent; despite himself, he felt sorry for Boris, whose life had changed forever, beyond his control, beyond his understanding.

But violence had been done, and there was no turning back. No apology could undo the fundamental change in the relationship. Boris had gone too far, and he knew it.

And so when Boris announced, the next morning, that he was

"disappearing for a few days," Moss figured he was trying to atone, by banishing himself.

"You don't have to," Moss told him.

"Actually," said Boris, "I do."

Moss became alarmed, wondering if Boris was building to some ultimate escape.

"Where are you going?" said Moss.

"Far away. Italy seems about right."

"Just for a few days?"

"Maybe a week."

"Don't go too long. You promised you'd be with her for the Big Event."

"So did you."

"So?"

"So, if I don't make it back in time, at least she won't be alone," said Boris, and then laughed at the look on Moss's face. "Don't worry, Moss. I'll be back. Five days, tops. Then you can go to L.A."

TWO DAYS LATER, Boris rose at dawn and drove to Boston in the Lexus, to catch a flight to New York, and then to Italy. To celebrate his own solitude, Moss decided to make a special treat for breakfast, the simple recipe for which had been tempting him for weeks.

With water and sugar he made the syrup; then he peeled three bananas, poached them in the syrup for five minutes and placed them on a serving dish on the counter. Then he uncapped a tall bottle of Calvados, held it up, tilted it and watched the golden liquid pour out onto the bananas—and remembered how his mother was eating a banana the morning she told him she was pregnant, and how she wanted him there for the birth, and he wondered if she meant *there,* in the room, while it was *happening*—he hadn't thought it, but what if? Wouldn't she want *someone?* He saw the room, the bed, her naked legs spread like the letter *M,* his letter, her gown drawn up above the hump of her belly, and her vagina, for lack of a better word, right there, the last thing in the world he should have to witness but which now thrust itself pungently into his mind: thick, curly dark hair, swirls of it, moist and matted nearer the center, that sticky pink opening from which he, too, had been born. Below that, her anus, dark animal hole, nestling on the white sheet. Clear blood-tinged fluids leak from her. A smell of water and mushrooms. She pushes so hard that the edge of a turd briefly dilates the ring of her anus and then pokes back inside. She screams. The doctor parts her labia with gloved fingers, revealing a gleaming blue surface pressing against the dilated slot, small and round as a jawbreaker, getting bigger now, a tennis ball, a base-ball—but no, go back—a better idea: she is still in the first stage of labor, he is at her side (holding her hand?), she is still properly cov-ered by her gown and the sheet, and he is placing his hand on her belly because she asked him to. (How big is it? Cantaloupe-size? Watermelon-size?) "Can you feel it?" she says. Yes, he can. The flesh is bloated and firm, he can feel vibrations through the layers of fabric and skin, or thinks he can. He pulls his hand away. (In real life he has not, of course, seen her full belly, could only picture it in black dresses, the kind she wore. He wondered how she walked, how her attitude toward her condition came out in the way she held her body in public. Did she hide it in modesty? Project it proudly in front of her? Over the months she had given him updates on how much weight she'd gained and how many inches around, not because she thought he cared, but because these changes fascinated and terrified her and she wanted someone to know that they were occurring, and that she couldn't stop them, that she was powerless against herself.) "Are you afraid?" he says, or, better, "Don't be afraid. It's going to be fine, Mom. Don't worry. I'm here." And he means it. She squeezes his hand, too nauseated to speak. And then he looks up and sees, in the doorway, a woman in blue scrubs who looks just like Danielle. But wait—it *is* Danielle! "Mind if I come in?" she says, in her chirpy caregiver's voice. She comes toward them, smiling. "I saw the name on the board," she says. "I couldn't believe my eyes! How *are* you two?" She even grabs Nina's foot affectionately, explaining that she had moved back to the city and gotten a job here, at this hospital, in Labor and Delivery, still her first love. Moss, speechless, instinctively embraces her and catches the scent of her shampoo, which drugs him momentarily with potent distillations of memory. They withdraw, and he looks at her, and he remembers, indeed has never forgotten, why he loves her. She can light up any room, even a hospital room. "This is unbelievable," he says. And though no one mentions it (could it be that he's the only one even thinking it?), somewhere behind Danielle's smile, far away but not too far, is the memory, the presence, of *her* pregnancy—the mischievous parallels would be too much for Moss if he thought Danielle were as sardonically aware of them as he. Fortunately, she has her own thoughts. She is on the job, not here to feel sorry for herself, or to hate him. She then announces that she will be attending the birth, or no, better, Nina asks her to—Nina takes her hand and says, "Will you stay?" This desire of Nina's to enclose the three of them together embarrasses Moss, but he knows she is only becoming more anxious with the increased intensification of her contractions. If she could, he thinks, she would place her hands on their backs and move them toward each other, and then to her. But this is only her delirium. Or is it his? Isn't it what he wants too? And now the doctor comes in and smiles heartily at Moss: "You must be Moss. You're just in time." She has the deep voice and tall athletic build of a female basketball coach and Moss hopes she doesn't ask him to help. She puts on a pair of rubber gloves, then pulls Nina's gown just above the hips, and now Moss can see, from above, the tangle of dark hair, so unintended for his eyes, and the doctor draws attention to Moss's discomfort by making light of it, saying, "You don't have to look—just hold Mom's hand." Moss obeys. He holds his mother's hand and looks at her face. Her eyes are closed. She grunts, moans, whimpers. The doctor positions herself between Nina's legs. Danielle puts gloves on too, with veteran professionalism. This is her element. This is her moment. Another nurse comes in. But Moss watches Danielle. She laughs at the doctor's jokes, but her eyes are sharp and alert, she sees everything, she is competent in the best sense of the word. "Here comes the head," says the doctor. Danielle places her hand on the inside of Nina's thigh, holds it back to widen the aperture. Moss can see a wrinkled blue-gray ball emerging in the doctor's hand. Nina's stretched labia shine in the light, encircling the waxing crown like the fiery rim of a solar eclipse. "You're doing great, Nina," Danielle says, and again Moss can hear his mother's yells, and he looks at Danielle and she looks at him and everything he ever felt goes out from him toward her, and she sees this, sees what he needs from her, and her eyes forgive him, even though, for her, there is nothing to forgive, for she has forgiven him long ago—*that* is what she tells him with her eyes, and that is all that needs to be understood, at least for now—and, looking down, he sees the born head, the patch of black hair, the ancient froggy face, the sealed eyes, the flat nose, the wide, downturned mouth, the entire head covered in some milky translucent film, thin as the skin of a soap bubble; and now the neck, the shoulders, the chest, the arms, everything blood-flecked and perfectly formed, the little live hands, the long gray umbilical cord, and then—"We've got a boy!" says the doctor, and Moss, staring at the penis, realizes that he could abide this only if Danielle came back to him—for then he wouldn't need to be needed by *them,* wouldn't have to agonize over what kind of son or brother to be, ran no risk of angrily cutting himself off from mother and child or else slavishly devoting himself to them at his own expense; he could accept the baby and the mother wholeheartedly and just be himself—

A fireball belched upward, knocking Moss back, the Calvados and the lighter flying from his hands. The bottle, which he had evidently emptied, smashed on the floor, and the fireball sucked itself back into the dish of bananas, leaving behind shreds of flame that adhered to the unfinished wooden cabinet that hung above the countertop. Moss blinked. He was unhurt, so far as he could tell. He stood up. He was okay. The fire was containable. All he needed was a towel or a blanket to beat it out. Or should he fill up a jug of water? He grabbed a dish towel from the drainboard and confronted the flames, which were slowly growing, expressing a defiance that Moss found strangely admirable. How far did they think they could go? He raised the towel and hesitated, as if checked by an intimation that a towel was not enough; and then he began whipping the sharp flame that was sucking on the edge of the cupboard door, even as it became apparent that the smaller trouble spots were flaring up faster than he would have thought, and he snapped the towel more frantically, but, as in a dream, his effort produced the opposite result of its intention: the cabinet had become shrouded in an increasingly uniform fire, the individual flames finding one another and coalescing, brightening on contact. Moss stared in fascination. What if he just let it burn? He could not believe it was real. But there was nothing more real or more devastating—he knew that. And yet he did not feel himself in immediate danger, even as the smoke began to fill the room. He thought: the fire extinguisher. It was in the pantry. He hadn't thought of it because he was sure he couldn't figure out how to use it. Instead he grabbed the phone from the kitchen table and dialed 911, but when the operator answered, he hung up on reflex. Why? He dialed again, and this time he said that his kitchen was on fire and that someone had better come fast. He hung up and stood there. The room had gotten appreciably warmer. What to do? Things were getting out of hand. He ran out of the kitchen to the other side of the house, to the room in which he'd been staying—there wasn't even a bed, just an inflatable mattress and some blankets (he thought to snatch up the blankets and run back to the kitchen, but it was probably too late)—and started packing his suitcase with the clothes that were strewn like lifeless bodies on the floor. Then he put on his shoes, took up the suitcase, which also contained the cash Boris had paid him, and walked down the hall to the front door, where he saw, through the haze of the living room, that the entire bank of kitchen cabinets was engulfed, the highest spires of flame now threatening the wooden trusses overhead. He watched for another moment, with no sense of his feet, then went outside, where he turned around and stepped back to behold the larger picture. Smoke had begun to seep through the seams of the shingled roof. Moss wondered how long it would take for the roof to catch—whether it would happen before the fire trucks came. And then it did happen: a flaming head poked through one of the holes, a formless creature emerging, diffuse and unslakable, its fiery feelers now crawling along the cedar slope. Moss acknowledged his authorship—the unique life of this fire, the fiendish murmur of its internal rhythms, its surge and glower, would not have existed without him, and this made it a thing of surpassing eloquence. Moss was terrified. Black smoke had risen above the treetops, gathering cloudlike against the white sky. Moss watched for another moment, then turned and walked away, with a strange composure—he knew where he must go.

The door to the Jeep was unlocked, as usual—that's how it was out here. Moss got into the driver's seat and reached underneath it, where Boris kept a spare set of keys.

He fastened his seat belt and slid the key into the ignition. Last month Boris had taken him out to some empty roads and let him drive, and there had been no serious incidents. Driving was not rocket science. Complete morons knew how to drive. Moss started the engine, put the vehicle in reverse and promptly backed up into a tree: there was a loud crash, but Moss in his seat belt was unharmed. He jerked the gearshift into drive and swung onto the gravel path that snaked around to the road.

19

MOSS GAZED OUT THE WINDOW AT THE FLIMSY-LOOKING wing that cut through the rushing vapors. He felt sedated, numb to things that should concern him. Nothing seemed real. Or rather, nothing seemed to matter. He wondered how long it would last. After driving, capably, to the airstrip in Maine, where he left the Jeep in a parking space, he had taken a small plane to Logan Airport, where he made three calls—one to Anton, one to Suzie Wolf and one to Boris, for whom he left a dispassionate message apprising him of the destruction of his house—and purchased a ticket to Los Angeles, whose green lawns and blue swimming pools now paraded below.

The plane landed safely and Moss entered the terminal, holding his suitcase. He was lost, given over to the glorious unknown. He would have to feel his way. And then he saw, amid a crowd of people waiting, a cardboard sign with MOSS written on it in red marker, held solemnly aloft by a tall spectral man with high cheekbones and stringy white hair past his shoulders, whom Moss recognized from a picture his mother once sent.

Anton saw him, held up his hand in Indian greeting. His eyes were sad. Moss held out his hand to him.

"Hey," said Anton, whose hand was cool and soft. "Congratulations."

"For what?"

"You're gonna be a brother, aren't you?"

Moss had almost forgotten. "Yeah."

"And people liked your script. So—congratulations."

Moss then remembered that he had a meeting at seven o'clock with Suzie Wolf and Josh Levitt, at some restaurant whose name he'd written on an airport napkin. Suzie had arranged it over the phone when Moss had called her, but somewhere on his journey Moss had forgotten about it, even though it was his whole reason for coming. With even a small Hollywood payday, he could go to another country (Mexico? Spain?) and support himself for years.

Anton led the way to his car. Outside it was warm and dry. Moss saw palm trees, a sure sign that he was in another world. Anton explained that the trees were sterile, imported from other climes. That explained why they looked so forlorn, Moss thought. They did not belong here.

Moss could not say the same for himself; he felt strongly that he was in the right place. Which, now that he thought of it, wasn't the same thing as belonging. He simply felt that his arrival here would produce consequences that could never have existed otherwise. Of course, this held true for any decision. Many times, Moss had stood on a corner, wondering which route to take to his destination, thinking that the rest of his life would be determined by his choice, each ticking second of action or inaction creating unknowable ripples in the future. The only thing to do, then, was be aggressive— Moss felt that now. Having conquered time and space, he wanted more, wanted another challenge. Walking with Anton in the haze of this new land, Moss realized that he could just as easily be somewhere else, that he had made a choice, and in so doing had claimed the place for himself, and therefore did belong, in a way that those who were merely born here did not. Anton, meanwhile, had the quality of being both estranged from, and integral to, his environment—he was like the trees: foreign, fruitless, calm and a little sad.

On the freeway, though, Anton drove fast, barefoot, squinting in the sun, his hair blowing all around him. There was life in him yet, perhaps even rage. Moss was open to all possibilities. He was in California now.

The loud beating of the wind discouraged conversation, but Moss felt a need to speak.

"I burned down a house."

"What's that?" Anton rolled up his window.

"This morning," said Moss. "I burned down a house."

"You burned down a house?"

"I did. I burned down a house."

"Whose house?"

"The guy," said Moss, "who got my mother pregnant. His name's Boris. It was an accident."

"What was?"

"The fire."

"What happened?"

"I was flambéing some bananas. And the flame just sort of torched up." Moss then recalled that the cabinet doors were smeared with cooking grease, from spatters and oily fingerprints. "It was a freak accident."

"Where was Boris?"

"On his way to Italy."

"I hear he's a friend of yours," said Anton. It was like an accusation.

"Not anymore," said Moss.

They arrived at Anton's, which, Moss reminded himself, had also been Nina's home. But when he got inside, he found no significant traces of her. This was Anton's place. Unopened mail and old record albums were scattered on the floor, and the piano was covered with sheet music and drinking glasses containing various evaporated substances. The sofa had a ketchup-encrusted plate on it, which Anton removed so Moss could sit. Anton then sat in the chair opposite; he crossed his legs, opened a small wooden box of Mexican design on the coffee table between them and pulled out a finger-thick joint, rolled with palpable expertise.

"You smoke?" he said.

"No, thanks," said Moss, who, the few times he'd tried the drug, had thought he was having brain aneurysms. "I've got that meeting in a couple of hours. You think you could give me a ride to the restaurant?" Moss pulled out the napkin on which he'd copied the name and address.

Anton looked at it. "Fancy place," he said. He lit the joint.

"Thanks for helping me," said Moss. "Getting my stuff to Suzie."

"It was out of guilt," said Anton, holding smoke. He exhaled at the ceiling. "Your letter made me feel like a real piece of shit. Little did I know Nina was busy consoling herself with your friend."

"I didn't know either," said Moss. "Of course, she wouldn't have done it if you hadn't cheated on her first."

"I wouldn't have cheated if she hadn't gone to see you on our goddamn anniversary."

"She came to see me," said Moss, "because you two had a fight."

"She came to see you," said Anton, "because you were having a nervous breakdown."

"What?"

"You broke up with a chick or something. You were coming unhinged. She was so worried about you that we had to cancel our plans."

"Worried?" said Moss, not understanding.

"Don't get me wrong," said Anton. "I knew she wanted to get away from me. But I figured she was getting pressure on your end."

"Pressure?"

"You missed her," said Anton, motioning with the joint, from which he presumably derived these insights. "She spends all those years in Europe, and then, when she comes back to the States, she lives as far away from you as possible. It makes sense that you'd try to get her attention."

"I bet a lot of things make sense to you," said Moss. "My mother told me about the books you read. You think extraterrestrials settled planet Earth."

"Yeah? Well, here's another one. You know the real reason Nina left me?"

"The real reason?"

Anton laughed raspingly. "Open your eyes, man!" he roared. "See this?" He bared his brown teeth, wiggled an incisor with his finger. "And that's not the half of it. My knees are gone. My back hurts. My hands hurt. Vision's going. Memory's going. I piss five times a night. I don't even piss—I dribble, and then only in spurts. I piss like an animal dies. And your mom, she saw what was coming. Soon she'd have to start taking care of me. And that is not an individual born to take care of anything."

This stung Moss—the judgment against his mother, and the suggestion that he himself had been victimized. It wasn't like she'd beaten him, or starved him, or chained him to a radiator.

"If she wasn't born to take care of things," said Moss, "then how do you explain her wanting to have this baby?"

Anton began coughing, hard, like he had a lung disease. "You mean you haven't figured it out?" he said, and hacked some more. "Hey, that's okay. You haven't been around. In my opinion, when she found out she was pregnant, she saw a chance to avoid the conflicts in her life. Having a baby would protect her from people's anger. Yours and mine, namely." He crossed his thin legs, leaned forward conspiratorially. "Without the baby, see, she'd have to deal with *us*."

"She has to deal with us anyway," said Moss, who was beginning to think that Anton was the one coming unhinged.

"Hey, don't worry," said Anton, as if Moss had agreed with him. "She's a fertile woman. That's how it goes."

Moss did not want to think about her fertility. "Can you give me a ride, then?" he said.

"A ride?"

"To my meeting."

"Why don't you just take the car?" Anton said, as if Moss should have thought of that. He reached into his pocket for the keys. "You know how to drive, don't you?"

THE GRASS WAS lush and viridescent in the gathering darkness, the air sweet with flowers and car exhaust, faint sexual poisons. The blackened palm trees towered silently against the pink electric sky.

Moss got into the Toyota. The car his mother had driven. She didn't even know he was here, visiting her old house, driving her old car. It was like he was inhabiting her life. Her old life. This wasn't her privacy, he thought; it was her past. A ghost world. But if she was beyond it, so was he. There was nothing for him here, at least not to do with *her*. He eased the car into traffic. The engine groaned amicably.

He turned onto a wide boulevard, the directions to the restaurant on the seat beside him. He saw Dr. Seuss trees, ramshackle Mexican walls, fast-food islands whose white lights burned with

the devotion of a refrigerator opened at midnight. The roads themselves seemed endless. He was in no hurry to arrive.

By the time he found the restaurant, he was twenty minutes
late. He pulled into the lot and parked the car between two hulking
sport-utility vehicles. It was only when he got out of the car and
caught his reflection in the window that he saw himself—his hair
was wall-socket wild, as if he'd just gotten out of bed, and his
T-shirt was stained with cooking juices and sweat, and still smelled,
like his hair, of smoke. Moss was not discouraged by the effect. He
was ready to make a deal.

Inside, he explained to the hostess that he was here to meet a
Suzie Wolf and a Josh Levitt. After a slight hesitation, he was led to
a table at the back.

Josh Levitt, standing to greet Moss, could not have been more
than five feet tall. He wore thick black-framed glasses and had fuzzy
reddish-brown hair, and was possibly younger than Moss, but with
an air of financial precociousness that made him seem much older.
Moss initiated a handshake that Levitt accepted cautiously. Then he
turned to Suzie Wolf, who was still trying to get out of her chair.
Moss was shocked to find that she was not only morbidly obese—her
face had a ring of fat around it, like an oval frame around a picture—but that she bore, beyond the fat, a passing resemblance to
Nina: the curly dark hair, the tanned, swelling breasts (packaged to
great advantage in her low-cut orange top), the hungry eyes, even
the bright shade of her red lipstick. Her handshake was decidedly
more vigorous than Levitt's, and her perfume, too, was bold and ag-

gressive. Moss could understand Anton's attraction to her—she was big and juicy, and young enough to be his daughter.

Moss then saw that both his dining companions had already been served—they had identical dishes, featuring some kind of small roasted bird.

"Sorry I'm late," Moss said, looking from one plate to the other. "Are those pigeons?"

"Affirmative," said Levitt. He grinned collusively. "Get it?"

"No."

Levitt scratched his ear, the smile frozen now. "*You* know. That scene where Bobby's so hungry, he eats that roasted pigeon with the Old Man?"

"Oh, I love that scene," said Suzie breathily. "It's like *The Old Man and the Sea.*"

Levitt, with an air of ceremony, tore a wing from his bird and handed it across the table to Moss. "For good luck."

"To success!" said Suzie, pulling off a wing herself. She looked like she could swallow it whole.

Moss took the wing from Levitt. The bone was sticking out. He brought it to his mouth and nibbled on the crisp salted skin.

"Order something," Levitt said.

"Thanks," said Moss. "But I'm not that hungry." With his teeth he ripped a sliver of meat from the bone and chewed. It wasn't much better than the pigeon at Beaujoli he'd maligned so ruthlessly in the press. He took another bite.

"Well, then," said Levitt. "I want to start by saying that I really like your ideas. The stuff about the father, and the cult, and the girl, what was her name?"

"Nutricia," said Moss.

"All that stuff's good," Levitt said. "But what I'm more interested in is the *journey*."

"I agree," said Suzie, looking at Moss expectantly.

"The journey?" said Moss. "You mean—when he rides the rails?"

"Exactly," said Levitt. "We need more to happen there. For instance, why can't he meet a girl along the way? We don't get any sex until page a hundred and three."

"It's a fabulous scene," said Suzie, leering voraciously at Moss. "It got me very hot."

"Thanks," said Moss, who had had Bobby bring Nutricia to a "crashing orgasm" with his "knowledgeable tongue."

"But it's not enough," said Levitt. "You have a plague of locusts at the end. Why not anticipate that fecundity with some wild sex in a boxcar?"

"I love it," said Suzie. She looked at Moss ecstatically. "Don't you *love* it?"

"So what does this mean?" said Moss, turning to Levitt. "If I add some sex, you'll buy it?"

Levitt didn't seem to hear him. "Give Bobby a partner," he said. "A woman. Maybe they're not even a couple at first. Or maybe they are, but then the relationship begins to crumble. And then maybe it's the *girl* who's captured for the human sacrifice, and Bobby has to save her—"

"Can we talk money first?" said Moss, trying to hide his annoyance. Bobby Boxcar didn't need a woman. He was fine on his own.

"Josh is giving you suggestions," Suzie said reprovingly. Her eyes were fierce. "If you want to make money, listen to what he's saying."

Moss's whole body tingled with a reminder of being yelled at as a child. In the next moment, one of the two cell phones on the table rang. Suzie's. She checked the number, got a confused look. "Excuse me, Josh," she said to Levitt, and answered uncertainly. "Hello?" A pause. "Oh, hi—here he is." Suzie held the phone to Moss, warning him with her eyes to make it snappy. Pigeon grease shone on her face, around her devouring red mouth. "It's Anton."

Anton? Moss took the phone. "Hello?"

"Hey," Anton said. "I just wanted to let you know that your mom's gone into labor."

"What?"

"She just called me. She didn't know you were here."

"Labor?" said Moss. He didn't like the sound of it. "Is she okay?"

"She couldn't get in touch with you or Boris. So she called me."

"But she's not due till next month."

"When you're finished with your meeting," said Anton, "you should go to see her."

"But—I'm here."

"You can catch a flight tonight."

"Are *you* going?"

"I can't," said Anton. "So just come back here when you're finished, and I'll take you to the airport."

"But—is she okay?"

"She's in some discomfort. Nothing to worry about."

"I'm not worried," said Moss. He was livid now. Couldn't she have waited another day? What kind of timing was this? Was he supposed to just drop everything and go? But why? What did she need him for?

He closed the phone, handed it back to Suzie.

"Is something wrong?" Suzie said.

Moss felt sick. He looked at Josh Levitt. "Why not pay me a little up front?" he said. "Not a lot. But something to show me you're serious."

"That's not how it works," said Levitt, glancing at Suzie for help. "I'm showing you I'm serious by meeting with you. But if you don't like my ideas—"

"Why couldn't we do this on the phone?" Moss said to both of them. "Do you know what it cost me to come out here?"

"Excuse me," Suzie said, emitting a deeper perfume, something chemical in her anger mixing sharply with her other essences. "No client of mine will show this kind of disrespect." She shoved a drumstick into her mouth, obviously the type who ate compulsively when she got upset. She kept talking. "Do you realize how lucky you are to even get this opportunity?" She looked like she might cry, or bite his head off, even as she chewed.

Moss couldn't look at her. He had to get out of there—money wasn't so important suddenly. He wanted to get into the car and drive. Already he could feel the world rolling out from under him in all directions, scalded by cars and lights. The gas tank was nearly full, enough to take him far, too far. He wanted to get lost in the dark. Maybe Nina would die, he thought. And the baby too. He didn't hate the idea, necessarily. He imagined his foot on the gas pedal, and the power of the engine traveling up his leg. The headlights would guide him, and the road would begin to rise: he saw rocks and cliffs, great hulking shapes, steep drops. Stars swarmed above. He followed the white lines that curved round and round.

Josh Levitt was saying something about how valuable his time was.

Moss envisioned himself on the other side of the hills, deposited into desert blackness. What would he do? Where would he end up? Maybe it didn't matter. The point was to be free, the way Nina had once been free, the way Boris wished to be free. Boris, who had probably picked up the message about the fire by now—he might already be on his way back home. The house might have burned to the ground, for all Moss knew, though it was more likely that the firemen had gotten there in time to save most of it. Fortunately, there wasn't much in the way of valuable furniture to be lost. And no one was hurt. And wouldn't insurance cover the damages? Even Boris, after the shock wore off, would have to acknowledge that worse catastrophes had occurred in his life.

Moss then noticed that Suzie's face had gone pale, and that she was holding her throat and gasping, or trying to gasp, for air. Her big eyes called out to him—him, and no one else.

"Frankly," Josh Levitt was saying, "I don't have to take shit from anyone—"

"She's choking," said Moss, standing up. He tried to think of what to do. Didn't he know?

"Shit!" said Josh. He made a move as if to slap Suzie's back.

"No!" said Moss. "Don't do that."

Josh froze, then looked around spasmodically. "Help!" he shouted. "Someone's choking!" He grabbed his phone from the table and dialed 911.

Suzie's eyes had widened to an alarming degree. Josh was yelling hysterically into the phone. Members of the waitstaff had come over, all of them equally unsure of what to do, until one waiter took charge and positioned himself behind Suzie's chair. He reached around her, just below the breasts, and was just able to clasp his hands together.

"No!" Moss shouted. "That's wrong!" He couldn't believe a person would attempt the maneuver without knowing how to do it, but that's what it looked like, and there was no time to take any chances. The waiter looked at him in astonishment—as with Josh Levitt, his confidence had been shaken by something authoritative in Moss's voice. Moss rushed around the table, yanked the waiter away by the arm and got behind Suzie. He strained to reach around her. He made a fist with one hand and covered it with his other. Then he pulled up her top to see where her navel was—Danielle had said to find the navel, then push upward an inch above it. But Suzie's navel was lost in folds of cold pink flesh, and so Moss placed his balled hands in an approximate place and thrust as hard as he could, grunting with the effort. It was impossible to get any power through all the fat, but Moss thrust again, and again, and then

Suzie's body went slack and she collapsed forward in her chair. Moss looked up and saw faces staring at him in horror. "Someone help!" he yelled. "We've got to get her on her back!" The waiter who had started the job stepped forward once again, and helped Moss lower Suzie onto the floor. Moss quickly got on top of her, straddling her hips as he clasped his hands and placed them on her navel, which was a horizontal line quivering like a nervous smile in the rolling waves of blotchy, clammy skin, and shoved again. Nothing. Moss remembered: open the mouth. He got off of her and knelt beside her head. Only now did he see that her eyes were closed, and this relaxed him some—it was the bulging, terrified eyes that had paralyzed him. He opened her mouth—Danielle had said to look to see if anything was there. But all Moss saw was a bluish tongue and yellow teeth glutted with silver fillings, and the black hole of the throat. He put his finger in the mouth, but would not go down the esophagus—he wasn't sure if it was procedure. Instead, he tilted back the head and pinched the nose—Danielle had said that at the hospital they used a special protective device so that you didn't have to come into contact with the patient's mouth, but Moss had no such luxury. He inhaled, then put his mouth to Suzie's mouth and breathed out. He repeated this, aware of the audience around him, which believed in him now, for he was their only hope. But when he looked, he saw that Suzie's chest had not expanded. "Can someone see if she has a pulse?" Moss yelled. He straddled Suzie again as the hostess knelt and placed her fingers on Suzie's wrist. Moss delivered another upward blow to the gut. What was he doing wrong? The hostess said that she thought she felt a pulse. Moss was sweating. He thrust yet again, and something flew up from Suzie's mouth and landed on her stomach, just above Moss's hands. It was a large piece of pigeon meat, which she must have sucked right off the bone. But it wasn't clear if she was breathing, and Moss climbed back off of her and dove to her mouth. He took in a chestful of air and pressed his lips to hers and exhaled—and he felt a hand in his hair, and heard a sound, and then his mouth filled with a hot bitter burning matter, and he jerked his head away, gagging, and saw the small wet chunks of brown vomit on Suzie's chin and neck, and her eyes were open now.

Moss stood up as Josh and others gathered around Suzie, who was asking what happened. Not knowing what to do, holding his breath against the putrid taste in his mouth, Moss ran to find the restroom. He reached a door marked *M,* opened it, ran to the sink and threw up. Then he turned on the water and put his mouth to the jet. He rinsed his mouth several times, spitting viciously. He hardly knew what he had done.

A moment later he was outside, running across the parking lot, to the car, the keys in his hand; and then he was on the road, driving, under control, even as the adrenaline screamed inside him and his experience fell away flaming like the first stage of a rocket. His mind was going too fast for his memory, so fast that it was a blur, a blank. He followed the signs to the airport, unaware of any plan, other than to keep traveling in the direction in which unknown forces propelled him.

20

AS SOON AS HE LANDED IN NEW YORK, MOSS CALLED ANTON and got the name of the hospital where Nina was supposed to be. Outside, at the taxi stand, he stood shivering in the predawn air, wearing only his T-shirt and pants—Anton would have to ship him the rest of his things.

A taxi took him to the hospital, which was way uptown. He hoped he wasn't too late. But too late for what?

Inside, the woman at the front desk looked up the name Moss had given—"It's my mother," Moss said, aware of a need to justify himself. The woman gave him a room number on the seventh floor.

In the elevator he closed his eyes, felt himself ascend. When the doors opened, he stepped out, unable to capture his thoughts. He was here—that was all he knew.

The room was all the way at the end of a long corridor. Moss took his time getting there. No one seemed to notice him.

To Moss's surprise, the door to Nina's room was closed. What did it mean? Moss stood there. Might she be in the middle? In the middle of having the baby? But that didn't seem likely. Moss clutched the door handle: he would open it an inch and peek.

He pushed the handle down, fit his eye in the crack.

She was lying flat on the bed, under a white sheet. Her eyes were closed and her arms were at her sides. Her stomach, covered by the sheet, looked much smaller than he had expected; he could not tell whether she had had the baby or not, though something told him that she had. He took a step toward her, and she opened her eyes and saw him. For a split second, their eyes locked, flashing with the primal recognition of members of a distinct species. "Moss," she said in a small voice, and smiled sleepily, beholding him with all her dreamy strength, he who had materialized from beyond. She lifted her hand to him, wanting him to come closer. He moved toward her, without words. She was pale, drawn, and looked neither young nor old. Moss put his hand out to hers. She took it and held on. Then she raised her head from the pillow, pulling him weakly to her. One heavy breast crushed against his shoulder as they embraced; he felt the glug of its food, heard a soft tuneless keening in her throat.

"Baby," she said. "I knew you'd come."

Moss closed his eyes and held her. "I'm here," he said. It was the truest thing he could think of, the only thing. "I'm here."

"I missed you so much."

Moss withdrew from her, searched her worn, radiant face. "Did you—have it?" he said. A fear shot through him. "What happened?"

She said, "Get one of the nurses to take you."

"Take me where?"

"To the nursery." Nina smiled tearfully. "To meet your sister."

Moss looked at his mother, and without any sign, without any cue, they both began to shake, silently at first, one standing and the other lying in bed, and then their voices came to them, and there was a moment when Moss wasn't sure if they were laughing or crying, and so he watched her, and she was, he saw, laughing, and so was he, and their laughter, so similar in pitch and rhythm, rose from them and intertwined, a fusion of language that was beyond the physical, and which threatened to overtake them, as had happened more than once in the past, when Moss had said or done something funny, to please her, tickle her, make her shriek, knowing her exact spot, and not even her tears could bring her so helplessly to her knees. Now *he* was the one going weak—he stomped his foot and doubled over, clenching his teeth and hugging himself as the spasms kicked inside him. Finally he caught his breath, and so did she, and the convulsions slowed, and they groaned and sighed together as they descended, giddily, from the clouds.

"So everything went okay?" Moss said, still breathing heavily, and not trusting their mirth, or the shiny happiness that had burst in him at the news that his sibling had arrived. He supposed he was relieved more than anything else, that no disaster had occurred. But he was not fully convinced. He wiped his eyes and shivered. "She's healthy?"

"Go see her," Nina said.

· · ·

ON THE WAY out of the room, Moss nearly bumped into a young nurse in pink scrubs. He stood in the doorway, facing her: a flicker of recognition passed between them. Moss had never seen her before.

"Hi," she said. "Congratulations!"

"Thanks," Moss said. "But I'm not the father."

"You're Nina's son, right? We've been expecting you."

There was something in the way she spoke to him that made Moss think his mother had said intriguing things about him.

He said, "Can you tell me how to get to the nursery?"

"Sure. I'll take you."

Moss looked at her name tag, which hung from a chain around her neck. Her first name was Joy. That was funny. Better she was here, in this unit, and not in Intensive Care. Above the name was her photo, a strikingly beautiful shot, a transcendent idea of her, of which she herself was a copy. But when Moss looked at her face again, he saw something new that the photo had showed him, and she became more beautiful.

"You'll need one of these," Joy said. "Give me your hand?"

Moss obeyed. She fastened a green plastic bracelet on his wrist.

She led him down the hall, her black ponytail bouncing behind her. She was quick and energetic in her movements. She looked over her shoulder and said, "I'm Joy, by the way."

"I'm Moss."

"I like that name. I've never heard it before."

"It was my mother's idea."

Moss became aware of other personnel in their midst, doctors, nurses, interns, technicians.

"Were you there?" he said, swallowing the small regret he felt for not having been there himself. "For the birth?"

"I was," said Joy, her bright eyes guessing at what informed the question. "Your mom did *great*."

This heartened Moss, who felt that Joy was including him in her praise.

"That's good," he said. "She's pretty tough."

They passed a window, through which you could see the babies tucked away in their transporters, which were parked at odd angles in the room. Joy stopped at a door.

"Just tell them you're the brother and give them your mother's name," she said, pressing an intercom button.

Moss felt a panic: was she leaving him? "Yes?" came a voice from the intercom. Moss turned to it. "I'm here to see Nina Messinger's baby," he said. "I'm the brother." The door buzzed. Moss opened it, looked at Joy. "Do you have time?"

"Sure," Joy said. "Let's have a look."

Joy knew which cart to go to—it must have been she who had wheeled the baby down here. For the first time, Moss could understand what was thrilling in this atmosphere, and what was humbling, and why some people were addicted to it. He thought, once more, of Danielle, felt what connected her to the past and to the future. The heroism of women. The midwife of history.

"Here she is," said Joy.

Moss looked down and saw a baby wrapped in a white blanket. He had never seen a newborn infant before.

She looked the way a sleeping baby was supposed to look. Arms above her head, hands by her ears, fingers curled. Hair, dark, not too much of it. Bulging eyelids, squat nose, slack lip, solemn jaw. Soft, blooming cheeks.

"It's amazing that they come into the world breathing on their own," Moss said. He was watching the nostrils, trying to detect movement.

"She's six pounds, seven ounces." Joy made a small adjustment to the blanket.

"So what happens now?" said Moss.

"When we're done visiting, we'll take her back to the room, so she can nurse, and bond with her mommy."

They were silent for a moment, gazing together at the baby.

"Would you like to hold her?"

"Me?" said Moss. He hadn't supposed it was an option. "I don't know—she looks sort of fragile."

"You don't have to."

"No," Moss said, with a sudden urgency. "I want to."

Joy scooped the baby up in her blanket—fearlessly—and brought her to him. Moss held out his arms.

"How do I do this?" he said. And then he was doing it. She had weight, reassuring weight. Moss smiled down at her, marveling at her skin, her little hands, her elfin ears. She looked like she was from another planet. A peaceful planet whose inhabitants spent most of their time asleep.

After a moment he turned and handed the baby back to Joy; their arms touched during this transfer, with the baby between them.

"What's her name?" Moss said to her as she placed the baby in the cart.

"I don't think we know yet," she said, her eyes on the baby. Then she turned to Moss. "Ready?"

Joy began to wheel the cart, and they headed down the corridor.

Just before they got to Nina's room, Moss stopped—he would let Nina and his sister have their bonding time to themselves, he decided. For now, he would go home, clean himself up, eat something and then figure out his next move. One thing he knew was that he had to keep moving—that was the main thing. He had given life to himself, and now he must listen to it and meet its needs. He, too, had a giant obligation.

"Tell Nina I'll see her soon," he said to Joy, and Joy smiled and said she would. Moss smiled back, and watched as she pushed the cart into the room. When she was no longer in sight, he turned and faced the length of the corridor, the elevators in the distance. He closed his eyes, opened them and started on his way.

ACKNOWLEDGMENTS

The author thanks Henry Bean, Amy Edelman,
Jonathan Jao, Jillian Quint, Kim Rosencrance,
Veronica Windholz, and especially
Jon Karp and Barbara J. Zitwer
for their help with this book.

ABOUT THE AUTHOR

PAUL HOND lives in New York.
He is the author of *The Baker*.

ABOUT THE TYPE

This book was set in Granjon, a modern recutting
of a typeface produced under the direction of
George W. Jones, who based Granjon's design upon
the letter forms of Claude Garamond (1480–1561).
The name was given to the typeface as a tribute to
the typographic designer Robert Granjon.